D1645708

Let's Jo

and Contact the Living

LET'S JOIN HANDS

AND CONTACT THE LIVING

RONNIE SCOTT AND HIS CLUB

JOHN FORDHAM

ELM TREE BOOKS
London

First published in Great Britain 1986
by Elm Tree Books/Hamish Hamilton Ltd
Garden House 57–59 Long Acre London WC2E 9JZ

Copyright © 1986 by John Fordham

British Library Cataloguing in Publication Data

Fordham, John
  Let's join hands and contact the living.
  1. Scott, Ronnie
  I. Title
  788'.66'0924   ML519.S3/
  ISBN 0–241–11794–1

Typeset by Input Typesetting Ltd, London
Printed and bound in Great Britain by
Redwood Burn Ltd, Trowbridge, Wiltshire

For My Mother

Contents

Foreword

I wrote this book because it drew together three enduring enthusiasms of mine. Firstly for jazz, which has given me more pleasure than any other art, as well as providing what has seemed to be a remarkably fitting musical score for urban living in the twentieth century. Secondly for London, and the transformations in it since the years of the Second World War. Thirdly for Ronnie Scott, a man who not only remains one of this country's finest jazz musicians but whose proprietorship of one of the world's most celebrated jazz clubs helped me to witness many of the legendary originals of the genre making music in an environment in which they could mostly feel relaxed, respected, often loved.

When Ronnie Scott began his career, serious jazz playing was in its infancy in this country, and for many years its British practitioners stood blushingly in the shadows of the mainly black American pioneers. As Scott approaches his sixties, much has changed. Players like Scott, with a deep respect for the music and its origins, have helped in every part of the globe to spread the word. If, as I have suggested, a childhood among Jewish matriarchs and the social upheavals of wartime London helped to push the subject of this story towards his life's work, social pressure lessens none of the achievement of it.

Though the condition of jazz in this country today has emerged from the work of all its performers and adherents, it's hard to imagine either the profile it has in 1986 – still marginalized, but a long way further forward than a quarter of a century ago – or the raised ambitions and hopes of its up-and-coming players which couldn't have been quite the same without Ronnie Scott and his partner Pete King. I hope this book goes some way toward expressing my gratitude for that.

Thanks are due, above all, to Ronnie Scott and Pete King

for their help, hospitality and cooperation. Also to all the people who helped me to tell this story, and especially to the following: Ron Atkins, Derek Bailey, Alfie Benge, Rachel 'Ray' Berger, Brian Case, Harry Conn, Joan Crewe, Tony Crombie, Jeff Ellison, Bernie Fenton, Nigel Fountain, Charles Fox, Ilsa and Nicholas, Benny Green, Coleridge Goode, Kitty Grime, Roxy Hoffman, Ted Hughes, Barbara Jay, John Jack, Bernard Kops, Nissel Lakin, Issac 'Mitch' Mitchell, Laurie Morgan, Julia Pascal, Mary Scott, Vic Schonfield, Stan and Jackie Tracey, Françoise Venet, Val Wilmer, Richard Williams, Cecil 'Flash' Winston, Robert Wyatt.

Thanks also to Theresa Allan for help with the research, to Neville Brody for the cover, to *City Limits*, to the *Guardian*, and to Kyle and Judith of Elm Tree Books for their forbearance. Love and thanks to Ros, to Vivien and to Fred.

Groucho Marx said to Greta Garbo when she rounded indignantly on him from under her hat, 'I'm sorry, I thought you were a fella I once knew in Philadelphia'. I sincerely hope that Ronnie Scott's friends and associates will recognize the man who travels the following pages. But such shortcomings as this book reveals are nobody's fault but my own.

John Fordham
London, March 1986

1 / Exiles

'I could see that Jewish people couldn't afford the luxury of being merely mediocre. They were like other people only more so. They were either angels or bastards and sometimes angelic bastards.' (Bernard Kops, *The World Is a Wedding*, 1963.)

'When the Jewish population have all made enough loot to take off for America, or Israel, then I'm leaving too. It would be turning out the light.' (Colin MacInnes, *Absolute Beginners*, 1959.)

Aldgate, London 1927

Of all the sounds that would turn a head, or raise an eyebrow, or stir a quiver of anticipation or disquiet in the East End on Friday 28 January – the clang of a tram, the sonorous hootings of big ships on the river, the bumping and clattering of goods trains in the docks, the babble of a streetmarket, the endless arguments of the out of work Jewish tailors waiting on corners for sweatshop jobs – the cry of a newborn baby worked its old magic on the members of one family in particular. Gathered at the East End Mothers' Maternity Hospital that day were the occupants of Number 33 South Tenter Street, a tiny terraced house at the southern edge of a labyrinth behind Aldgate station, not more than a quarter of a mile from Tower Bridge and London's Western Dock, and in the heart of one of the biggest Jewish communities in Europe.

The East End was basking in the afterglow of its visit from the Prince of Wales that week (the local paper warmly greeted the Prince's enthusiasm for 'finding out something about the real lives of the people who will one day acclaim him king') an honour not permitted to pass entirely without question in the district, however, especially amongst the knots of Russian exiles in the doorways and the little restaurants still claiming personal acquaintance with Trotsky. Elsewhere, the great city was going about its business, dancing teachers offering proficiency in the Charleston and the Black Bottom in the small ads of newspapers, scullery maids seeking the £30 or so per annum the job occasioned, Mr Baldwin declaring from Downing Street that he was the 'loneliest man in the country'. And at the East End Mothers' Maternity Hospital, Ronald Schatt was born to Joseph Schatt, musician, and Sylvia 'Cissie' Schatt, saleswoman, of South Tenter Street. Ronald was the couple's first and only child. They had married at the end of August 1926, when Jock was twenty-three and Cissie twenty-five – and four months pregnant.

Joseph Schatt, a handsome, elegant man with humorous eyes, was a dance band saxophonist, and a good one. He had served an apprenticeship that had given him an intimate knowledge of popular music. It was one that he continually added to as the years passed, building a repertoire of classics that would be proof against the most awkward requests from the floor. He played the alto, with the sweet, pure tone that was fashionable for the day, and was convinced for life that only with such rudiments could the instrument be properly played.

His profession was one of the most glamorous of the 1930s, the previous decade in Britain having seen a startling boom in popularity for a predominantly American music that was capable of superficially cauterizing the wounds of the Great War. Bandleaders with gleaming tonsures and immaculate tail-coats would lead phalanxes of section players like perfectly drilled armies through repertoires at once elegant and exhibitionistic. The dance band player was popular everywhere. For Joseph and Cissie Schatt, this wasn't an unmixed blessing.

Joseph was a man people remembered. He was sharp, a fancy dresser, a practical joker, a gambler, a shrewd Jew in an unwelcoming world, and he knew the score. He was one of countless gifted members of his race for whom the careers of overnight fame – notably, as far as the East End was concerned, boxing and music – were the route out of the ghetto, most of the more august professions being virtually inaccessible to Jews at the time. He travelled widely to play, and around the time of Ronald's birth was leading a palais band in Scotland, the Glasgow Plaza Band. Like many of his generation – and the one that followed – Joseph Schatt thought it prudent not to work under a Jewish name. He was always known professionally as 'Jock Scott'.

For Cissie, Jock's style and the demands of his working life were both fascinating and unsettling. The house at South Tenter Street became, in her mind, a traditional Jewish home with the birth of Ronnie. Cissie was always close to her mother and stepfather and to her brother Mark, a compulsive gambler forever on the verge of the deal that would bring the New World to their doorstep. Jock Scott loved the races too, and spent a fortune on them over the years.

Jock was descended from a Russian Jewish family, a community turned into refugees in the 1880s when anti-Jewish riots in southern Russia and Poland – followed by laws that crippled Jewish business – drove them across Europe to seek sanctuary in the West. Some were joining relatives already living in the Jewish ghetto of the docklands of London's East End. Most were heading for America. Some stepped off the boats in London en route to the States and never left. Some thought they actually were in America. The docks bore witness daily to their tribulations, lost souls straight off the ships into the arms of disbelieving relatives, if they were lucky. Bustled chattering down grey alleys, through seething marketplaces, sweatshops, past the modest premises of hopeful jewellers, tailors, restaurateurs, even brothels run by Jewish mamas and their daughters. The most celebrated establishment was in a neighbourhood that the locals ironically dubbed 'Christian Street' because there wasn't a single *goy* living in it. The area was populated with exiles exchanging imprecations and anecdotes in the cosmopolitan shorthand of Yiddish, or a mixture of Yiddish and Cockney. The language itself was an inspiration to musicality – so many of its meanings emerged from intonation as much as vocabulary.

For a Jew, it was a good time and a bad time to be born. While Cissie was waiting through the last days of her confinement, the *Daily Express* was asking 'How Long Can Fascism Last?'. But though unemployment in Britain touched a million and a half, London was doing well at the end of the 1920s and many of its Jewish community knew it. The entrepreneurs of the ghetto were geniuses of popular taste because they were starting from scratch, understanding a marketplace the dynamics of which could be measured simply by consulting the needs of mothers, fathers, brothers, sisters. The Joseph Lyons organization became the virtuoso of street-corner catering, Marks and Spencer's of downmarket luxury. The Grade brothers, music-hall tap dancers both, ended up showbiz tycoons.

Survival required a volatile mix of risk and family stability. For Jock Scott, it was important to believe that life would – given a few lucky breaks – pan out fine. Though he moved in the more respectable circles of dancehall and hotel enter-tainment ostensibly, he continued to live much like a *kletz-morim* in evening dress, a travelling player.

Thousands of them had come to Britain and America as the migrations went on. They represented a rich seam of Jewish musicianship that had developed out of the obligation to assimilate non-Jewish culture in order to survive, clarinet-tists, fiddlers, mandolin and dulcimer players who could play polkas for the locals, waltzes for the aristocracy, but be able to reel through the authentic repertoire for barmitzvahs and weddings. Jock's brother Dave was a violinist too, and played successfully in the dance bands.

Both sides of the family were bursting with opportunists, resourceful people apprenticed to the art of riding with the waves on this strange sea, and navigating it with mixed results. Aunt Julie and Uncle Muchie – an olive-skinned, dark-eyed, gypsy-looking couple who bore unmistakable signs of Cissie's Portuguese ancestry, who ran a hotel in Brighton. There was Uncle Harry, who made what living he could at the Brighton race-tracks, and who was to serve prison terms for fraud and con-artistry; Uncle Mark who never had a job, forever borrowing money from Cissie to back another cert. Uncle 'Gypsy' Rafie wore a bandana and a gold earring though nobody could trace much Romany ancestry in *him*; he sold racing tips for sixpence a throw down Petticoat Lane.

But the hazard in the path of that journey that Cissie had seen herself as taking with Jock loomed only too soon. He wasn't ready for domesticity, and soon proved it. Cissie travelled to Glasgow one day in 1930 or 1931, where her husband was at work. Perhaps she was already unsure. Cissie found Jock with another woman, and all the blandishments and charm that her husband could later unfurl, just the kind that had sparked a love for him that would never really die, were not enough to persuade her to find a way around what seemed to her that most irrefutable betrayal. Cissie was a mother now, and felt that her child needed a kind of security that Jock would find hard to grasp. She asked him not to return to the family house shortly afterwards, and began divorce proceedings.

For the young Ronald, Jock had always been a shadowy figure in early childhood, though there were glimpses that stayed with him. One night Cissie took the child to see Jock play with a band that he had in the East End, sat Ronnie at a restaurant table, heard the ever-bouyant man sound as convinced as ever that everything would be all right, that it would be worth another try, heard herself insist that it was all too late.

But a presence with which Jock filled the little East End house was the saxophone. It is one of the most beautifully designed of all musical instruments, a sensuous sculpture throwing flashes of light around the room. Its memory lingered on after he had gone and by 1931 Jock had gone for good, swept off into the tempestuous dance band scene, into the celebrated Jack Hylton band and then into the outfit led by Hylton's wife Ennis, whose signature tune was 'This Is The Missus, Just Look Her Over'. Jock eventually lived with Ennis Hylton until her death in the early 1950s. He was not to reappear in his son's life until the boy's teens – when Ronnie Scott was on the verge of following his footsteps into showbusiness.

The East End years were brief, but intense, a blur of colourful images: Uncle Rafie down the Lane, Ronnie's hand gripped fiercely by Cissie's mother, Nana Rebecca, Uncle Rafie pretending not to recognize his nephew in the urge to add authenticity to the act, saying 'hello little boy, come over here and help me give these tips to the gentlemen', little Ronnie scuttling to and fro and wondering not so very much later why his Uncle Rafie wasn't as rich as Croesus if he knew so much about the horses. A policeman came to the door one night to tell the family that Nana Becky's husband Samuel had died, an event that distressed the young Ronnie greatly. Great Aunt Leah, who lived in a tenement nearby and had a withered hand, saw her sailor son repeatedly at the foot of the bed, the one who had been blown to pieces in the Great War. Ronnie's great-grandfather was secretary of the local British Legion branch, a man with a copperplate hand into great old age. And Ronnie remembers the visit with Grandpa to the Portuguese synagogue in Great Alie Street when he was five – music, song, the passionate chanting of the cantor! Bearded old men in black, musty clothes, dust, history.

The household in South Tenter Street was hardly orthodox, but Nana Becky guarded as much of the tradition as could decently be observed – candles were lit on Friday nights, and respect for the fast of the Passover maintained.

After Jock's departure, Cissie's job as a saleswoman at the Jewish-owned Aldgate department store Burstein's (it later became the Houndsditch Warehouse Company and exists to this day) was the sole support for the household. But Cissie met her second husband whilst working there, a tailor called Solomon Berger. Sol was the diametric opposite of Jock Scott in every conceivable way. Hardworking, straightforward and businesslike, he resembled a Jewish Herbert Morrison in his horn-rimmed spectacles, and he took instantly to Ronnie. Sol and Cissie were married when the child was eight, and not long after Ronnie's stepsister Marlene was born. The boy was fascinated by the new arrival, watched her mother play with her for hours. The family soon began, like many London Jews before and after them, to follow the well-worn paths out of the ghetto of the docks – and just in time, with the Mosleyite race riots only just behind. Stoke Newington and Stamford Hill were more promising, greener and more forgiving parts of town for those who could afford to make the trip.

Though music was still not a part of the young Ronnie's world he did discover it in the family's Stoke Newington flat. Two brothers – much of Ronnie's age – lived upstairs in the house. One played the guitar, the other the alto saxophone. Paul Bennett, the saxophonist, later became a professional. Bennett's influence, which permeated the building, may have awakened dormant memories of the glamour of a musical life in a child otherwise preoccupied with aeroplanes and racing cars; the former became a nightmare in later years, the latter a perpetual fascination. Ronnie Scott went to Hebrew school in Stamford Hill to study for his barmitzvah, but the war intervened before he was to take it.

August 1939 saw the family in Bognor on holiday when war was declared, and Sol and Cissie feared returning to the family house since no-one knew then whether the onset of hostilities with Germany might not mean that that country's war machine would commence to decimate the capital from the air the very next day. Aunt Annie and Uncle Muchie's hotel in Brighton seemed like a safer bet.

For a twelve year old, Brighton was a pleasant enough place to be, and young Ronnie played hookey from school for much of the summer. The war seemed to him not the threat of loss and trauma that it was for his parents. Ronnie wanted to be the rear gunner in a bomber, and was fascinated by aviation and aeronautics. When the family moved back to London in 1940 (this time to Edgware – and the blitz began on the very same day, an event that none of them could entirely believe was a coincidence) the young Ronnie Scott began a course at Hendon Technical School for what seemed the first step on the route to conquest of the skies. He enrolled for a once-a-week appearance at the 410th Edgware Squadron of the Air Training Corps into the bargain, spurred on by a regular march to Hendon aerodrome with the irresistible promise 'you're going to fly this week' – one that never materialized.

But something altogether more compelling was soon to replace the ever evaporating promise of flight and the Grand Prix motor racing triumphs in the books he voraciously consumed. On the way to school one morning, Ronnie Scott bought his first musical instrument. In the window of a junk shop was an ancient cornet held together with black tape. Though the cornet didn't work, the boy was proud to take it on for five shillings. A little later he came by a soprano saxophone the same way. Like the cornet, it was barely good enough to extract a sound from, but it worked well enough to produce a handful of phrases that added up to something recognizable as a tune. Sol and Cissie were delighted, and they could see how keen Ronnie already was. If this was what their boy wanted to do, then there was no sense him being held back by second rate equipment. And if Cissie was troubled by the possibility that young Ronnie might turn into a man in the image of the father he hardly knew, she wasn't showing it. She went to Archer Street, the West End open-air labour exchange where the commercial musicians plied their trade and took some advice from old friends of Jock's, men she had known from the dance bands. After some thought, she and Sol then bought Ronnie the prize to end them all. It was a silver-plated Pennsylvania tenor saxophone with a gold plated bell. Sleek and smooth and gleaming as Jock's had been in the dockland house so long ago, soft yielding pads under pearl inlays, as sensuous as a human form and yet as thrilling in its mechanics as an aeroplane, a miraculous conjunction of wires and levers and flaps capable of producing a sound – somewhere between that of the brass instruments and reeds – which more or less defined the dance band era. It was also the instrument of Jewish social life, performed on by balding moustachioed men with twinkling eyes, delivering the pop tunes of the day, mixed phlegmatically in with the music of the Jewish dances. It was the instrument that had gleamed behind the lace curtains in the moody lighting at the Phoenix Theatre in Charing Cross Road when Cissie had taken Ronnie there because the Jan Ralfini orchestra was playing – and because Jock was somewhere in the saxophone section. Even though Cissie was still clearly in love, she never went backstage or sought him out.

There was also the world of the saxophone that Ronnie Scott did not yet know, but when he discovered it would devour it so voraciously that his companions would be astonished by his skill in absorbing the music of the best saxophonists of the day. Sidney Bechet, the great Creole musician, had transferred from the clarinet to the soprano saxophone, playing a music of sweeping passion that could make you shiver. But it was Coleman Hawkins, the saxophonist who had come up with the bands of Louis Armstrong and big-band leader Fletcher Henderson who had virtually created the tenor, single-handed. He had rescued the larger horn from the wilderness of sensationalism and special effects it had been relegated to, and turned it into a vehicle for warmth, sardonic humour and a kind of brusque tenderness.

Ronnie Scott thus found himself catapulted into a musical

age in which the sighings and flouncings of the dance orchestras were increasingly being charged with a new and irresistably exciting ingredient. 'Hot' music. Jazz. The first recordings of a young trumpet genius from New Orleans, Louis Armstrong, had trickled into Britain in the mid-1920s, and a newspaper, *Melody Maker*, had come into being the year before Ronnie's birth, to cater for both the regular music business and a buff's readership of 'hot jazz' lovers, the devotees of the genuine article. And in the year he was born, and not a five-minute walk from the South Tenter Street house, Britain's first specialist jazz record shop – Levy's in Whitechapel Road, an establishment founded by a dealer who had been selling records in the local streetmarkets for years – opened in response to the growing popularity of a music that had been forged by another ghetto community thousands of miles away.

What British fans experienced as the 'hot' quality of jazz was unmistakable, if imperfectly understood. It was the fierce glow of a music thrown up by the experience of recently emancipated slaves migrating from the southlands to the northern cities and in the process accelerating the rambling, conversational tempo of back-porch folk-blues into a taut and clamorous urbanized band music that sounded like the clang of trams, the badgering of streetmarkets, the climaxes and cadences of street-corner badinage, the stridency of marching bands, the pragmatism and casual tragedies of the blues.

But to most Western whites, jazz was not much more than an interesting musical accident valuable mainly for those bits of its rhythmic originality that could be given poise and a fashionable refinement by the elegant dance orchestras. It needed 'improving', it was a phenomenon altogether too crude and feverish for those of more tender sensibilities. Its creators, by popular acknowledgement, were still 'niggers' or 'coons', a description you might generally hear from bandleaders, critics, politicians. When Ronnie Scott was six months old, the dance-band leader Bert Ambrose was performing a work at the London Palladium called 'Heart of a Nigger'. An outcry about its derogatory overtones saw it altered, discreetly as they thought, to 'Heart of a Coon'.

But in Ronnie's early childhood, jazz began to get a real foothold in Britain. Though the white Original Dixieland Jazz

Band had toured the country successfully years before, and the great Sidney Bechet had appeared during the 1920s, the visits of Louis Armstrong and Duke Ellington to London in 1932 and 1933 were unquestionably a turning point. Armstrong had triggered a bewildering mixture of responses, from *Melody Maker*'s 'tremendous force in modern dance music' to the *Daily Herald*'s account of an 'untrained gorilla . . .' who 'might have come straight from some African jungle'. The *Herald*'s correspondent observed as if in self-sufficient explanation that 'the young Jewish element at the back were enthusiastic'. But the pressure to campaign for the authentic originators of the music was coming from one of the dance-band musicians. Bandleader Jack Hylton had brought Ellington over. The dance-band artists were a mixed bunch – immigrants, survivors of purges, inheritors of the music hall traditions, artisans of the business who knew their way through the tunes and the keys like a cabdriver knew the back doubles – they knew a good thing when they heard it. That world – where 'entertainment' was being laced by a 20th century musical revolution from a source considered incapable of serious art – was where Ronnie Scott was headed.

The East End youth clubs were the place to start. The notion of a 'teenager' wasn't invented, so you were either at school, or you were at work, or looking for work, and in the clubs there was the chance to talk to somebody older than you about what it might be like, try to wring out a feasible future from the fantasies of the *Wizard* and *Hotspur*, find out what adulthood meant from somebody maybe six months older over a game of billiards. Clubs like the Stepney and the Oxford and St George's had games rooms with billiard tables, gramophones and records, as well as a dance hall. Kids who could sing stood the best chance of getting a break and a chance to entertain their friends – and maybe even take a step on the first rung to the big time.

Ronnie encountered them all going their different ways in the urgent, self-motivated, adventurous atmosphere of the Jewish community. Sonny Herman, a youth club trombonist, became a rabbi in Amsterdam. Mike and Bernie Winters, youth club regulars, came up through the music halls and variety shows. Vidal Sassoon went to the Oxford and St George's, where Ronnie Scott spent much of his teens. And for Ronnie's father to have been a professional saxophonist was glamorous, but not exceptional. Tony Crombie, the young furrier's apprentice who wanted to be a pro drummer and who formed a lifelong friendship with Ronnie Scott from those days, had a cinema organist for a mother, a drummer for an uncle and a father who was an instinctive, if rudimentary piano player.

To learn to play like a dance-band musician was an irresistible ambition in the early 1940s. The ground-work was hard, but you could buy stock arrangements from the sheet music shops for a shilling apiece and there was no shortage of older kids who knew just that little bit more who could help you along. Sol and Cissie could see that Ronnie was determined to take his new hobby very seriously indeed.

Ronnie Scott had lessons with Vera Lynn's father-in-law, Jack Lewis, who taught the dance-band saxophone from the front room of a house in Stamford Hill. Lewis was a genial old man, anxious to help a youngster as obviously keen as his new pupil. Lewis's own son was a musician, and a succesful one – he had also married one of the biggest names in Tin Pan Alley. Jack was a realist. Knowing what your instrument could do and what it couldn't, not getting fancy ideas, getting the best of that lush, romantic sound that the tenor seemed to be made for, that was the secret. Ronnie made the difficult journey from Edgware to Stamford Hill once a week for six months, and felt he was beginning to understand the subtle potential of the instrument. He was a quick learner, and a good mimic. He had also learned to play 'Honeysuckle Rose', which could get you a long way.

The circuit of Ronnie's existence from school to Jack Lewis's house and back to the East End on Saturdays to the clubs now embraced a London increasingly ripped apart by the war – but still gloriously unthreatening to a child confident of immortality. In the summer of 1941, unsure of his future but by now in love with the silver and gold Pennsylvania tenor, Ronnie left school and got a job in an establishment that seemed to promise a more useful education as his interest in music grew. He went to the Keith Prowse Organisation, the biggest company in London dealing in records, instruments and sheet music.

Ronnie Scott started his working life as a packer in the

basement of the Prowse Coventry Street store but hated it. The staff took pity on him and he was sent to the Kensington High Street branch and put on the record sales desk. He sold a lot of records there, listened a great deal and helped himself to some that ended up on the gramophone in Edgware – one of the few twelve-inch discs that Tommy Dorsey made, Benny Goodman records, the swagger and bravura of 'Sing Sing Sing' by Benny Goodman. Ronnie moved from Keith Prowse to Lou Chester – Dance Band Instrument Suppliers in Soho's Rupert Street, a shop run by an ex-dance-band trombonist. It was a storeroom job again, but by this time Ronnie's rudimentary expertise on the saxophone was beginning to win him occasional gigs on the East End youth club circuit. Dances, weddings and barmitzvahs ensured that a sax-playing Yiddisher boy needn't feel neglected. And there were soon enough of them to ensure that store-clerking for Lou Chester would be the last daytime job that Ronnie Scott would ever need to have.

London was a town bursting with the desire to survive. Entertainment was a therapeutic form of war-work, helping to make every laugh, every moment of euphoria a bigger and better one because it might just be your last. Bandleaders knew it was possible, because they had seen it with their own eyes, that serious revellers could be dug out of bomb damaged houses and still make it to the clubs and dance halls with the dust still in their hair, patched up, determined to put it out of their minds. It was risky for everyone, but if you were a Londoner, you might as well be in a club as anywhere, if you could afford it. Many couldn't, and discontent was rife between poor Eastenders, badly hit by the bombing, and the more fortunate West End.

In the East End, Ronnie was beginning to hang out with kids who were already on the brink of showbusiness, and some of them even habitues of that glamorous underworld of the Soho dives. Flash Winston, a diminutive, fast-talking young drummer was one such, already working the West End and Tony Crombie, the reluctant furrier, would get a taste of the action by carrying Flash's drums to gigs. Crombie himself, a little older than Ronnie, soon began to work, notably in the Bouillabaisse, a black club that presented a mixture of swing-based jazz and calypso music. The West End was the magnet. All the semi-pro, thirty-bob-a-throw gigs on the wedding-and-barmitzvah round would be just treading water compared to the irresistible life of the professional.

They more or less camped out on the club scene. Hanging around those beckoning doorways at night, peering down rickety stairways into seething, mysterious basements, lurking around back entrances. Catching the last tube home, or missing it and spending the rest of the night in the Lyons Corner House, drinking tea, hearing tales of the night's work from one of their number lucky enough to be playing, catching the first train of the morning out to the suburbs. Cissie didn't especially like it, but wasn't going to hold her son back.

That square mile was run on hedonism and fast turnover. Soho then was the nearest London could get to the twilight world of fringe life in Chicago and New York. The licensing laws in these one-room drinking clubs (home for what were usually described as 'bottle parties') were that the clients were supposed to have bought or ordered their drinks twenty-four hours before their visit to the premises. This didn't often happen, but as fast as the police would close one establishment down its organizers would reappear somewhere else. Stark, dirty and run-down in the day-time these dim and smoky rooms at night were a focus for every kind of drifter and square peg who didn't, or couldn't, relax in polite society. London's small West Indian community and the passing black seamen from the docks came in. So too did servicemen on leave with no homes to go to, GIs, crooks doing deals, black marketeers, billiard players, blue bloods slumming it.

And because it was a scene in which so many wired and nervy people, speeding on the ever-present proximity to death were fixing and manipulating and patching up their lives, it was also a scene in which the young musicians, ignored by all but the true fans, perched attentively at the edge of the bandstand, had an immense amount of freedom. The tradition was when you heard the whistle of the bombs that the band kept playing, unless it was *very* close.

With the anxiety and exhilaration, and the long hours,

came drugs. The clubs were like sweetshops; variations of speed and heart stimulants intended for servicemen at the end of their tether, benzedrine inhalers dismembered and dropped into teacups, marijuana. Availability and adventurousness were leading the new generation to experiment with narcotics seriously for the first time in Britain.

London was being forced to change in many other ways. Though the inescapable truth that bombs were no respecter of social class had helped to melt, at least temporarily, the worst of the country's social taboos, others were growing. By the late summer of 1942 the war had brought 10,000 black American servicemen to the country. They had received a mixed reception. MP Tom Driberg had asked Winston Churchill in the Commons in September of that year 'whether he is aware that an unfortunate result of the presence here of American forces has been the introduction in some parts of Britain of discrimination against negro troops.'

Churchill seemed hardly impressed. The argument went as far as a confused and rambling Cabinet discussion in which the Colonial Secretary, citing the case of a black official on his own staff now barred from his regular restaurant at the insistence of white American officers patronising it, elicited this response from Churchill: 'That's all right. If he takes his banjo with him, they'll think he's one of the band.'

The Cabinet eventually endorsed a document that made fitful noises about deploring discrimination against the defenders of democracy but nonetheless discouraged 'close contact with English home life or English women'. Some American soldiers were even reported to be separating West Indian troops with white wives as they walked along the streets. Black soldiers – from the States and from the colonies – found themselves in many cases fighting for a strange kind of freedom.

The social stigma of contact between black troops and local women created a vacuum rapidly filled by prostitution. Clubs like the Fullado, where Tony Crombie played some of his first engagements, was a marketplace for transactions between black American servicemen and white hookers. But musicianship was a passport that worked everywhere.

The clubs were a haven for both the Archer Street professionals and the feverish congregation of teenage hopefuls following them around. Where the early evening would pass to the accompaniment of the clink of decanters in the plush restaurants, the steady swell of small talk, the after-hours low-life atmosphere would be a tumult of noise, blandishments, importunings, marijuana, indulgence, survival, villainy. The club owners welcomed the informality of the musicians' way of working, bustling around Soho all night with their instrument cases, dropping in and out of clubs, playing a few tunes, moving on. After all, if somebody wanted to turn up and play for the hell of it, they didn't expect to be *paid* as well.

Ronnie Scott, fifteen years old, began to be one of them. He knew his grip on the music was tenuous and that playing the tunes was more complicated than it sounded, but you had to start somewhere. And as he began to come to the West End regularly, he began to look out for Jock, wondering what his father would be like, watching the pavements from the top decks of buses, knowing that this was his patch, glimpsing this or that elegant, grey-haired figure, a man with an instrument case, wondering how he would start a conversation if he found him.

One night toward the end of 1942, in a sudden rush of renewed confidence about his understanding of the tenor Ronnie Scott came 'up West' and asked for a blow with a band run by drummer Carlo Krahmer. In a musical world where most of the practitioners were hard-bitten professionals with no time to lose and little appetite for fancy ideas that wouldn't pay the rent, Krahmer was both a pro and an enthusiast. In almost every respect he was a rare bird in an environment already crackling with eccentricity.

Krahmer was approaching thirty at the time, a prolifically busy performer and bandleader making the best of the hyperactive club scene by running bands at many of the London dives and legendary for operating several gigs in the course of the same night. What made Krahmer's negotiation of this obstacle course more remarkable was that he was almost totally blind, unable to drive and obliged to hump his kit around the city on the buses and the underground, though he partly solved the problem by leaving bits of innumerable kits all over town. He was a one-man recycling agency for every kind of commodity that London's now substantially itinerant population was anxious to convert into cash – ties from America, records, musical instruments. He was rumoured to be the first exponent of the art of hi-hat playing amongst the city's drummers, a 'cymbal man' in a forest of snare-drum rollers, rimshot artists and boom-boom bass drummers reared on the swing players. And he had courage. In an altercation one night with the owner of the Gremlin Club, Krahmer was felled by the aggrieved party despite warnings from the proprietor's minders that his opponent couldn't see. Krahmer was spirited, energetic, and loved music – and he was a jazz enthusiast. He had a collection of thousands of records, he kept pace with what was happening in America, and he had an ear for musicians who grasped the spontaneous and invigorating spirit of jazz. Krahmer later recalled that first encounter with the East End boy with the tenor, remembering, 'He's got a good sound, this lad; sounds promising, make a note.'

Ronnie Scott began knocking on the door of the music profession at a time when its composition was changing. The great age of the big bands was passing, partly as conscription and the dwindling male population was knocking serious holes in the lineups, and partly because of their immense overheads in a time of austerity that was to last well into the 1950s. The shift meant that the balance imperceptibly moved in favour of the younger players. The old bandleaders needed their services, fancy ideas or not, and if the youngsters wanted to stretch out, play a little more jazz, then maybe they'd have to be allowed to.

The war slowly turned in the direction of the Allies. Those journeys on foot that Tony Crombie and Flash Winston had taken, walking back from the West End clubs in a blazing city, amidst rubble and falling masonry, firemen at the end of their tether, walking where a cab couldn't take you because the roads were impassable, were becoming a dimmer memory. Londoners felt united, and felt the beginnings of optimism too, though not everyone could share it. A local young black woman, Amelia King, from Stepney, was refused entry to the Women's Land Army in 1943 because the farmers had objected to her colour. Future tensions in the nation's life lay mostly dormant beneath the massive obligation of the war.

Ronnie Scott's love affair with the music business grew. It wasn't simply the music alone, the seductiveness of what it might be like to unpack the Pennsylvania on the bandstand in front of an expectant audience, warm it up, adjust the reed, run effortlessly through the hits; it was the atmosphere, too, and the people.

Ronnie Scott ran into Krahmer again in 1943. The band-leader had remembered. He recalled that kid with the big sound, quick on the uptake, that raw recruit with consuming enthusiasms, awkwardly but determinedly borrowing what-ever he could from all the tenorists he could hear. Krahmer was running the house band at the Jamboree (later to become the Flamingo) in Wardour Street. His six-piece was short of a saxophonist for a fortnight, a delay in the arrival of the replacement.

'Would you like the gig?' Krahmer asked the young Ronnie Scott. The boy enthusiastically accepted but told the older man that his playing wasn't in the same class. He didn't know the tunes, he wasn't familiar with his horn in all the keys, he was certain he'd be lost at the first chorus.

Krahmer wasn't bothered. He liked Ronnie, and could see something of Jock Scott, whom he knew slightly, in the young man. 'All you've got to do is sit there with the saxophone,' Krahmer said.

The first night at the Jamboree was a dream come true. The atmosphere was irresistible. When he had to play, it was only to busk his way through 'Don't Be That Way' or 'Tea For Two', bits of blues. Much of the time, when players who really knew what they were doing would arrive to sit in, Ronnie Scott would get off the bandstand and listen, fasci-nated. Since Carlo Krahmer was a devotee of jazz and knew the music well, to be in his band and to hear him talk was to make contact with what this unruly and spontaneous music was really all about. But what counted most was that for a fortnight, at sixteen years old, having played his horn for only eighteen months, Ronnie Scott knew what it was like to be a professional, in a professional's band, working in a West End club.

He went back to Edgware and told Sol and Cissie all about it. He was in the music business. He was following Jock. Cissie knew that this handsome, humorous, strong-minded boy with an increasingly freewheeling confidence about his future was beginning to resemble uncannily the father he could barely remember. She knew that they would meet, sooner or later.

2 / Sweet Bird of Youth

Monday afternoon in Archer Street. At the height of business you couldn't see a square yard of pavement between the elbowing, badgering, gossiping men. Familiar faces struck familiar deals. Newcomers mingled, carrying instrument cases to demonstrate their speciality. It wasn't unheard of for drummers to be found edging anxiously around the pavements with a snare tucked awkwardly under one arm. Interrogations, investigations and pleasantry were indistinguishable – 'what are you doing?' . . . 'where are you working?' The hairdresser, reared on the rag-time bob, was shortly to have to reconstruct his business to accommodate the 'rebop' cut. Relaxation was the pin-table in the tobacconist's, the one where a gig king (master-fixers of the one-night stand) would take up office in the doorway. In the cafe, the proprietor would watch his more expansive customers anxiously while one would mime a solo, instrument in the imagination, teacup loosely swinging from a fretting finger. From the newspaper shop, where *Melody Maker*'s London sales were at their best, men in box-shouldered, double-breasted suits would crane for a glimpse of a Windmill Girl in the dressing rooms across the street, until shooed unceremoniously away by the white-haired old lady whose premises were ritually put to this unelevated purpose. Sharp operators disinclined to overspend developed an elaborate system of codes by which to economize on the inexperienced and avoid rocking the boat with old hands; 'it's worth two' they would say within earshot of the glowing young performer just hired on the expectation of nothing more – while the three fingers spread on the thumbed lapel of those double-breasted jackets would carry the real message. It was a world of commerce, not art. It was the nerve-centre of a service industry.

Sometime in 1943, Ronnie Scott got to hear of the departure of a tenorist from the house-band at the Bouillabaisse. The bandleader there was Clarry Wears, a rhumba-king in the West Indian community, and Tony Crombie was already a drummer at the club. Ronnie Scott got the job.

The club was run by a man called Bah, an athletic-looking black man who had lost half an ear in a fight. Many of the young white musical community played there, including the trumpeter and pianist Denis Rose, an artist sophisticated beyond his years, musically immensely knowledgeable and an acquaintance of Crombie's from Sundays spent in Petticoat Lane, listening to the latest American imports on the record stall. The music didn't require jazz, merely a vigorous rendition of dance tunes but Ronnie Scott's powerful sound suited the repertoire. And from Rose, he began to appreciate subtleties of construction in music that he had never known existed.

The Bouillabaisse didn't last, closing down and then reopening as the Fullado, another black club that encouraged jamming and a loose interplay of musicians. Crombie continued to be house drummer. Ronnie Scott took to visiting Archer Street regularly. And when he was seventeen, and in the midst of debating with himself the pros and cons of a dance-band job at a local venue, the Cricklewood Palais, Cissie at last arranged a meeting for Ronnie and Jock in an Archer Street café. The passing years had deadened much of Cissie's resentment and her desire to help her son, the musician, overcame what remained. Jock was respected in the business and well-connected. He might be able to help.

Ronnie was initially shy at the meeting with Jock, who turned out to be exactly as he had imagined him, a youthful, expansive man with humorous eyes, dapper and sharply dressed. Jock could see a headstrong quality in his son, the qualities of a natural musical leader that might emerge too soon for his own good. 'Just read the parts,' Jock urged Ronnie, as he explained about the Cricklewood offer. 'Don't try to lead the saxophone section.' Jock was convinced Ronnie was too impulsive for his own good, but the boy found his father's earnest solicitations ironic, since as yet he could barely read music.

The scene was thick with heroes. At the Potomac in Piccadilly and the Princes in Jermyn Street – both plush West

End restaurants for those on more than a footslogger's pay –
two bands alternated sets since the establishments backed on
to each other. One was run by the Belgian trumpeter Johnny
Claes, the other by a glamorous local tenorist Reggie Dare.
Dare was everybody's idea of the romantic dance-band
musician, a towering blond with a lush, sensuous sound on
ballads, a swaggering, grandiloquent manner of delivery and
considerable popularity with women – which reputation, in
those days, led to earnest speculation about aspects of the
Dare expertise not immediately apparent on the bandstand.
He seemed everything a musician ought to be. What was
also striking was that the tenorist allowed the musical fortunes
to rest heavily on his own shoulders – it was unusual for a
saxophonist to work simply with a piano trio at the time, since
saxophone solos were still regarded in dance-band circles as
attractive as long as they were brief. Dare had a big influence
on Ronnie Scott.

Johnny Claes was a different kind. He had a powerful
trumpet sound, fierce and vigorous, not unlike Roy Eldridge.
But a combination of musical farsightedness and all-round
adventurousness made his band a suitable receptacle for
transfusions from the emerging revolutionary jazz on the
other side of the Atlantic. For a start it was a nine-piece – a
remarkably flexible unit within which to combine the
colourful harmonic possibilities of whittled-down big band
arrangements with the alertness and manoeuvrability of a
small group capable of highlighting soloists. When the
Potomac opened, Ronnie Scott went to audition for Claes.
The Belgian made as striking an impression as Reggie Dare
had done. He drove fast cars (he was later to drive at Le
Mans, and Ronnie Scott came across him in a Grand Prix car
at Silverstone only a few years later). He went to Jermyn
Street for his haircuts, had family money, believed that the
presentation of the band was half the battle – which last
axiom powerfully influenced Ronnie ten years on when he
was to be a bandleader himself.

The Belgian was friendly, and liked the young man's sound.
But, as with Krahmer before, to move from an orthodox
dance-band setting to one in which at least some experimenting with improvisation was possible, was a big step.
Ronnie Scott continued to be adrift with the materials,

couldn't read the scores and was trying to get by on sheer instinct and whatever devices used by the professionals he had been able to pick up.

It wasn't long before the chickens came home to roost. Claes invited Ronnie Scott to sit in at the Potomac for one night, get the feel of the band. The experience shattered the young recruit's confidence. The music was too complicated and busking couldn't carry him through it. Claes gave him every chance but knew it was too soon. 'Look, son,' the Belgian said. 'You sound fine, but we really need someone who can read.' It was a disappointment but Ronnie Scott knew that he was right, felt that if anything he was being let down gently. To escape from the club that night was a profound relief.

There was always the palais-band world to fall back on. He took a job at the Royal, Tottenham, in a band led by Les Ayling in which Diana Coupland – later to move into acting – was the vocalist. The clothes-conscious Ronnie Scott hated the work because it required the wearing of little grey bolero-jackets he knew that Crombie and Rose would crack up at. He kept his connections with the East End.

Since the end of the 1930s, the opportunity to hear Americans live in Britain had disappeared because of a Musicians' Union ban, a state of affairs that lasted well into the 1950s and which occasioned considerable sectarian argument in the music business. The diverting of shellac into the war effort similarly meant that the release of new records was all but drying up by 1944. The effect of these obstacles, though, was to make the mystique of the American music scene all the more compulsive. In that year, Scott and Crombie went to Levy's record store where there was by now a tiny recording studio. An ad hoc assembly of unevenly talented friends recorded 'My Blue Heaven' and 'Blues in C Sharp Minor' on an acetate. The second side was actually a blues in C minor but Harry Morris – the garrulous, wisecracking street-hustler who never played an instrument but loved the company of those who did – preferred the inflections of being able to announce on the recording: 'from one kind of blues to another, "Blues in C *Sharp* Minor" in a mid-Atlantic accent.

The next year, a chance with Johnny Claes came again. The band was leaving the West End residencies and going on the road; it needed a new tenor player for the job. Ronnie Scott was now faster, more familiar with the repertoire, more flexible in the keys. Claes was impressed and took him on. The alto player Jerry Alvarez took the young man aside. 'You'll learn a lot from Johnny,' Alvarez said. It had been his recommendation that had persuaded the Belgian to listen to Ronnie Scott a second time.

The band was a revelation. Not least because of its drummer Freddie Crump, an extraordinary black vaudeville performer from Richmond Virginia who had come from the States with the Blackbirds show in the early 1930s and stayed on. The possessor of an elephantine drumkit unplayable by any of his contemporaries, hand painted in white with black diamonds on the bass drum, the perspective entirely out of joint, Crump's antics were a showstopper. He could produce a deafening, monsoon-like noise from massively overweight cymbals that other musicians swore blind were made from the conning towers of submarines. He could play the kit as well with his back to it as facing the right way round, his heel producing a thunderous barrage from the bass drum. He could produce percussion sounds from the kit, from his teeth, from just about any solid object in the possession of nearby members of the audience, and he would sign off what he called his 'ack' by skidding face-first across the stage on his stomach, diving into the orchestra pit and emitting one last celebratory crash on the pit-drummer's cymbal. Though a minute figure of slender build, Crump could generate the sheer volume of a man twice his size, and he delivered it all with an unflagging affability. Tony Crombie was astonished by him. He never revised his original opinion that Freddie Crump was one of the most startling drummers he ever heard anywhere, even including Buddy Rich.

But, strong as the musical impression of Claes' Claepigeons was, the impression of life on the road for a seventeen-year-old was stronger. Ronnie Scott had never left home for long periods before, never been able to consider the freedom and uncertainties it offered. He grasped the former whole-heartedly and made that first tour one of the most exciting periods of his career. Road life for bands involved intermi-nable hours spent in buses and trains, on journeys made harder by the war years, but the circuit of tatty hotels and

digs run by landladies who had in many cases been looking
after touring musicians for years was new and full of promise
to a young player. On a stopover in Middlesbrough, Ronnie
discovered with his landlady's daughter just what it was that
the older musicians had joked about and sometimes been
anguished, chastened, maudlin about. In the front room, by
the coal fire, Ronnie Scott discovered sex and a pursuit in
life that would be as exhilarating, treacherous, revealing and
unpredictable as the affair with the Pennsylvania. Denis Rose
was practising Harry James licks in the next room, his face
contorted with the effort of playing James' vibrato. As the
fire died down, Rose quietly played 'You're A Long Long
Way From Home'.

The Claepigeons featured several of the sharpest and most
restless and inventive young players on the local scene, many
of whom had heard enough of what was going on across the
Atlantic to be certain that the musical future for the palais
bands would offer them little. Claes operated more of a jazz
policy than was commercially sensible at the time, but he
would experiment endlessly with new ways of selling it,
through stunts with lighting, routines for his players,
anything that would make the band stand out.

But though Claes was a man with a feeling for the future,
he could not visualise it as clearly, nor understand the forces
at work in its music as instinctively, as the second trumpet
player, a guru in the making, Denis Rose. He had drawn
Tony Crombie into clubland, transcribed the 'V-discs' taken
from American broadcasts and reduced them to simple principles that his less sophisticated colleagues could make sense
of.

Rose, a tall, cadaverous figure with enormous bush-baby's
eyes in a bony face, looked an artist from the crown of his
Homburg to the tips of his two-tone shoes. He was a sharp
operator, too, like a cross between a faintly imperious Fred
Astaire and an extra from a Hollywood gangster movie. He
was the total jazz musician in a jazz world so short of real
resources and insight. But he was a West End lad too, a
survivor, at ease with the criminal fraternity, an inspired
teacher, a listener to anything and everything and consistently and helplessly himself. Musically he had a mixture of
intuition and natural comfort with structure, and a fund of

knowledge culled from hour after hour spent in the Keith Prowse record shop, from opening time to closing time playing disc after disc, making notes, making sense of it.

Rose had been called up for the Medical Corps but deserted and hid out in Soho. Though the war was winding down, Germany had saved its energies for a last counter-punch. In the winter of 1944, a new call-up had demoralized those who remained at home, but the Allies were badly shaken by von Runstedt's off-the-ropes campaign at the Battle of the Bulge. The newspapers were once again full of tales of survival and of the not-so-fortunate being pulled from those prim terraces in which the V1s and V2s had suddenly and unceremoniously ripped a hole, like an abruptly extracted tooth. A musical hero who had left a resounding impression in London during his work in Britain with forces bands, Glenn Miller, went missing in an aeroplane and was never found.

The following year, though, genuinely promised that long-imagined deliverance and both citizens and soldiers could only hope, in that offhand manner of those for whom risk had become a daily condition of life, that fate wouldn't deal them a bad card so near the end of the game. For Ronnie Scott, Denis Rose and the young London jazz musicians in search of inspiration, the closing months of the war found them thrown ever more closely into the company of the visiting Americans in the forces bands, which were exempt from the Ministry of Labour ban, and the experience made them all the more curious about the culture on which was founded so many of their dreams.

The Americans were only too aware of their impact. If the Benny Goodman band had included even half of the Americans who came through London during the war years claiming to have performed with it, it would have been big enough to perform a Mahler opera. But the Sam Donahue band – an American forces unit under the direction of a hardened pro – was the real thing. Donahue and his musicians would congregate at a Soho club called the Nuthouse, where Carlo Krahmer had a band.

Sam Koontz Donahue was a tenor saxophonist and occasional trumpeter from Detroit, a man four-square in the tradition of big-band swing who was later to front a recreation of the Tommy Dorsey band in the early 1960s after the trombonist had died. Donahue never went down in the record books as a giant on his instrument, but in the jam-packed atmosphere of the Nuthouse, to an audience only distantly familiar with the finer points of jazz, in an ambiance of servicemen and hookers stumbling on doctored whisky, the American could unleash the first romantic surf-rolls of 'Body and Soul' and the club would be in reverential silence. For the Donahue sidemen, a long way from home, finding music an invaluable calling-card and the status of their home-land a surefire hit with the local players, there was no shortage of reverence. Men like Denis Rose, Ronnie Scott, pianist Tommy Pollard and guitarist Pete Chilver, would congregate at the all-night Lyons Corner House in Coventry Street, meet the Americans there, learn ideas from them.

One London club that became a magnet for the musicans among the American population was the Feldman – later to become the 100 – in Oxford Street, an establishment opened by a wealthy businessman for the benefit of his infant prodigy sons, familiar to Ronnie from the streets of Edgware, where they were local heroes. Victor Feldman – nicknamed Kid Krupa – was playing the drums with professionals when he was only seven, and the club was frequently a showcase for his remarkable talents. The club also attracted Americans on tour like Art Pepper, then an unwilling military policeman, a clean-cut, Italian-looking twenty-year-old and a gifted and precociously experienced saxophonist who had already cut his teeth in Benny Carter's band and worked with legendary figures like Dexter Gordon whilst still in his mid-teens.

Pepper had been playing in a military band at a conva-lescent centre for injured servicemen on their way back to the States or back into the war. He was the epitome of what all the London musicians wanted to be, a sophisticated messenger from the music's homeland, and his poise and fluency on the alto astounded Ronnie Scott, who one night made a point of congratulating the young Californian on his artistry. Pepper simply said, 'If you liked that, you should hear Charlie Parker.' As yet, Parker was just a name.

In the late spring of 1945, the press carried two items of information that were of particular interest to Ronnie, Sol and Cissie. In April, *Melody Maker* ran an item on the Claes band that concluded, 'Scott is undoubtedly one of *the* tenormen of the future'. And the following month, the same paper, under the headline 'Ring Dem Bells', hurled itself unselfconsciously over the top. 'In this great symphony of discord', the editorial ran, 'VE day is the coda. Soon, the drums of war throughout the world will be stilled and the calm fluting of a peaceful theme will be stated for the world orchestra to play. May it be in full harmony.'

The Second World War was over. Cissie had shaken Ronnie awake on the morning the news broke. It was a public holiday, everyone was heading joyously into town to celebrate. Ronnie had marched around Trafalgar Square with his saxophone, Denis Rose accompanying with the trumpet. Then the two of them had gone to the East End. Because of the docks, the streets of their childhood had taken a merciless hammering. Relief would be sweeter there than anywhere else in town. In Petticoat Lane, a piano was wheeled on to the street. Ronnie Scott and Denis Rose performed with it while Flash Winston played the drums and the East Enders danced around them. The Royal Family visited the East End to pay its respects.

London had turned into one gigantic party. Outside Buckingham Palace and in Downing Street they thronged in their thousands. At West London magistrates court, Mr Paul Bennett declared 'It goes against the grain to send anyone to prison today.' Londoners slept in the parks that night, or danced home to the suburbs in the early hours.

Through the war, people had grown used to hearing music brought to *them* – in the factories, in the forces, at public concerts. These changed expectations brought a boom in the dance-halls. And after the invasion of American culture that had hit the nation since 1942 young people wanted jazz.

Of all the younger bandleaders likely to benefit from the emergence of a new and more demanding audience, the best equipped was undoubtedly Ted Heath, a trombonist who had made a mark with the outfit of the dance-band specialist Geraldo but had broken away when offered the chance of a series of BBC broadcasts with a band of his own. He soon proved he was capable of fronting a highly commercial blend of the power, noise and drive of the thirties swing orchestras, but by adopting a policy of hiring front-line instrumentalists with a leaning toward modernism, his band had a contemporary edge that made it a surefire hit.

Ronnie Scott was keen for a change. On his nineteenth birthday he found himself already respected in his profession, making money, the apple of Sol and Cissie's eye, still living in that tiny bedroom overlooking the garden in Edgware. But he was pulled between the conflicting demands of the showbiz appeal of making it big and the knowledge that there was so much to do on the saxophone that he had hardly yet begun. In Heath's band there were two musicians who knew Ronnie Scott's playing and understood his potential. One was Jack 'The Beat' Parnell, a spectacular young big-band drummer and the nephew of impresario Val Parnell (the music press of the day would describe him in terms like 'ace-high drum stylist') whose party-piece solos were a climax of the Heath act. The other was Dave Goldberg, a Scottish guitarist growing increasingly fascinated by the sporadic news of jazz revolutions taking place in the States. Both men recommended Ronnie Scott to Heath, and the young tenorist went to audition for the band at the BBC's Aeolian Hall.

Ronnie Scott was still convinced he didn't know enough. Much of the development of his playing had come from the making of instinctive connections improperly understood. He was not a fast reader of music, and he had an appetite for personal embellishments that might not endear itself to a man as preoccupied with the finished product as Heath clearly was. But that day the fates were with him. He handled Heath's brash, pumping arrangements comfortably and the bandleader's lead altoist Les Gilbert had no hesitation in going over to his boss and giving the young contender the nod.

Ronnie Scott found his acceptance hard to believe. Even more of an unexpected gift was Heath's offer to him when he went to the band's Albermarle Street office to sign up. 'The money will vary from week to week', Heath began ominously, 'but you'll never earn less than £20 a week.' In 1946 it was a fortune. And since the band was in growing demand throughout that year, often they earned much more. They performed for a movie, *London Town*, with Kay Kendall. They did a Scandinavian tour, the first time Ronnie Scott had ever been out of austerity England – breakfast on a continental railway, unlimited supplies of eggs, butter, three different kinds of bread. Being a snappy dresser in a business where appearances counted for a lot, Ronnie Scott took to spending much of his new found wealth on made-to-measure suits in the latest square-shouldered American styles, shirts bought from musicians coming off the transatlantic liners. More conservative columnists on *Melody Maker* were soon to bewail the takeover of the music business by 'rainbow-tied, over-dressed, super-padded, loud-talking and queerly tonsured youths'.

If the war had changed the music that people wanted to hear, and the places they wanted to hear it in, it had also changed the way musicians wanted to conduct their business, a controversy that would affect the way that Ronnie Scott himself would work only a few years later. The brilliant young trombonist George Chisholm had written in *Melody Maker* toward the end of 1945 that the age in which the maestro was entitled to expect unquestioning obedience from musicians was passing, and that the music business would have to accept the fact that more and more young players would want real participation in the policies of the bands they played in, or break away and run cooperative bands from scratch. Ted Heath had replied to Chisholm in December 1945, saying that he believed in consultation with musicians but insisted on the right to run his own show. The Labour government that had unexpectedly come to power in 1945 had unquestionably been carried on an awakened hope that the loosening of British class divisions that had been glimpsed during the war years could be legislated out of existence in peacetime. Growing restlessness among young musicians was merely a reflection of the mood of the times, a recognition that they were in an industry like any other, and helping to make their employers rich. And as they hung out together in the corner-houses and after-hours joints, listening to records at Carlo Krahmer's flat in Bedford Court Mansions, the germ of independence took root.

But the war still had a trick to play.

Early in Ronnie Scott's stint with the Heath orchestra, he got his call-up papers for the army. By this time, any appeal that the institution might have had – the opportunity for adventure, to leave home, to strike out in the company of kids his own age – had been replaced by his opportunities as a professional musician. But the music business knew ways around what seemed like inescapable obligations to more respectable citizens. The Heath musicians knew a doctor in West London who could take care of such unpleasant surprises. In exchange for £20, the physician – a shambolic figure with a fastidious Alec Guinness voice, horn-rimmed glasses, cigarette ash covering his lapels – would maintain that a patient he had only just met was known to him for years, and moreover clearly unfit to travel on account of nervous stress, or persistent headaches. Schooled by an expert, Ronnie Scott went to an RAF medical examination at Uxbridge, wearing Dave Goldberg's enormous overcoat down to his feet, unshaven, speeding on benzedrine. If the medics knew he was a leadswinger, they didn't let on. Now that the war was over, the really dedicated layabouts were more trouble to the forces than they were worth. Ronnie Scott was rejected for service with His Majesty's troops.

But with Ted Heath's troops, he felt at home. Not that the music particularly appealed to him, but the lifestyle was luxurious and players like Goldberg and Parnell were obviously interested in experimentation. Moreover, Ronnie Scott was in love. He had met a girl called Joan Crewe, pretty, dark and unassuming, a builder's daughter from the Caledonian Road, at one of the Monday night shows that the Heath band used to perform at the Hammersmith Palais. She was sixteen, Ronnie was eighteen. He was a star in the most popular dance-band in the business, and he became her first lover. Soon they were going everywhere together. She joined the jazzmen's circle, as anyone in a relationship with one of them was more or less obliged to do, trying as best she could to keep up with the relentless nightlife, the long hours in the all-night cafés, and still get to work the next morning. She taught Ronnie Scott to dance, expressing astonishment that someone who could play dance music so naturally hadn't a clue about where to put his feet. They would practise jiving, Ronnie stopping and starting in unexpected places and insisting in response to Joan's perplexed look, 'There's two more beats yet before the end of the bar'; her laughing and saying, 'We're dancing. Beats in the bar have got nothing to do with it.'

Ronnie Scott never took Joan to meet Cissie and Sol. Though Cissie didn't make as much of an issue of it as some Jewish mothers Ronnie knew, she wanted him to marry a 'nice Jewish girl'. But Joan's parents liked Ronnie, found him funny and charming and were impressed by such early success. They wanted the couple to marry too, couldn't really see, as the relationship grew and was clearly the most serious partnership in the young lives of either of them, why they didn't formalize matters. Ronnie had money and prospects, Joan had been at work from the age of fourteen; they were obviously deeply attached to each other but Ronnie distrusted the idea of marriage, and when Joan became pregnant the couple opted not to go ahead – a recourse that for a woman frequently amounted to the price of a sexual relationship in those days of unreliable birth control. 'I didn't regret it,' Joan would say later. 'It takes two to tango. But I knew I couldn't go on like that forever.'

The affair lasted for most of the next decade, though its conclusion would be stormy, and for the first time in his life break Ronnie Scott's confidence in the certainty that things would always pan out all right. Nothing that ever happened in the household under the care of Cissie and Nana Becky had ever made him doubt it.

The Heath band used to play Monday nights at the Hammersmith Palais, Ronnie Scott getting the spotlight on a solo rendition of 'I Surrender Dear', played in a hybrid style of the broad brush-strokes of the swing-era tenorists and the more complex and ambiguous variations of the modernists. This was a method much used by popular American saxophonists like Charlie Ventura. Parnell had frequently talked about forming a breakaway band of his own, and one night at the Palais Heath asked Scott if he had been invited to join – and if so, what his answer would be. The young man said he would go if Parnell wanted him, and then bit his lip. Heath was not really the kind of man to whom you could make such casual declarations. The bandleader looked momentarily aggrieved, but said nothing more. It was risky to take such a gamble. Over half the Musicians' Union's 4,000 members had no regular employment at the time, and certainly wouldn't consider lightly relinquishing such a prestigious job as Heath's. For the moment Heath bided his time and Scott continued to be one of his star soloists.

Dave Goldberg shared a flat with fellow-guitarist Pete Chilver in Phoenix House, a rabbit-warren of tiny apartments above the Phoenix Theatre in Charing Cross Road. The two men had become obsessed with the fragments of material that had been finding their way out of America, and Chilver in particular was making rapid headway at developing the guitar style of Charlie Christian – a young swing-band musician who had been a star soloist with the Benny Goodman orchestra, pioneered revolutionary techniques for the new electrically-amplified guitar, played rapid single-note solos like a saxophonist and made sensational use of fast chord-changes to add rhythmic drive to the band. Christian had died of tuberculosis five years previously and had barely recorded, but the work of the young New York musicians developing a musical antidote to the swing orchestras in which they were obliged to find employment rang a bell with British players resigned to doing exactly the same. Goldberg and Chilver made friends with two black American artists – L. D. Jackson and Cornell Lyons, 'The Businessmen of Rhythm', then performing a song-and-dance act at the London Palladium – who had brought over with them some of the latest American recordings. From Jackson and Lyons, they heard stories of the 52nd Street nightclubs and thought of them as Mecca. London had been lively during the war years, but nothing like this. Even Paris, a city already regarded by many black American artists as something of a natural home because of its relaxation about race, seemed better endowed. After all, the French discophile Charles Delaunay, visiting London after VE day, had asked *Melody Maker*'s Max Jones: 'If I'm here for only two or three days and say "Take me to a place where I can hear English jazz" what will you do?'. Jones had not been able to find a reply.

One January Sunday in 1947 Ronnie Scott, Tony Crombie and Pete Chilver, with the bassist Lennie Bush and Laurie Morgan (a fast-developing young drummer who had first met Ronnie in the Fullado Club during the war) were at Carlo Krahmer's Bloomsbury flat for one of his informal record sessions. Art Pepper's hint to Ronnie Scott two years before that there was a musician at work in the States who had magically made sense of all the half-grasped visions and dammed-up energies of the dance-band players had simply lain fallow, pushed to the back of his mind by the excitements of life with Claes and Heath in those crowded years.

This was to be no ordinary session at Krahmer's. One record in particular was to be the focus of the afternoon's listening, though as it was unpacked from its functional brown-paper sleeve and placed on the turntable, Ronnie Scott could not yet know that the impact it would leave with him would last a lifetime.

Out of the crackle and hiss came a sudden unison chorus. The tune they were playing seemed familiar, though far more urgent and driving than the idiom from which it had been borrowed and reforged. It swung easily, with that arrogant relaxation Ronnie Scott already knew as a trademark of American jazz. And at the end of the ensemble introduction arose something utterly different, a sound so bursting with life and tumultuous harmonic complexity as to be unlike any kind of saxophone playing Ronnie Scott had ever heard. It was a seamless flow of variations on the chords that never faltered, never repeated, that were perfectly shaped, shot through with the blues, and which would clearly have swung irresistibly even if all the soloist's colleagues had left the studio.

The tune was 'Red Cross', a Savoy release of a last minute adaptation of the chords of 'I Got Rhythm', cut to fill out the closing minutes of a three-hour recording session intended to be a vehicle for the unspectacular vocal talents of Art Tatum's guitarist Tiny Grimes.

The alto saxophonist was Charlie Parker.

'The history of jazz can be told in four words. Louis Armstrong, Charlie Parker.' (Miles Davis)

'Bird was like the sun giving off the energy we drew from.' (Max Roach)

Overnight, life with the Ted Heath orchestra felt like standing still. At the time, and subsequently, many musicians of Charlie Parker's generation reported that hearing Bird – or Yardbird – for the first time was like suddenly being able to recollect a dream, being able to see the clinching move in a game of chess, suddenly finding a locked door swing open before you. It was the solution to a problem that most young commercial musicians had only been able to experience as restlessness and frustration. It was not the music of the future, it was the music of its time, and when Ronnie Scott heard it he knew it was the only way to play.

He began, tentatively, to introduce as much of Parker's approach as he could understand into his own work. Denis Rose began to dissect the mysteries of the Americans' transformation of chord patterns, constantly transcribing the music of the new idiom from discs on to paper. Frequently the basic shapes of the old swing-era hits were used – 'I Got Rhythm', the underpinning of 'Red Cross' was a favourite. Another Parker composition 'Scrapple from the Apple' was the same tune, but with a counter-melody, taken from 'Honeysuckle Rose'. The music was a remoulding of everyday tools of the trade, but it had a sardonic edge too, a way of saying to the old bandleaders: 'You think you know this, but you don't.' Where the most basic chord structures would have sufficed for bar after bar of a dance tune, the revolutionaries would substitute new and complex variations that would add subtle colourings to the harmony even though not departing from the same tonal centre.

A name evolved for this new music. It was a piece of onomatopoeia taken from its jittery, headlong momentum. It came to be known as bebop, or rebop. The latter version was the one in widespread use at the end of the 1940s.

In the winter of 1947, soon after that astonishing day at Carlo Krahmer's, Ronnie Scott's new inspiration led him to try one of Parker's favourite – and most conspicuous – devices on the Heath orchestra's version of 'Stars Fell On Alabama'. He played part of the solo in double-time, not entirely sure of the technicalities but carried ahead by sheer exhilaration, the notes flying and ricocheting over Parnell's steady swing. After the show, Heath was clearly furious, though he would rarely express his resentments face to face.

A little later, Ronnie Scott committed the cardinal sin of missing a Heath gig. The band had been playing in Liverpool, and the musicians took the night train back to London for the following day's show. Ronnie Scott was in adventurous mood, however. He had never been in a plane, suddenly fancied the idea, and booked into a Liverpool hotel overnight, planning to come back to town in style the next day. Snow-storms closed the airport, and the twenty-year-old Scots tenorist Tommy Whittle was quickly brought in to take the missing saxophonist's place. Shortly after, Ronnie Scott received a brief note from his employer, informing him: 'Your services are no longer required.'

Whittle took Ronnie Scott's place. *Melody Maker*'s report on 22 February 1947 ran: 'Scheduled to join Ted Heath on Monday next is atomic tenor-stylist Tommy Whittle. He takes the place of the outstanding young tenorist Ronnie Scott who leaves Heath this week.' But alternative work, at least of the bread-and-butter kind, wasn't hard to come by. The same paper was announcing very soon after Ronnie Scott's arrival in the band of trumpeter (and later DJ) Jack Jackson at Churchill's, a West End restaurant, 'He is now in the kind of environment where he can take all the solos he wants.' It wasn't strictly true. Pete Chilver and Laurie Morgan were in the band, and the musical direction was more chaotic than deliberately open-minded. Jackson was something of an old style bandleader, as was his co-leader and pianist Hamish Menzies, and disliked the tendency of bop-influenced players to carry their variations on the theme through an apparently endless string of choruses. Jackson and Menzies were also frequently fatigued by the generous hospitality of Churchill's, and would on occasions be simultaneously instructing the band to play completely different tunes.

Scott and his friends also played with pianist Jack Nathan's band at the Coconut Grove in Regent Street, but the work was mostly dull and enlivened only by whatever attempts they could make to live it up in the West End. There were a lot of biking fans amongst them – bassist Joe Muddell, saxophonist Harry Klein, and Ronnie himself, who had a Triumph Tiger 100 – and the monotony could always be broken by racing the machine around the backstreets in the intervals. It was during this period that Scott and Johnny Dankworth would visit the White City to watch the speedway, and Scott took Lennie Bush to Silverstone to see Johnny Claes race. Ronnie Scott would head the Tiger 100 home to Edgware in the small hours, often sitting on the pillion so that he could lie flat toward the handlebars like a racer. One night he got home to find he'd negotiated the whole trip with the propstand lowered, which could have spun the bike like a top if he had cornered at a tight angle. He sold it not long afterwards, convinced that going fast on four wheels had to be a better bet.

The young pioneers knew that they were floundering, and wasting valuable time. All that they could make of the new American genre was a rough approximation to its superficial qualities. They knew little of the culture from which it had come, little of the city that had become its home and whose vibrations it apparently reflected, and the union ban meant that there was little prospect of hearing its high priests anywhere in Britain. The only loophole was the technically American territory of the airforce bases, a device increasingly used after the war, but the camp entertainment officers were unlikely to start booking such a fierce underground music as Saturday night entertainment. The Londoners knew that there was a shot in the arm to be had for their condition, just a plane ride away. They were all out there, on every street, in every club. Dizzy Gillespie, Charlie Parker, Lester

Young and Coleman Hawkins, back to back, side by side in the basements of brownstones in the heart of non-austerity, unrationed, superhip New York.

Laurie Morgan chatted it over with Chilver one night in the bandroom at Churchill's. Chilver said, 'Let's go over there, see what it's all about.' Morgan was so keen he sold his car and his drumkit to raise the fare. He already had some contacts in the States – a woman he'd known in London had married a GI and left with an open invitation for him to visit the West Coast, and Americans he'd met on tours of the airforce bases had promised the same. Tony Crombie and Ronnie Scott decided to go under their own steam and Crombie got in touch with the editor of the *Musical Express and Accordion Times* (a forerunner of the *NME*) to see if the sale of some articles on the New York scene might help to subsidize the journey, and arrange some accreditation that might help with reluctant club managements into the bargain. The paper accepted, but Ronnie Scott hadn't saved much of the proceeds of his prosperous year with Heath, so the journey's overheads had to be pared to the bone. The cheapest flight to New York was by Icelandic Airways – a method that took the best part of twenty-four hours.

But the exhaustion of the journey evaporated quickly. It was an experience as different from everyday life as arrival on another planet. It was New York just the way it had been described those nights in the Coventry Street corner-house and the Feldman Club, but bigger, faster, noisier, wilder. Hershey bars, pineapple drinks, butter, modern shirts, ties. The 52nd Street buildings frequented by, as Ross Russell described in his biography of Charlie Parker, 'studios for sign painters and silkscreen operators, mail order drops, import-export concerns run out of a hat, offices for private detectives and teachers of the piano and saxophone, darkrooms shared by photographers who prowled Broadway nightclubs with Speed Graphics.' Scott and Crombie took a cab, dumped their luggage at a rundown Greenwich Village hotel called the Marlton on West Eighth Street and took off into town.

In the days that followed, New York willingly gave up its secrets – tensions and euphoria so much bigger than getting a three-inch down-page write up in *Melody Maker*. If they weren't playing they were listening or arguing or shouting,

going around in bunches singing riffs and licks. They encountered dedication and devotion in the States. They found that
Bird was the Messiah. People would turn in jobs to follow
him around the country. They recognized that Bird's *sound*
– quite apart from his lightning fingering and tumbling
phrasing – lay in gospel music and the blues, though much
of its sophistication was drawn from that musical genius's
absorption of European orthodox devices. It seemed to be
the voice of an emerging consciousness in post-war youth.
But above all, it was the sound of *America*. The sound, the
hum, the background noise of Edgware or Stepney, or even
Archer Street, was not the same. As the older generation
had always said, New York seemed to be the place with no
traditions and no respect. But it was a place where, over the
preceding century, most of the experiences of the world
seemed to be pooled. The result was dynamite.

The New York jazz clubs tended to occupy basements or
abandoned ground floors of the brownstone. They were
popular and they made money through fast turnover – many
would be cleared of punters every half hour or so and a fresh
audience brought in. Of all the 52nd Street joints, it was The
Three Deuces that impressed Ronnie Scott the most. It was
a cramped establishment at the Sixth Avenue end of the
block, run by a young Jewish jazz fan called Sammy Kaye.
Three cards spread in a poker hand was its emblem and
adorned the entrance. The doorman was a man called Pinkus,
who wore a commissionaire's peaked cap and an overcoat,
and always smoked a cigar. 'Come on in folks. You're just in
time for the complete performance,' he would say to all and
sundry, regardless of what stage in the show it actually was.
When Ronnie Scott met Pinkus years later he was still doing
the same job and insisted: 'I'm the happiest man in New
York.'

Charlie Ventura's band was in residence on the Londoners'
first trip, featuring the idiosyncratic trombone playing of a
regular Woody Herman sideman, Bill Harris. Ventura, a
white swing saxophonist in the style of Chu Berry, had found
a modern context for the idiom in a music halfway between
swing-band sensationalism and bebop. Harris's trombone and
the crackling drumming of Dave Tough were enough to
convince Scott and Crombie that they were in the right town.

But it wasn't simply the music, it was the venue, and the street. Even in the war years, when Sam Donahue had entranced the regulars at the Nuthouse, London had never supported such establishments dedicated to music lovers as these.

Scott and Crombie went everywhere in pursuit of music, knowing that their financial affairs made time short. They heard Duke Ellington's orchestra playing the interval show at a Broadway cinema, and Lionel Hampton's band at the Apollo Theatre in Harlem, where they were the only whites in the crowd. They got themselves photographed on the balcony of the Roseland Ballroom, looking like a couple of apprentice Mafia hitmen. They heard the full impact of the new vocabulary of jive-talk, a language developed to shut intruders firmly out, just as the growing fashion for wearing dark glasses at all times of the day or night was designed to do. To be hip, or not, that was the question. If you could dig the music, you were probably not a square. If it was a knock-out, or even a gas, you were halfway there. Laurie Morgan developed variations of his own. 'Steady, Waldo' he would insist, to no-one and for no reason in particular.

Morgan and his non-playing partner Harry Morris (who had a photography arcade in Soho, looking like Chico Marx behind the unwieldy 1940s cameras) had gone out to the West Coast and Morgan remained there for months, much of the time at the Westlake Music College. He met Bird fans there, played the records long into the night with them, discs on which the Parker solos were worn out with repeated listening. Scott and Crombie meanwhile were running out of their meagre funds within a fortnight. A visit to Ronnie Scott's Uncle Phil, one of Jock's brothers who worked at a tailoring establishment called Bond Menswear on Times Square, won them an evening of elaborate tales of the money he made as a gambler, but when it came to trying to secure a loan it was a gamble he wasn't remotely interested in. They had an open ticket back by sea, but the Cunard office told them that the boats were booked, that they would have to wait at least ten days. The two lived on coffee and doughnuts for the rest of their stay in the magic city, came back broke and sleeping rough on a shabby vessel called the *Ernie Pyle*. But the unglamorous return journey couldn't take away the taste that New York had given them. They couldn't wait to go back.

When Ronnie Scott got back to London, in the mid-summer of 1947, it was to find that *Melody Maker* were to sponsor a public recording session at the EMI studios on Sunday 29 June, and that 128 British musicians had been given the job of choosing a series of pick-up bands made up of what they thought were the leading musicians of the day. The tenors were Ronnie Scott, Reggie Dare and Tommy Whittle. Ronnie Scott performed with Woolf Phillips on trombone, Pete Chilver on guitar and the lyrical blind piano player George Shearing, later to become an expatriate to the States. *Melody Maker* recorded that Scott wore red, white and blue socks, which it took to be a patriotic gesture following his absence abroad, and played an elegant rendition of 'Blue Moon'. He also performed alongside Dare, his old hero.

Only five years had passed since the days when he would have found this company awe-inspiring, but America had changed all the young players who had made the trip, and many more were shortly to follow. For Ronnie Scott, absorption of new influences was happening so startlingly fast that it was in danger of swamping the musician he might uniquely be. America had been the experience that completed his transition into a natural front man for his musical generation, a change that he would always rigorously deflect himself but which was increasingly acknowledged by those who came into contact with him. It could only be a matter of time before he would lead a band of his own. Jock Scott's cautionary advice that he shouldn't try to run the show had applied to young men of an era gone by. The war had ensured that.

Opportunities quickly came, sooner than Scott could have anticipated. The *Queen Mary*, refitted after its emergency service as a troop-ship, and now as spanking new as on its maiden trip, was due for its second honeymoon on the Transatlantic run and needed musicians to form the several bands booked for the voyage. Drummer Bobby Kevin was forming one that Scott was invited to join. Johnny Dankworth was its young alto player, a twenty-year-old as well, from Highams Park in Essex, who had started his musical life as a classically trained clarinettist, developed an interest in jazz and impressed Art Pepper as one of the most promising musicians emerging in Britain on those nights at the Feldman Club in the last year of the war. Dankworth took to the alto after hearing Charlie Parker's 'Cherokee' on the BBC's 'Radio Rhythm Club' and had quickly made a reputation for himself on the unfamiliar instrument. Playing dance-tunes for the revellers on the *Queen Mary* was a small price to pay for the trip.

When the boat docked in New York the response was sensational. But for the musicians on board there was something quite different to celebrate, a return to the fountain-head of the music that obsessed them. Laurie Morgan knew that the ship was bringing those pilgrims of his outward journey. He didn't bother to go to the quayside. He went instead to 52nd Street, stood outside The Three Deuces and waited. Within an hour, the Englishmen rounded the corner. Scott, Dankworth and their friends were raring for another tour of wonderland. Kansas Fields, a drummer who had befriended Morgan, took them into Harlem. It was as if Ronnie Scott had never been away and England seemed like a country you could hold in the palm of your hand. Dankworth offered his cabdriver a $20 bill for a two-dollar fare, and the driver vanished in a cloud of dust. Not all that needed to be learnt was musical. Ronnie Scott did half a dozen trips in the *Queen Mary* during the following year. One night at The Three Deuces, Miles Davis and Charlie Parker were together, the young trumpeter nothing like the faltering and hesitant newcomer of the recordings of the period. But it was still a one-way traffic. The impasse remained and back in Britain the union ban still held out. Dizzy Gillespie's Orchestra was due to visit at Ted Heath's invitation in March 1948 but wasn't allowed to play. Music press headlines of the gig in Copenhagen declared: 'Tense, neurotic – but it's DYNAMITE!'

The future steadily beckoned nonetheless. Early in 1948, Denis Rose and Harry Morris opened a short-lived club called the Metropolitan Bopera House and Rose led a sextet there with Ronnie, Dankworth, Tommy Pollard, Lennie Bush and Tony Crombie. For Ronnie Scott, it was now one of a host of opportunities.

Whatever the circumstances Scott was always bursting to play, and would frequently appear as a guest soloist with local rhythm sections as well. There was a refuge for converts to the bop school such as Ronnie. From October 1947 he had become a regular performer in the band led by Tito Burns, who had made an unusual mark as a bebop accordion player. Pete Chilver and Denis Rose were in it and the band was a convenient hiding-place for them. Burns was a bebop fan at the time but later lost confidence in being able to make the music commercial. Stoke Newington Town Hall was one of the band's ports of call. In Jack Oliver's semi-pro band, which played there too, was a stocky, humorous, easy-going young tenorist called Pete King. Scott and King met only fleetingly then, but formed a lifelong friendship in the years to come.

When the young players came back off the boats they were, as Laurie Morgan would later put it, 'boiling with music'. The problem was that there weren't many places to let off steam and if you did it on somebody else's time you were likely not to be asked back.

One solution to the problem was a tatty basement called Mac's Rehearsal Rooms in Windmill Street, opposite the Windmill Theatre. Since it was so close to Archer Street, the young boppers would book the room on Monday afternoons and pass the word – surreptitiously – that playing would be going on there for anyone who fancied a little animated relaxation. Regulars there were Scott and Dankworth, Tony Crombie, Laurie Morgan, trumpeters Hank Shaw and Leon Calvert, bassists Lennie Bush and Joe Muddell, pianists Tommy Pollard and Bernie Fenton, altoist Johnny Rogers, with occasional visits from Denis Rose. It rapidly became a focus for jam sessions. And it caused a stir in Archer Street. Laurie Morgan would keep his drumkit in the Piccadilly left-luggage office, available for use at the drop of a hat. Secret messages would be passed. And when they would *play*, curious faces would pop round the door, anxious to listen or blow.

So much curiosity was aroused that the ever-vigilant Harry Morris convinced the others that a golden opportunity was being missed by neglecting to charge the listeners for the privilege. Events at Mac's Rehearsal Rooms became more frequent. Both Dankworth and Crombie led bands there, augmented from time to time by visitors. And because there were ten musical 'regulars' plus Morris who became the unofficial manager and doorman, the establishment was dubbed the Club Eleven on its opening on 11 December 1948. It was the first club in Britain to present a solely jazz repertoire, with a policy devised entirely by a co-operative who were also practitioners themselves.

At night, life in the club was the perfect definition of bop style and exclusivity. Much of the dress was American-derived, for those who could afford it the drape-back jackets with aggressive shoulders, pegged cuffs, Billy Eckstine shirts, lurid ties with a big knot. Cecil Gee's was the outfitter that specialised in the genre. Detractors of the lifestyle – and that was almost everybody not intimately involved with it, in particular the adherents of the new cult of traditional New Orleans jazz that was gathering steam in South London and Kent – spoke disparagingly of it all, sardonically dismissing the hipsters and their 'fruit salad' ties. There were plenty of other variations. Corduroy bags were popular, prismatic sweaters, waistcoats. Thelonious Monk's polka dot bow tie was also much imitated (the two bands at the Club Eleven had red and blue ones respectively) and so were cravats. Music was for a more sophisticated young clientele – taking unintentional advantage of the fact that the university popu-lation at the end of the 1940s had reached an all-time high, partly due to the return to studies of forces personnel back from the war.

There was nothing prepossessing about the environs of Club Eleven in those days. Visitors descended the wooden staircase opposite the Windmill to find themselves in a cramped, low-ceilinged room with a bandstand at one end, dimly lit by bare bulbs. A few battered sofas passed for the soft furnishings. But on a good night the Club Eleven could be the wildest place in town. Young women who became regulars at the club developed their own styles of dancing to cope with the breakneck tempos of bop, twirling elegantly at half speed, backs straight, so much more graceful and cool than the jitterbuggers that had preceded them, twirling dirndl skirts.

On either side of the Atlantic, the real meaning of the bop revolution was coming out. Where Louis Armstrong's generation had become minstrels, gone along with racism and risked the label Uncle Tom, Lester Young's had sidestepped it and become Bohemian, retreated into another world with its own language; it had its own mores, its own mode of dress and – as it turned out – its own kind of self-destructiveness in the bid to pretend that second-class citizenship was a status that could simply be shut out. But the beboppers were different. The sound of the music was fierce, urgent. Pioneered by Kenny Clarke, bop drumming took the beat from the bass drum to the top cymbal (a more varied, flowing and sensuous approach) and left the bass, tom toms and snare for accents. The metronomic quality of the swing bands was thus disrupted at a stroke. Thelonious Monk, an unorthodox and untrained pianist soaked in gospel played percussively with his fingers splayed, used unconventional chords, and welcomed bop as a way of freezing out strangers, musicians who, by his standards, weren't really serious.

In early 1949 Ronnie Scott and Johnny Dankworth got a chance to sample Parker's work at even closer range. They were invited to the Paris Jazz Festival where many of the heroes would appear. It was a golden opportunity, but Scott nearly didn't make it because he discovered that his passport was out of date whilst waiting at the airport to leave. 'We can let you through,' said the customs officer to Ronnie Scott's frantic imprecations. 'But you'll never get off at the other end.' Like the invitation to join the army, official obstacles were not always impenetrable to musicians who knew the ropes and were used to finding the short-cut. In addition it was the unstable post-war period, a time of black-marketeering, graft, of knowing the right person to call. After some urgent telephoning, Scott eventually tracked down a passport official after hours. It only took a fiver to get the passport problem fixed and shortly after that the young saxophonist was heading for the appointment he was already a day late for – and discovering into the bargain that the delay had put him on to a plane heading into the worst storm he was ever unfortunate enough to fly in. By the time Scott, altoist Johnny Rogers and Dankworth found themselves in a small club in St Germain, busking gently through a semi-bop repertoire, all the effort started to be worthwhile. The word came that Charlie Parker was on the way. When he arrived – a large, shapeless young man with a fitfully angelic look that dissolved the startlingly world-weary impression of his shambling appearance – he was followed by an entourage of acolytes. He joined the band, borrowing Dankworth's alto, roared through an uptempo bebop standard, insisted on playing no more choruses than his fair share to the chagrin not only of those who had come to watch, but to those other performers on the stand who knew that he was light years out ahead.

Dankworth discovered, standing next to Bird, that the saxophonist at close range was an unbelievable phenomenon. He rarely needed a microphone, could – as bandleader Thad Jones once remarked – 'seal every crack in the wall' with his sound. Ideas tumbled from him, even when he was exhausted, in bad mental shape, or drunk. Dankworth said later that his alto felt as if it had been transformed by Parker's handling of it, seemed as if it had somehow been 'opened up'. Parker's wind came up from the gut, his stomach muscles could be made so taut that he could resist a full-blown punch in the stomach as if it were a playful tap. Moreover, he had served an apprenticeship with the orchestras, was used to making a big impression in big venues.

It was what made Jock Scott, who sporadically bumped into his son in Archer Street, able to admire the boy's achievements without always understanding them. 'Come down to our club one night,' Ronnie urged him. 'See what it's all about.' 'Maybe I will,' Jock would reply. 'But it's not really my cup of tea.' He never came. People outside the charmed circle found bop hard to take then.

Ronnie Scott's admiration for the long-lost father who had suddenly come back into his life, a man who was widely respected in the same line of business, might have been expected to help propel the two into the closeness they never had a chance to find in earlier years. But it was harder for them to establish a rapport precisely because they were doing the same work – but in such profoundly different spheres. The difficulties presented by a difference of generations that both men could experience musically as well as socially were brought sharply home to both of them over the episode of the *Caronia*.

The *Caronia* was a cruise liner booked for a round-the-world trip in December 1949, starting with a series of journeys between New York and the Caribbean. Jock invited his son to join the band. Ronnie, attracted by the idea of such an exotic journey and by the thought of getting to know his father better, agreed. The ship sailed from Southampton to pick up its passengers, then from New York to the West Indies and back. Jock Scott was a veteran of the boats. Nevertheless, he found that the bad side of London life could not be entirely forgotten simply because the circumstances had suddenly become so idyllic. On his first night on the *Caronia* the head barman invited him to his cabin for an introductory drink. 'What's your name?' the sailor asked. 'Jock Scott.' 'Pleased to meet you. Makes a change from these fucking Yid bandleaders.'

Jock was perfect for the work not least because of his voluminous memory for the repertoire. But though he was an irrepressible joker, he had his diffident side too, as did his son. The *Caronia* cruise was for millionaires, and there was only one class – first. The sidemen repeatedly asked Jock to make more of an effort to persuade the customers into parting with tips – 'They're good bungers, these people,' Jock's partners would say. 'You have to chat them up a bit.' 'I don't want to do that,' Jock said. 'It's not my style.' They talked him into it eventually. When one of the Americans next approached the bandstand to request a tune, the bandleader took the direct approach. 'Do you want the five dollar version or the twenty dollar version?' Jock eventually enquired. He was reported to the purser for it.

Ronnie got bored with the journey and argued with Jock. Apart from the band's bassist, Pete Blannin, and Harry Conn, a saxophonist, the other musicians were all of his father's generation. Congenial company to Ronnie Scott then meant people to whom you could talk about Bird, and Diz, work out licks and complicated chord substitutions, share what had become an obsession. The only virtue of the trip had been the opportunity it offered to visit the New York clubs once again. Ronnie had sat with Harry Conn one night listening to Charlie Parker and a gentler white West Coast saxophonist, Lee Konitz, and the older man had said of Parker: 'I prefer the other guy.' 'You'll learn,' Ronnie had said pityingly. 'You'll learn.' But when the *Caronia* docked again at Pier 90 on the return journey from the Caribbean there was a letter from Joan Crewe, expressing boredom in no uncertain terms about spending a life waiting for him to return from one far-flung assignment or another. It was the final straw. Ronnie decided to cut the job short and come back to London. This was no pushover. Becoming a bandsman on the boats required a good deal of bureaucracy – technically the musicians became merchant seamen for the duration of the cruise, and were answerable to the purser. Ronnie Scott swung it with a piece of typical East End ingenuity. He got his mother to send a wire from London saying 'Grandmother dangerously ill – come home at once.' He then went across the quays to the *Queen Mary* which had also docked, and was due for its return trip to Southampton. He looked out Ray Feather, the tenorist on the *Mary* and buttonholed him with the tempting question: 'How do you feel about going round the world?' Feather accepted. Then came the persuasion of the officers on both ships, and his father. Jock didn't believe a word of it and was furious at what he believed was a combination of deception and ingratitude on the part of his son. They had a heated argument about it. The confrontation exposed all of Ronnie's ambiguous feelings about his father. 'My mother's told me all about you' he eventually shouted at Jock in desperation. 'You can't have a go at me.' It wasn't even true. Cissie had never spoken disparagingly of Jock. Ronnie regretted that outburst for the rest of his life. As for Jock, he even wrote a letter to the Musicians' Union in London demanding Ronnie's expulsion from it, but tore it up on second thoughts. Ronnie was headed home.

Back in London, Club Eleven continued to be the place to be. It wasn't only a jamming and socialising haunt for local artists, it was a refuge for visiting musicians as well. Benny Goodman, Ella Fitzgerald and the composer Tadd Dameron all appeared in the audiences there. Dameron was returning a social call that Scott and bassist Pete Blannin had made on the *Caronia*'s stopover – when Miles Davis had arrived in the middle of the evening, taken one look at the two Londoners and growled to Dameron 'what you doing with these ofay cats?' Club Eleven was so popular, and yet so poorly endowed, that a move was becoming increasingly necessary. In April 1950, they took a bold step, shifting the premises to number 50 Carnaby Street, one of the hippest thoroughfares in London, as it was to be again a generation later. It moved into a disused night club, as shabby as Mac's, but somewhere to take the music to, and somewhere to hang out. The doorman was Charlie Brown, a black ex-boxer and the landlord of 10 Rillington Place. Musicians and fans ate there, played cards there, drank there, played.

New premises occasioned a stab at a new policy. It might be worth trying to get some of these visitors to actually perform at the club to raise its profile. But the whole subject was a minefield at the time. The legendary saxophonist Sidney Bechet had illegally played a concert in defiance of the Ministry of Labour's and the Musicians' Union's strictures in November of the previous year and the men who brought him in were convicted and fined in June 1950. Nevertheless, it might be that if they got a big fish on the hook, they could then argue the pros and cons later.

They sent an invitation to Billie Holiday. The optimistic young proprietors of Club Eleven sent an offer for $250 for a week's work and accommodation. But, unfamiliar with the manoeuvrings of the Tin Pan Alley fixers, they didn't mention the air fare. They didn't know the singer's whereabouts either and sent the request care of the West Coast jazz magazine, *Downbeat*. Knowing Lady Day was involved with hard drugs, they dropped various hints in the letter that all her requests could be met, but the invitation fell on stony ground.

Meanwhile, Ronnie Scott continued to grow as a British musical celebrity. The saxophonist, and subsequent writer, Benny Green later recalled the day at Sherry's Ballroom in Brighton when he was playing his first professional assignment and discovered that Ronnie Scott had arrived on the balcony of the hall. Scott's reputation poleaxed Green. The saliva dried up in his mouth and he couldn't play a note.

Back in Club Eleven, trouble was brewing. Ever since the war-years and the American 'invasion' drugs had been part of the scenery. For those living from day to day in a city under attack, edging along a highwire of nerves it was bad enough. For musicians in that world driven moreover by a boiling desire to crash through a sound barrier to the sublime, to play as well as their heroes, to play as well as each other and better, some drugs were an aid to stamina and concentration. They could, as Laurie Morgan put it, 'shorten the distance between not knowing and knowing something.'

Much of this trouble centred on the pianist Tommy Pollard, who was one of the first of the circle to become dependent on hard drugs. Pollard was a brilliant musician, who understood the circumlocutions of bebop as well as Rose did and was genuinely 'inside' the music rather than simply covering its mannerisms. But he was already a heroin addict and the habit was leading him toward the fringes of the criminal fraternity.

The night of 15 April 1950 promised nothing out of the ordinary. Ronnie Scott was playing Parker's 'Now's The Time', with his eyes closed as was his frequent habit. When he opened them he found that the club was teeming with police. A massive uniformed sergeant almost blocked his vision.

The scene was chaotic, close to farce. Ronnie Scott had cocaine in his wallet, and no chance whatever of disposing of it. Denis Rose headed frantically for the stairs, hoping to escape from the club's lavatory window, and Scott saw him again a few seconds later being carried back down by two policemen, his feet not touching the ground. Rose already knew he was in big trouble, since his unannounced absence from military service wasn't going to go down well with any other charges he might find himself up against. Everyone was carted away to Savile Row.

The night in the cells was rescued by the fact that many of the miscreants were jailed together, and that Flash Winston was present, who treated the whole thing as an opportunity for a solo performance. It had been helped on its way by the behaviour of the police themselves, obviously unfamiliar with the intricacies of this kind of arrest. One of the confiscated items was a matchbox used for smoking roaches, with a scorched hole in it where the joint would be inserted. The station sergeant had declared authoritatively to a constable, to the barely concealed hysterics of the accused, 'See that. They sniff it through there.' Mario Fabrizi, the Italian Cockney who was to win fame as Corporal Merryweather in *The Army Game*, was one of those in the cell as well, and similarly took the opportunity to milk the situation. Winston took to crawling across the cell during the night and banging on the door, croaking 'Water, water!' They all found it hard to believe that they hadn't been suddenly abandoned in the middle of a Marx Brothers movie.

When the case came to court the following morning, it suddenly looked more serious. The magistrate knew nothing about the jazz life, or about jazz clubs, and seemed to feel that he was standing between the nation's moral future and the schemings of a collection of dangerous subversives. 'Musicians and Seamen in Early Morning Raid' trumpeted the *Evening News* in alarm. 'Police Swoop on a Soho Bebop Club!'

Sol and Cissie had been petrified by the news and realised the music business had changed since the dance-band days. They distrusted the obsession with America and the idols that Ronnie and his friends had chosen to follow, but they still trusted him. They knew he wasn't a drug addict. He had tried heroin and it had made him so sick, vomiting and struggling for breath, that he had thought he was going to die and swore never to touch it again.

For Joan Crewe, it was different. Through the circle of musicians, she had already encountered the drug and took to it, as she later admitted, 'like a duck to water.' It could blind you to feeling, make you indifferent to sadness, preserve the euphoria of the nightlife, the energy of the music, the anarchic originality of the company, long after your natural reserves would have run out.

She had tried to keep it from Ronnie, but it was a hard habit to hide. When he found out, he would repeatedly examine her arms to look for the marks and she would try to cover up by using the same point over and over again. 'Marry me and I'll stop using drugs,' Joan said to Ronnie one day. 'Stop for three months and I will,' the musician replied. She didn't and couldn't. Ronnie Scott had even gone to Caledonian Road police station to ask if there was anything the law could do.

Joan came to the court to meet Ronnie and the others after the case. Uncle Mark was waiting there too. He came over to the girl and asked, 'Are you Joan?.' She nodded, 'Who are you waiting for?' 'I'm waiting for Ronnie.' Uncle Mark twisted the conversation. 'Don't you think it's time you stopped waiting? He's never going to marry you, you know.' Joan was still stinging from that barb when Ronnie Scott and the others left the courtroom. She had never wanted to be Jewish so much in her life.

4 / It Won't Always Be Like This

'Denis thought it was all childish. As the elder statesman, he always thought we were silly, getting stoned out of our minds, thinking we were *God*.' (Laurie Morgan to Kitty Grime, *Jazz At Ronnie Scott's*, Hale, 1979.)

'How do we know that Jesus was Jewish? He lived at home until he was thirty. He went into his father's business. His mother thought he was God Almighty. And he thought she was a virgin.' (Jewish joke)

Club Eleven's landlords were not unfamiliar with the courts. They recommended a lawyer to the defendants, whose case was due to come before Justice Daniel Hopkins at Marlborough Street Court. The rumour that Hopkins suffered from gout came as little consolation. 'Maybe we should fire the lawyer and get a chiropodist,' Winston opined.

When the case came to sentence, it looked bad at the outset, and all twelve miscreants convinced themselves that prison was inevitable. Hopkins' position was ambiguous. On the one hand, he was clearly of the view that any form of drug usage was taking its adherents and anyone who came into contact with it to the brink of perdition. On the other, he was citing the previous good behaviour of all the young men before him, of their education, of the high standing of some within the music business, of their prospects. London's modern jazz scene was obviously a mystery to him, however.

'What's bebop?' the magistrate enquired of the officers of the law.

'It's queer form of modern dancing,' Chief Inspector Brandon of Savile Row had replied.' 'A negro jive.'

'This sounds a queer sort of place to me,' the magistrate reflected. 'A very rum place.'

But in the end it came down to heavy fines, and Ronnie Scott and his partners were back on streets they had come to believe they wouldn't see for months.

Club Eleven closed a few months later. Somehow, the heart had gone out of it and no-one was especially surprised. The explosion of the discovery of bebop was already three years into the past. They had all discovered how much they wanted to play it. But they hadn't yet worked out *why*. Many British musicians of that generation never did.

The players had cut themselves off from the 'peasants'. They withdrew into the nihilistic rebelliousness that characterized the early Cold War years, a disaffiliation common among alienated white youth. They were wild, arrogant, frightening to some in their private languages, hyperactive lifestyle, frequent insensitivity to women who weren't their mothers, aunts or grandmothers, and the breathless obsessiveness of their version of American jazz – a version that possessed very little relaxation. For men like Monk and Bird it was a different story. They, and many of their contemporaries, were only truly themselves in performance.

Morgan and Rose were both unhappy. Morgan thought that there was little *romance* in it. 'In a jungle,' he would say later, 'you can pick an orchid and another one grows while you're watching. In a greenhouse it's much harder. That was the difference between America and Britain.' Morgan thought there was a religious and spiritual dimension to the black American experience that confounded the most sophisticated grasp of technique. He felt that the players in Britain didn't listen to each other sufficiently and didn't, in the end, support each other. Unhappiness with the inheritance of a borrowed culture almost made him give up the drums.

Rose felt much the same as Morgan. After a period of years in which he had been a cornerstone in the development of some semblance of credibility for British bop, he ceased to feel that the jostling for music-business work, and the delicate politics of juggling a progressive music policy with the expectations of promoters and dance-hall managers, would hold out much more appeal.

Some bandleaders grasped the nettle of taking bebop to the dance-halls, and generally adopted a conciliatory stance, usually employing a vocalist to sing the hits when required: Dankworth, Tito Burns, the pianist Ralph Sharon and Kenny Graham – a gifted and highly original tenor saxophonist and composer – all took bop-oriented bands around the halls, though Burns' heart increasingly ceased to be in it; he and his singer wife Terry Devon moved steadily back toward showbiz. Carlo Krahmer was by now acting as a chronicler of the work of his younger colleagues, having established a record label – Esquire – with his wife Greta and an old friend, drummer Peter Newbrook, who had been his deputy in the wartime days when Krahmer had gigs all over town and frequently double-booked himself. As dedicated collectors, they were convinced that a market existed for the new British jazz and recordings made by the independent American companies – neither of which much interested the existing duopoly of Decca and EMI. Esquire set about recording Ronnie Scott and Johnny Dankworth, Krahmer's old vibra-phone pupil Victor Feldman and many other local players – as well as beginning to re-press foreign recordings. The activity brought Charlie Parker, Dizzy Gillespie and Miles Davis to British ears. Esquire even released modern classics by Alban Berg and Schoenberg. The early Esquire releases were through a mail-order record club that sold ten-inch 78s for ten shillings, twelve-inch ones for fifteen.

Krahmer signed Ronnie Scott to the label at the beginning of 1951, and the tenorist recorded extensively through that year. But anyone who had heard him in the Heath days would have barely recognized his sound. The muscular swagger of the Ventura influence, compounded by swing players like Flip Phillips and local heroes like Reggie Dare had mostly disappeared. Ronnie's tone was now delicate, muted, fragile as an alto being played by someone trying not to wake the occupants of an adjoining room.

Though hearing Charlie Parker had been a revelation as a way of approaching jazz, Ronnie Scott had not tried to absorb Bird's technicalities as assiduously as Dankworth. And when a 1948 recording of the Woody Herman band demonstrated

to him the utterly different skills of Stan Getz, a white Philadelphia saxophonist of his own age who had derived his style
from Lester Young, Ronnie was hooked. Out of the rich,
swaying sound of an American big-band at the height of its
confidence, at the end of sonorous, downward-spiralling reed-
section passage, the brass elbowing insinuatingly into it, came
a sound as delicate as a breeze in branches. It was Getz on
the classic 'Early Autumn', playing a brief but gem-like solo
ending in a coda like a flurry of falling leaves.

Ronnie Scott allowed the Getz influence to claim him
utterly, recording tunes like 'Too Marvellous For Words' and
'September Song' for Krahmer two years later with that light,
airy sound, the notes blown like bubbles gently pushed into
space. The ease with which the saxophonist absorbed
influences had much to do with his effortless affinity with
swing and the art of inflection that in jazz transformed the
often rudimentary materials inscribed on a stave into music
of vibrant beauty. As with the unerringly accurate
impressions of movie stars of the day with which Ronnie
Scott entertained his colleagues, he had no trouble mimicking
anything he could hear as a player either. The knack won
him many things – regular occupancy of the 'top tenor' slot
in the music-press polls for being what amounted to Britain's
very own stand-in for an American, the admiration of his
colleagues and the fans. But even in those days, deep-seated
lapses of confidence would grip him. Coupled with that early
ascent to the top of the music-business tree that seemed of
such ambiguous appeal to squarer pegs like Denis Rose and
Laurie Morgan, the path to finding an original voice for
himself on the instrument was that much harder.

In April 1951, Scott found himself performing, not in the
adventurous outfit he had anticipated Jack Parnell leading,
but in the pitband of a West End musical featuring variety
stars Tommy Trinder and Pat Kirkwood. The show was *Fancy
Free* at the Prince of Wales Theatre. Considering the number
of sophisticated musicians in Parnell's band, the requirements
of the assignment were like exercising greyhounds in a telephone box. Apart from Scott, Derek Humble, a brilliant
altoist in the Parker mould was in the lineup; so too was Phil
Seamen – a drummer who was to become a legend, both as

a player and as a wild and finally tragic eccentric. The repertoire, two shows a night, was cripplingly banal.

Inevitably, the boredom caused chaos in Parnell's all-star outfit. Trumpeter Jimmy Watson took to escaping through the emergency exit into the pub outside the theatre, and for him the stint developed into a desperate bid to break a record of his own making, the ordering and consumption of a pint and return to his seat in the space of a 12 bars rest. Watson would also declare: 'I'm coming up' in a reverberating stage whisper to his colleagues, make his way on hands and knees to the piano, bite pianist Max Harris firmly in the leg and make his way back. Later in the run, as a variant on the exercise, the saxophone section would stop him returning as the cue for the brass entry drew ever nearer.

All this horsing about was bound to get its come-uppance. The brass section had taken to firing paper pellets at each other from the mouthpieces of their instruments, Seamen responding by increasing the firepower to a catapult. One night Trinder bounded blithely onstage for his solo spot, a mixture of gags and song and dance routines that had been his trademark from vaudeville days. On the cue of his catchphrase 'You *lucky* people,' his act was thrown into disarray by the impact of a missile from the orchestra which the comedian was hard put not to take personally. The musicians kept their jobs, but only just. The show ran for over a year before the Parnell band finally did what its members had been hoping for – it went out on the road. Highlight of the show was the drum duet between Parnell and Seamen. It was on this tour that the real quality of the band for which Parnell had left the lucrative Heath gig could really be heard. Seamen, Humble, Scott and Parnell himself were clearly not simply imitators alone, and the shows played to ecstatic crowds.

High regard for Parnell's outfit won it some prestigious and lucrative work, including acting as Lena Horne's backing ensemble on the singer's tour of Britain in 1952. American singers were not uncommon on the circuit in Britain in the 50s, because they were not covered by the terms of the Ministry of Labour/Musicians' Union embargo. Ms Horne brought with her a pianist, Arnold Ross, who fitted in comfortably with the Parnell musicians both professionally

and socially. Scott and Derek Humble were already enthusiastic gamblers, in the former's case an inheritance from the
East End legacy of Uncle Mark, Uncle Rafie and Jock himself.
They introduced Ross to the clandestine pleasures of the
illegal gambling scene in Britain at that time, it being an era
before the invention of betting shops, the country being
riddled with underground premises dedicated to the cause,
many of them receiving a diplomatic warning phone call from
the local police before the arrival of periodic raids designed
to show the flag. Whilst in Glasgow on the northern leg of
the tour, they took Ross to Billy Bell's betting shop in the
basement of a forbidding tenement building. Ross won a
comfortable sum, which occasioned one of the establishment's
minders visiting the party of musicians and balefully insisting
that they 'come up and see the boss'. They were convinced
that the Billy Bell gambling emporium was going to welsh
on its obligations by the simple means of killing its creditors.
When they got to the proprietor's office, he turned out to be
a jazz fan and an ex-saxophone player. For the rest of the
season in Glasgow, that individual arranged for the band's
more energetic members to be picked up from the hotel in
the mornings and taken to his golf club. Gamblers and jazz
musicians, united by uncertainties and the haziest of career
prospects, frequently felt as if they were somehow the same
breed.

But the only way to get one night stands into the engagement book was to get yourself heard around the country. That
meant radio broadcasts. And the route to radio broadcasts
was commerciality. Radio music was flooding uninvited into
people's homes. There had to be some kind of calling-card.

There were two ways to be commercial. One was to play
the hits of the dance band circuits, since an entirely home
grown repertoire wouldn't work with fans keen for Ameri-
cana. The other was to use a vocalist, preferably one that
looked good as well as sounded good. Most of the band
singers were women, though not all, and it was the palais
band singers of the early 1950s who made it in the early Hit
Parades before the coming of rock and roll. Parnell's choice
for a singer was Marian Keene. But Marian Keene was
married to a tenor saxophonist, Ronnie Keene. The price of
her services was a job for the two of them. Parnell got round

the problem by firing his second tenorist, Pete King. The resulting row changed King's career. Though he had already left Parnell's band to return to the life of a tenor soloist, it changed Ronnie Scott's too.

King was a laconic, squat, deceptively ponderous man with the demeanour of a fight referee, a Cockney who had come up in semi-pro bands in Stoke Newington, and encountered Ronnie Scott as a guest soloist on the one night stands the place used to offer to celebrities on Thursday nights. King had later turned pro, played in the outfits of the popular black bandleader Jiver Hutchinson, British swing veteran Bert Ambrose and the rising young saxophone star Kathy Stobart. He was popular and his treatment at Parnell's hands – even though the bandleader had shrugged, 'There's nothing I can do' – rankled with his partners. On the coach back from King's last gig with Parnell at the Colston Hall in Bristol, saxophonists Derek Humble and Kenny Graham, Seamen and trombonists Ken Wray and Mac Minshull had gone to Parnell, sitting in the front seat of the coach as the bandleaders always did, and handed in their notice. By the time the bus arrived at Alsop Place, Baker Street, the Parnell band was in tatters. King was profoundly moved, and said as much to the press.

January, 1953. 'What the fuck're we going to do?' was the question that opened the New Year for the ex-Parnell musicians. A group of them were sitting in an Archer Street café called the Harmony Inn. It was a popular refuge, particularly when it rained, when every musician in the vicinity would try to squeeze in. Run by a Czech by the name of George Siptac (all the musicians remembered it because it was cat piss spelt backwards) a man who knew little enough about jazz but knew the market value of all the customers. Siptac knew that Ronnie was a rising star. He regarded himself as something of a social service in those unpredictable days, and it wasn't uncommon for him to put meals on a slate that he knew would never be settled for those musicians who were in bad trouble.

The musicians were friends, much of the same age, jazz lovers who had had too few opportunities to present their discoveries to the public in suitable surroundings, and they were open to any suggestion. Ronnie Scott had left Parnell before the row, and was playing in a quartet in which Tony Crombie was the drummer and Lennie Bush the bassist. A combination of that band and some of the ex-Parnell men might lead toward a sound that Scott had banished to the back of his mind since those exciting adolescent days with the Claepigeons. Cooperative bands were much in discussion. Nobody was rich, but nobody's needs seemed markedly greater or lesser a priority than anybody else's. They could share and share alike. Scott recalled Claes' band, how the front line had been so flexible but could sound like a much larger outfit than it really was. But as an admirer of Stan Getz and Gerry Mulligan as well, he liked the idea of a baritone saxophone to deepen the sound. Unexpectedly Ronnie Scott invited Benny Green, a musician he had met the previous year on a one night stand at a Manor House club. Green, another veteran of the wedding and barmitzvah circuit, wrote later that to the average dance band musician this outfit 'smacked strongly of syncopated Marxism' because of the unconventional way that it was run. What was worse for the band's detractors inside the music business, it looked highly likely to clean up. It was a dance-band but a dance-band charged with jazz. Trumpeter Jimmy Deuchar had written many of the arrangements and proved to be a startling original at adaptions of bop phraseology into the smoother lusher sounds of the dance floor.

After the mixed attractions of Club Eleven days, Jock Scott was now unhesitatingly proud of his son. Sol and Cissie were ecstatic. After all, the band were a smart bunch. They wore blue suits with check waistcoats, which Sol – whose textile business was flourishing – had made for them all as a gift. Blue plexiglass music stands with their names inscribed were intended to glow romantically in the backlighting. Ronnie Scott, who was unchallenged in the leadership of the outfit, despite its egalitarian constitution, was businesslike in the public relations. He told *Melody Maker*, 'This is first and foremost a commercial band.' He was understandably nervous of any arty label, knowing Tito Burns had regretfully concluded in 1948 that the public for a purist contemporary band couldn't keep the wolf from the door. 'Idealistic thoughts of playing jazz only are out. The formula will be pop tunes with the melody predominant.' 'I have the last word on musical policy,' Ronnie additionally informed the paper's correspondent, Max Jones.

But before the band was ever really tested on the road, a unique opportunity materialized, an event of such magnitude in the British music calendar as is hard to conceive of now, or even three years after it happened, when a jazz story could no longer be guaranteed front page space in the music press after the coming of rock 'n' roll. Though the Musicians' Union and the Ministry of Labour still held their old line about American imports, fate took a hand that broke the spell.

The winter of 1952/3 brought widespread flooding to Britain, a major disaster for a country trying to haul itself to its feet after the war. American impresario Norman Granz, a tireless promoter of a frequently sensationalized jazz that nonetheless employed the music's greatest originals and provided the world with an opportunity to hear them at first hand, offered his 'Jazz At The Philharmonic' roadshow to Britain as a fundraiser for the recovery effort, in which respect the show would be unaffected by the ban. Granz was clearly the perfect promoter for the job, since his tours were known to gross $5 million at times even in the 1950s. He also paid well, insisted on a racial mix wherever he played and was utterly professional, even down to handling much of the dogwork of administration himself. A star-studded gig was planned for the Gaumont, Kilburn on 8 March 1953. The Musicians' Union and the Ministry of Labour concurred, as long as the visitors would undertake not to play any other gigs. The Ministry would not issue work permits, so concerned were they to emphasize the unique status of the concession, but what they called 'entry notes'. Ronnie Scott was booked to play on the first half of each of two concerts on that Sunday, the day after the nine-piece was due to make its debut on a series of Manchester warm-up gigs, at venues with names like the High Street Baths Ballroom and the Lido Palais de Danse. He would thus find himself playing opposite artists like Lester Young, Oscar Peterson and Ella Fitzgerald, illustrious liaisons not experienced by Britons since those distant, dangerous, glamorous days of the bottle party clubs and the Coventry Street Lyons Corner House meetings of the small hours.

In the music world, the visit of Granz's musicians took

precedence over everything else. Both concerts sold out, and the gigs raised £4000 for the Flood Relief fund. Fans queued for hours for tickets outside the Gaumont State, whose manager declared: 'In 26 years in showbusiness I've never seen anything like it.' A young fan from Willesden, queueing in the early hours, said to a reporter, 'I want to see American jazzmen. I'm mad at the Ministry of Labour for banning them.'

Jazz at The Phil gigs in those days were fast, loud and aggressive. A Ronnie Scott sextet – not the full nine-piece that was currently in rehearsal – with three other local ensembles warmed up the show, Scott himself playing at the top of his form, energized by the momentum of the occasion. Then the Granz musicians began with a slamming version of 'C Jam Blues', set rolling by a furious, thumping beat from Oscar Peterson's piano. From Peterson's first tumultuous chords, Benny Green recalled that the entire mysterious world of jazz that seethed across the Atlantic and which was denied to local musicians and fans alike was suddenly revealed to him. He realized exactly what the ban on American players had really meant to the developing sensibilities of the British jazz players, how the conceptual difference was a gigantic chasm unbridgeable by the most studious attention to tutors and transcription from discs.

It was a sweating, relentless and breathless show, in the barnstorming JATP tradition. Flip Phillips, a fast and boisterous swing tenorist made a powerful impression, at the expense of Lester Young, the real legend, who was by 1953 in serious decline. Journalists were merciless about Young's performance, notably Mike Nevard in *Melody Maker*, who called the saxophonist's playing, 'a pathetic parody . . . an empty shell of a man . . . a whisky drinker who makes a lot of witty remarks.' Young had been in low spirits throughout the visit, refusing to sightsee with the others, maintaining his distance, playing well below his earlier genius, but still the object of immense affection from the British fans and musicians, who besieged his dressing room. 'How's Billie Holiday?' Young would be asked by the glowing visitors. 'Lady Day?' Young would struggle to remember. 'Many moons, no see. Still nice!' 'Hope you'll be back soon,' somebody said. 'I don't think so,' Young prophetically replied. 'Man, I'm so tired.'

Whatever his shortcomings on that gig, Young impressed himself on Scott and Crombie. He was gentle, softly spoken, had a melancholy, spaniel-like face and a strange way of carrying his saxophone while playing, holding it to one side as if trying to hide it – the legacy, it was said of playing in cramped Kansas City clubs where the audience was so close they didn't give you space to hold the horn out in front of you. When he played, his sound was a delicate, mournful, plaintive tremor – though never sentimental or maudlin; it frequently resembled a voice about to break down in tears. Playing with a plastic reed on a battered saxophone with an unsuitable mouthpiece made no difference to one of the most affecting and emotional artists in all the music. Scott went to Young's dressing room where the American demonstrated to him the mysterious 'false fingering' whereby the same note could be created at different positions on the horn, with subtle variations of tonality in each. He opened a pewter pot, the one that had appeared in so many photographs of Young, usually described as containing beer, muttering 'Bells'. Like snakes in a basket, a cluster of joints nestled in the bottom. Ronnie Scott did not then know what was happening to Lester Young's personality and found him simply to be the virtual definition of a bohemian artist, speaking in a language that was not of the everyday world.

The American was hardly into his mid-forties at the time but alcohol and constant marijuana smoking had not only affected his playing and his temperament. His experience of drafting into the army (he was held in army detention on drugs charges for a year) was a period of utter misery for him, leaving him paranoid and hostile. It was also troubling him deeply that the group of white players – led by the young Stan Getz – from the Woody Herman band who had so idolized Young as to attempt to replicate his every breath and nuance were becoming increasingly successful at selling a style that he, as the pioneer, was finding it harder and harder to perform properly. Young died six years later, returning from his self-imposed exile in Paris to New York for his last months. Ronnie Scott had found Lester Young a 'beautiful man', and was a dedicated admirer of the American's innovations. It was not obvious to Scott then that the other-worldly fascination which the black innovators so often seemed to occasion was part of their smokescreen against an unforgiving world – one that frequently killed them in the end.

In some ways the JATP performance came as a shock to British musicians and to their fans. Correspondents wrote to the music papers with varying degrees of disenchantment with their local heroes. 'How my British idols have crumbled' wrote one to *Melody Maker*. Another declared 'three facts stand out. 1) That English musicians should return to their elementary text books and check up on the meaning of the word "dynamics". 2) That Ronnie Scott held his own with both of the American tenor players. 3) That at last I know what the critics mean when they say that we do not possess one real rhythm section in this country.' Granz himself said after the performance 'a lot of your musicians said at our concerts that they could do better musically. Maybe. I didn't hear much of them. I heard some warmed-up Getz and Shearing.'

Nonetheless Ronnie Scott went back, elated and inspired by the experience, to preparing his new band for road life. It had been an exciting week for him. In addition to the JATP show and the debut of his band, he had also won the *Melody Maker* tenor saxophone poll for the fourth time since 1949, clocking up 1,596 votes against his nearest rival, Tommy Whittle, with 472.

For guidance, it helped to remember his recent past. Johnny Claes had been convinced that the right presentation was essential to break the ice of an uncommercial sound. Freddie Crump had been a one-man icebreaker all on his own. The world of Archer Street, so close to the Windmill Theatre, was where budding comics like Peter Sellers, Spike Milligan, Alfred Marks and Michael Bentine went – all fresh out of the forces, their sense of humour honed on a mixture of pre-war music hall routines and the anarchic vision of those who had experienced that mind-warping mixture of absurdity, jingoism, ideals and death in the battlefields. Ronnie Scott therefore borrowed some of that highbrow clown Dizzy Gillespie's act to expand his contribution as the front man – like announcing his intention to introduce the members of the band and then proceeding to introduce them to each other, or stumbling around a darkened stage with a cigarette lighter to recreate the blackout. Declaring: 'And now, an unexpected appearance by Toulouse Lautrec,' lowering the mike three feet and abandoning the stage. It all helped to make the nine-piece band take off, which it did with a vengeance.

'Ronnie had a lot going for him,' Pete King reflected later. 'He was young, good-looking, bright; he had a good dress sense. He was made to be a bandleader.' After the Manchester tour, the band began to travel the country in a run-down bus without a heater or radio, bought from British European Airways and driven by an ex-boxer called Les Bristow. Bristow's antecedents didn't bear too much going into, but the fact that he had been a serious contender for the southern area light heavyweight title had endeared him to Ronnie Scott, a keen follower of boxing as most East End boys were, when Bristow came to the Wimbledon Palais to ask the bandleader for a job as a roadie in the opening weeks. Bristow thought the musicians were soft and tried to instil in them a concern for their physiques, at one stage even attempting to get them to run behind the bus in quiet country lanes. The road manager's ringcraft was firmly brought home to Derek Humble, an irrepressible clown who didn't always know where to stop. Bristow one day landed some of his sporting experience in Humble's face in exchange for the saxophonist's terrifying habit of pulling an overcoat over the head of the driver whilst the latter was piloting his charges at full belt through the hedgerows.

The boredom of road life was dischargeable by any means. With Bristow's encouragement, they took to carrying cricket equipment, and Blackheath was a favourite stopping point in the summer months to pursue their inelegant version of the elegant game, though Derek Humble quickly gained a reputation as a demon fast bowler.

Scott found his gambling to be a handy pastime as well. He would always maintain to the others that it wasn't an obsession for him the way it was to some of those in his family, but it was a serious preoccupation, as members of the band discovered whenever the coach was in the vicinity of an appropriate venue, such as Doncaster. Bandwagon time was also a dimension measured partly by the invention of new vocabularies. Like the recently-demobbed comics working at the Windmill, much of the raw material of the day, extensively drawn from forces humour, was unsurprisingly based on gags about other races, mingled with as much New York jive-language as the players could remember and a good deal of all-round surrealism culled from Marx Brothers movies. Those movies portrayed a world that appeared to function exactly in the way that the musicians perceived theirs – where a small group of sharp operators moved through life like quicksilver while 'normal' people just stood round scratching their heads. Jimmy Deuchar, the quiet Glaswegian trumpeter, was famed for being able to draft out the charts for all the members of the band on a new addition to the repertoire, simply in the time between the outfit's departure from London at nine in the morning and arrival at the venue, and irrespective of whatever mayhem was going on in the bus throughout the journey. They had absorbed both the skills of the Archer Street professionals and at least some of the more iconoclastic inclinations of the American boppers, and they quickly began to be a hit with the public.

The solace of the house in Edgwarebury Gardens was never far off. Many of the members of the band could sense how much it meant to Ronnie. There was always the comfortable figure of Nana Becky, whenever the young bandleader or any of his partners just happened to drop by, always anxious to make them feel at home. 'I just made this cheesecake especially for you, lads,' she would say in the face of the most unexpected visit. 'Come right in and have some.' SSh knew tttthat her grandson was doing well. That was all that mattered.

But it wasn't exactly the kind of success you could contemplate retirement on. Scott brought his old enthusiasm to Green's attention one night in 1953 at the Orchid Ballroom, Purley, in response to an unquestionably modest return for a night's work. The two men were engaged in trying to divide nine into £14.6/5d. Scott announced that he was planning on investing his share of the nine-piece's overall profits in the launch of a jazz club. 'What profits?' Green enquired. 'It won't always be like this,' Scott replied. 'Not every date will turn out to be like this one.' Green mercilessly recorded that in a sense, Scott was right – at the following week's gig, at

Acton Town Hall, they realized £12.10/6d. 'It is not really surprising that it took Scott another six years to realize his ambition,' Green wrote many years later.

This was not, however, a status that was obvious to the BBC, an organization to which all new bands were beholden for the exposure air-time brought. The Corporation auditioned the Scott nine-piece in the summer of 1953 for its jazz shows and turned it down flat. There was uproar in the music press. The fact was that the Corporation just didn't like modern jazz and was doing its best to keep it away from the public. The band, however, was rolling too fast now for this to be much more than a temporary setback.

Though the momentum of the Ronnie Scott Band was impelled by music and youth, it had an enthusiast behind it who understood the hard realities of the music business far better than the performers, however worldly they might imagine themselves to be. The enthusiast was Harold Davison, a would-be music business entrepreneur who had come out of the RAF with a passion for jazz and a conviction that with proper attention to details and some serious professionalism there was no reason why some money shouldn't accrue from it. Davison had started his business as the manager of a popular swing and 'jump' band led by a guitarist, Vic Lewis. He had served with Lewis in the air force and had subsequently taken Johnny Dankworth under his wing as well. With inclinations in the direction of business rather than blowing, Pete King had begun working with Davison during the latter's association with the Jack Parnell band and had even been on a scouting expedition for the manager when *Fancy Free* was being run in in Birmingham, checking on the first appearance with the Dankworth band of a young singer called Cleo Laine. Despite the Parnell bust-up, the splinter group nevertheless had no hesitation about asking Davison if he would represent them as well. He lent them the money to buy their bus, and was an endless source of advice, encouragement, and frequently hard cash over the years to come.

It was sometimes a confusing relationship for an agent, even though he was not much older than his charges. All the unruly energies exhibited by young men and women in the front line of the music of the moment could be difficult to square with the philosophy that the customer, if not always right, has at least got the option to take it or leave it. Davison, like most managers likely to succeed, therefore, became preoccupied with the complications of keeping his artists in line. When the offer came for the nine-piece to play at the Sculthorpe American forces base it seemed like a great opportunity since British groups rarely got the chance to play such venues. Since they were also technically performing on American territory and thus outside the reach of the Musicians' Union ban, Davison also scented an opportunity to make ground for himself and his organization for the days when the blackout would finally be lifted. He was convinced that the squeeze couldn't last forever. After all, that very summer James C. 'Little Caesar' Petrillo, the American musicians' union leader (an ex-trumpeter and another veteran of the Jewish weddings circuit) had proposed an experimental trial period of twelve months in which there would be a free exchange of British and American players. Hardie Ratcliffe of the British Musicians' Union turned it down, arguing that there was no such thing as a free exchange when American musicians were so much more popular in Britain than British players could possibly be in the States. But a dialogue had been opened.

Nonetheless, since forces bases did not provide the luxury of dressing rooms for visiting performers, on its arrival at Sculthorpe the band was obliged to change in the administration offices. Benny Green discovered a supply of the unit's letterheaded notepaper and he and Scott devised a letter to be delivered to the luckless Davison, purporting to come from the unit's commanding officer. It accused Scott's band of every variation of unprofessionalism and offensive behaviour that might be assumed to drive the manager to tearing his hair out. The musicians, the letter indignantly protested, had turned out to be specialists in fraud and larceny as well as the dance repertoire of 1953 and had even made unwelcome suggestions to an officer's wife. It was hardly the kind of behaviour that a host country might be expected to display to its guests and what was the management's opinion of it? They posted the letter on the base that night and went on with the week's gigs. But Pete King got an urgent call to visit Davison's office and found him with the letter in his hand. Davison's world seemed to have fallen apart. Putting it right wasn't the easiest thing that King had ever attempted.

Nevertheless, Davison's instinct to use the forces gigs as an ice-breaker in the transatlantic impasse was understandable. Connections were made then – particularly with the band of Woody Herman. Herman was impressed with Scott and Victor Feldman, going as far as to say to them 'if you ever want to come over to the States and join the band, it would be nice to have you'. Feldman took up Herman's offer two years later.

One night at the Folkestone Leas' Cliff Hall the band discovered Art Baxter. It had experimented with a number of vocalists, including Barbara Jay, a lively and flexible performer who was later to marry the tenorist Tommy Whittle; and Johnny Grant, a relaxed, Perry Como-like singer. For Barbara Jay, who was with the band for the longest stint of all its female singers, it wasn't an entirely happy occasion. Members of the band admitted that the outfit once went through an entire day's auditions of girl singers entirely unsuitable for the band to get a laugh out of their discomfiture with the repertoire as much as anything. Barbara Jay knew she really had no role to play. All the young men in the outfit wanted to play jazz; and they weren't overly respectful of womankind either. A singer was only necessary for the commercial dance tunes that they played as their passport to the circuit, and as such was generally undervalued. Barbara Jay later acknowledged that she had sometimes had to conceal the tears of her isolation from the young Turks.

Art Baxter found it easier to cope with. He was singing in Folkestone with the Jan Ralfini Orhcestra, the outfit that Cissie had taken Ronnie to see all those years ago when Jock was in the lineup. Baxter had a good voice, an extravagant and mildly camp stage presence, and an attractive informality in his presentation – he would sit on the edge of the stage and take the audience into his confidence in a manner that was rare at the time.

Moreover, he was a hilarious and outrageous companion, which quickly endeared him to the Scott men. His finale was the song 'Somebody Loves Me', which he delivered with as much indignation as coyness on occasions – if the audience didn't like him, he'd leave the stage directing V-signs at it. When he unexpectedly cropped his hair during a tour, the band thenceforth referred to him as the 'Singing Coconut'. Baxter, who was later to make occasional unscheduled appearances at Ronnie Scott's Club wearing such unconventional attire as a ballerina's costume, and from time to time with equally unconventional adornments – such as Coca Cola bottles – attached to his genitalia, was nevertheless, for all his expansiveness, a man of deep and unexplored insecurities. When the nine-piece rapidly began to make an impact on the polls, the opportunity came to play a pollwinner's concert at the Albert Hall opposite the Heath Orchestra, the Jack Parnell band and others. Baxter didn't show for the sound check or the rehearsal, and eventually a telegram arrived for Ronnie Scott: 'BAXTER NEEDS COMPLETE REST – BACK AUG 11'. It purported to come from a doctor, but everybody knew it was from the singer himself. One night at the Palladium Baxter had been so paralyzed with fear in the wings before his entrance that he only got on stage as a result of being hurled into the spotlight by Les Bristow.

But if the ups and downs of such volatile ingredients in the band were manageable in short doses and in after-hours anecdotes, they could create havoc on the road. Scott himself later came to believe that most bands would have a year of vitality, a year of levelling out and a year of deterioration. The course of the small band went pretty much that way. Touring would force changes, it was always unavoidable. A man like Art Baxter on a long coach journey could be a mixed blessing. The boy on the tricycle from the Edgware streets, the prodigy Victor Feldman, replaced Norman Stenfalt, and Feldman's arrival made possible a drum routine between himself and Tony Crombie that regularly raised the roof on the gigs. It had shades of the two-drummer routines that Ronnie Scott had witnessed in New York's Apollo Ballroom. Then Crombie left to start his own band.

Phil Seamen replaced Crombie in Scott's band. Like Crombie, he was that rare thing, a British drummer who had an instinctive and sympathetic grasp of what swing really meant, and a warmth in his playing rare on the instrument

– an effect partly gained by a subordination of technique to the musical atmosphere. Seamen's talent was such that he could have dominated the British jazz world for the next three decades, but alcohol and junk prevented it, and his unreliability throughout the 1960s lost him high-profile opportunities. But he remained one of the best-loved and, in his way, most respected of local percussionists. In the early 1970s, not long before his death, at a drum convention in London Buddy Rich paid just such a tribute to Seamen. Though the drummer had a hard time struggling to his feet to acknowledge Rich's gesture – not a man given to casual praise – the audience of hundreds of drummers cheered him to the rafters.

In the summer of 1955 the nine-piece broke up. It made its last recording on 13 April of that year with an EP that contained 'S'il Vous Plait', 'Pearl', 'This Heart of Mine' and 'Jordu', the last a nod in the direction of the cloistered but glowing sound of the Miles Davis band that had so affected Dankworth in its development of chamber-jazz pieces that had struck such a chord with the college-boy's instinct for a music that could somehow be both adventurous and yet not upset your parents. Many would later say it was the disease of many of the young British jazz artists of the day, and of later days. You could be a day-tripper into rebelliousness in Britain in the 1950s. You could smoke a joint, and go home to mum for supper, just the same as you could grow your hair long and cut it when the going got tough in the Britain of a decade later. Many black Americans, most notably Charlie Parker, never had that choice. A rebelliousness that was no more than the fling of youth wasn't promising as the catalyst to an artistic change of any real substance.

For Ronnie Scott, 1955 was also the year of another kind of parting of the ways. Joan Crewe abruptly left for the United States, in the tenth year of that relationship which had begun as a teenage romance at the Hammersmith Palais as a euphoric London returned to peace. Work on the road with the nine-piece had taken Ronnie Scott away from Joan a lot, and she had become seriously dependent on heroin and principally preoccupied with those who used it and those who could obtain it. Her original ignorance of what the outcome of such a dependency might be was shared by almost all of those experimenting with it at the time. Scott was grateful that his own flirtations with it had proved so completely unseductive.

Joan was also coming belatedly to the conclusion that Ronnie Scott would not marry her, or, in all probability anyone else. Uncle Mark had been harsh but right that day after the Club Eleven court case. And she felt guilty about the responsibilities of their relationship, as if they all fell on her. 'Don't force me to marry you, Joan,' Ronnie had said to her once. Her mother had even had the banns read in church. This was leading nowhere. Ronnie Scott wanted a boy-meets-girl encounter to last half a lifetime. But for a girl, there wasn't so much time to play with. She met a young American saxophonist, Spencer Sinatra, in Britain with the Stan Kenton orchestra. Sinatra was also a junkie, which drew him and Joan together, and while the nine-piece was touring, they began an affair.

When he discovered it, Ronnie was frantic. At twenty-seven, it was the first time anything like this had ever happened to him. Rational thought fled. He rang Kenton, Sinatra's boss, and told him that the saxophonist was a junkie, not particularly to Kenton's surprise. He heard of a flat in the suburbs of London where the couple were meeting, went there one night in a rage and confronted them both, ending up struggling noisily but without much impact with Sinatra on the floor. Sinatra returned early to the States, maybe because of Scott's complaint to Kenton. But Joan Crewe followed.

Ostensibly it was for a holiday, to see what America offered and maybe consider a new start. When Sinatra met her in New York he proposed that they should marry at the end of that week. Joan was surprised by the young saxophonist's urgency. 'You didn't come all this way just to see the sights did you?' Sinatra asked her. So far from home, and so close to the American's enthusiasm, she found it hard to refuse.

Her departure had been a severe blow to Ronnie. Until she was gone, he had not considered what life might be like without her. He sold everything he could quickly dispose of to raise the fare to the States. Since the Club Eleven raid, he had always considered that it would be hard to get an American visa, but five years after the event seemed a sufficiently long period of atonement and the Embassy eventually gave him the nod. But when he got to New York he had no idea where Joan and Sinatra had gone. He was able to trace the saxophonist to an accompanist's gig in a strip club, followed him from work, got on the same bus and sat at the back, feverishly rehearsing what he would say, whether there would be a scene or another fight, whether he would be able to talk Joan into coming back with him.

Sinatra went to an all-night restaurant and met Joan there. They sat at the table as Scott approached. He had no idea what he would say, but was surprised that much of the fury died down in him. In the end they hardly spoke at all. 'I hope you'll be very happy together,' he eventually said, and left the restaurant with hardly another word.

Ronnie Scott tracked down his old playing partner Victor Feldman, who was by now playing with the Woody Herman band in Lake Tahoe in Nevada. Crossing the States on buses, hanging out with Herman's sidemen, talking music again, helped him to handle the bewilderment of suddenly finding himself in America for a reason that had ceased to make sense. Joan Crewe later had two children with Sinatra, her family in the Caledonian Road moved to New York to be near her, and when Sinatra suddenly died some years later, they helped her to look after them. Ronnie flew home after a brief but diverting interlude with the Herman musicians. He had to reconstruct his life – and work out where to start again musically as well.

For the jazz community at large, 1955 was a year to ponder such things. News came through in March of that year that Charlie Parker had died in New York. His last months had been a nightmare. Overweight, racked with ulcers, living on stimulants and spending whatever money he could lay his hands on on drugs and booze, he had begun regularly to foul up his gigs, even firing the entire band and walking offstage in a gig at New York's Birdland and attempting suicide by drinking iodine immediately afterwards. Parker died in the Fifth Avenue apartment of the European jazz fan the Baroness Pannonica de Koenigswarter on March 9 at the age of thirty-four. The Baroness, a Rothschild, was immediately implicated in rumours of an affair with Parker in the downmarket press; in fact she was one of the saxophonist's few real friends. One-time sportswoman, pilot, private in the Free French Army, the Baroness had grown bored with her later years as a diplomat's wife and set up residence in Fifth Avenue's Hotel Stanhope, where she put her wealth at the service of the city's (mostly black) jazz musicians and acted for all the world like an old-style European patroness.

The graffiti artists defiantly wrote 'BIRD LIVES' on the Greenwich Village walls and subways. It was the strongest reminder of the world that Laurie Morgan had discovered in his journey of 1947, in which Bird was the Messiah, the leader to be followed to the ends of the earth if necessary. Parker's journey led to madness, chaos and death. His music, however, came to sound more beautiful, rounded, generous-spirited and loving every year, as the abrasiveness that seemed to be its primary feature when it first burst upon the world was gradually eroded by time. Ross Russell, in his inspired biography of Parker, quoted the words of the critic of Stockholm's *Orkester Journalen* who perceptively remarked after the saxophonist's death: 'Together with Jackson Pollock, Dylan Thomas and James Dean, he became a symbol of protest for a whole generation. It is easy to see how these four artists shared the same rebellious mind and desperation.'

5 / Teenagers

'This night the switchboard lit up like a Christmas tree. Dewey would play "Blue Moon Over Kentucky", then turn it over and play "That's All Right Mama". It was just those two sides for the rest of the evening. Finally Dewey said "Get that guy down here!" ' (Wink Martindale describing Elvis Presley air-plays by DJ Dewey Phillips in 1956 from Albert Goldman's *Elvis*, 1981.)

'Maybe our forefathers couldn't keep their language together when they were taken from Africa but this – the blues – was a language we invented to let people know we had something to say. And we've been saying it pretty strongly ever since.' (B. B. King to Val Wilmer, *The Face of Black Music*, 1976.)

In the summer of 1955, Ronnie Scott decided to form a big band. It was always a difficult temptation to resist, a rare opportunity in a predominantly miniaturist idiom to perform a music that packed a more substantial punch. The pitfalls were well known. They were cripplingly expensive to run, logistically difficult to organize, and if personality conflicts had been troublesome with the small band they were likely to be that much worse with a big one. Yet, they still had glamour and clout. Ronnie Scott loved the power of the brass, the lissome undertow of the reeds, the explosive swing of a good big-band drummer – a task that he entrusted to the volatile but inventive Phil Seamen. Other sidemen from the old Parnell band days were drafted in. Jimmy Watson, the trumpeter who had passed the idle moments on the Tommy Trinder revue with visits to the pub between the trumpet breaks, Pete King and Ken Wray from the nine-piece.

It also featured a man who came from very different origins

from the Archer Street players who made up most of Ronnie
Scott's circle of musician friends. Joe Harriott, a Jamaican
altoist who had come to Britain in 1951 when he was just
twenty-three years old, was already raising eyebrows as a
Parkerish saxophonist; nevertheless he clearly had ideas of
his own and an original way of adapting Bird's phraseology.
On a good night Harriott was a player of immense fire.
Though he worked for a period in the Crombie band, where
his soulful sound fitted perfectly, he had little sense of the
prospects of making a niche for himself in the music business
and put his spiky, unsentimental style on to the anvil of
experimentation. His playing was never cool and sounded,
as he often did himself, on the verge of an explosive outburst.
Harriott, like many of the black Americans who were to visit
Britain in the coming years, was a man who demonstrated in
his life and its mixture of euphoria and reverses that the
world simply looked different, and mostly less welcoming, if
it was being viewed from behind a black face, and that was
that.

It was never the same as the nine-piece had been, from
the moment of its debut performance at the Samson and
Hercules Ballroom in Norwich. Harold Davison, normally a
prudent man, had thought the big band a good idea even
though the overheads were reflected in the doubling of the
personnel, though Scott himself later said the scheme was
'one of my worst ever'. The less charitable thought that its
most intense and creative activity was its poker school, famed
for the unblinkingly dispassionate physiognomy of Harriott,
and trumpeter Hank Shaw's touchingly prudent habit of
instantly posting whatever winnings he would make to his
wife. But musically, it was living proof that an assembly of
diverse talents doesn't always make a living band, and it
might have been the insecurity of the outfit's musical perspective that sowed the seeds for the unrest that was frequently
under its surface. Harriott was unhappy with being second
alto to Dougie Robinson. Trumpeter Dave Usden and Phil
Seamen even fought publically on the bandstand in Morecambe on New Year's Eve 1955 and accompanied the ensemble's final rendition of 'Should Auld Acquaintance Be Forgot'
with a three act opera of shouting, deprecations, abuse and
all round indifference to the perplexed revellers. It was not

a happy ship, and the most surprising feature of its voyage was that it took so long to go down. Scott called a halt shortly after the Morecambe débâcle, and went back to working with Tony Crombie. But he also put his toe in the water of promotion again, something he had not considered since the days of Club Eleven.

The dream of a club in the 52nd Street style was still strong. If it was to be done, it had to be somewhere in the West End. Soho in the early 1950s was the place where the fringes of almost every human activity could find a home – it was an oasis for those who didn't, or couldn't make sense of respectable morality, acceptable arts, conventional standards of behaviour, sex, self-indulgence and dress, mainstream religion, the right manner of speech or ethnic background. It was also an oasis for those who didn't give a damn about the law.

In the 1950s, the West End was dominated by a self-styled 'King of the Underworld', Jack 'Spot' Comer. Jack Spot was a big, vigorous, cigar-smoking Jewish East Ender (he had fought Mosley's blackshirts in the thirties) who had owned Soho clubs that had given a good deal of work to jazz musicians. At the Modernaires in Old Compton Street, Flash Winston had a group as a piano player, performing what Spot and the gangsters indulgently called 'yer Heebie Jeebie music'. There was no doubt in such places about who was in charge. Spot's office telephone was actually in the music room itself and a wave of the hand from him would be enough to bring musicians and dancers to a silent standstill as he carried on his business, the whole atmosphere snapping back into action like a restarted film as soon as he replaced the receiver – this charade would go on a dozen times in a night. Denis Rose worked for a while in Spot's club too. Rose had always been fascinated by the underworld, though his occasional unreliability was a serious risk with such employers. One night Spot told Rose: 'You'll never work in the West End again,' when the pianist and trumpeter was two hours late for a gig. The rest of the band recalled playing 'Please Don't Talk About Me When I'm Gone' at the time.

Spot eventually retired after being cut up by the rising generation of younger operators in 1956, and bought a bowler hat and furniture business off the Gloucester Road. Though fights would occasionally happen in his clubs, and a good deal of unexplained action went on that the musicians knew better than to betray, serious intimidation was not really Spot's way. He got results by fixing deals. He made accommodations with other gangs that the new generation, like the Krays, would only deal with by violence, a pursuit they had an undisguised affection for. Soho was about to come under new management.

In Gerrard Street, in the heart of London's Chinatown, there was a shabby and dimly lit basement owned by a small time Soho businessman by the name of Jack Fordham. During the war it had been a bottle-party club, and later a refuge for cab-drivers for cards and coffee, and a 'near-beer' joint, in which male customers would be encouraged by the friendliness of attractive waitresses to spend a fortune on non-alcoholic drinks in the mistaken assumption that the waitresses might become still friendlier at the end of the night. Since such places didn't come to life until late in the evening, they were frequently hired at other times to act as occasional jazz venues. Scott and Pete King hired it once or twice in 1956 and half-heartedly considered old plans. But 1956 was also a year for other diversions. It was the one in which the old supremacy of Archer Street was to be finally challenged.

American rock and roll first hit Britain in the middle 1950s. Bill Haley's cleaned-up version of blues shouter Big Joe Turner's 'Shake, Rattle and Roll' had crept into *Melody Maker*'s new bestseller charts by the Christmas of 1954, the movie 'Rock Around the Clock' featuring Haley and his Comets arrived in 1956 and the singer followed it up with a tour of Britain the following year. Elvis Presley's first record, too, was a similar borrowing of the Mississippi blues singer Arthur 'Big Boy' Crudup's 'It's All Right Mama'. For Ronnie Scott and his musical contemporaries, still assuming themselves to be the young generation but now approaching thirty, the revelation of a new audience for a new music, whose practitioners and fans were barely out of their teens (and especially a new music that seemed to be simply a louder and more amateurishly performed version of the black urban blues music that they had known for years through jazz) was a difficult thing to take seriously. But the changes were unmistakable.

Melody Maker had taken to printing the best selling ten records of the week in order of popularity, so at last the criterion of success of a Tin Pan Alley song was no longer being judged on the sale of sheet music, a telling indication of the extent to which the transistor radio had become prime mover in music-business economics. The newspapers reported teenage fans rioting at showings of Haley's movie. Young Londoners like Bermondsey-raised Tommy Steele (originally Tommy Hicks) were already driving the fast sports cars and enjoying the trappings of success that went with being on top of the tree, and they performed for an audience that was economically attractive to the music business for the first time – an audience for the most part under sixteen. As George Melly pointed out in his recollections of the period, the fans for a successful dance-band solo singer like Dickie Valentine would have seemed young until then – maybe between eighteen and twenty-five. But this was different. A changing Britain was ensuring that the sentiment, cosy emotions, repressed sexuality and blandness that character-ized the kind of pop music that had emerged from the dance-band era was about to receive a hammering from which it would never recover. 'Teenagers' were here.

The war had brought it about. Austerity Britain, the Britain of self-sacrifice and patient duty, seemed about to be swept aside forever, partly as a result of American investment in European reconstruction, which had sunk $12 billion into fuelling an economic boom in France, Britain and Germany particularly. British exports skyrocketed. Meat rationing was finally abolished in 1956. A new and impatient generation needed new icons, new dreams. The children born in the height of the Blitz were born to parents who had decided that for their descendants it was all going to be different next time around. More people had more money to spend on themselves and each other; on refrigerators, cars, washing machines, televisions – and on their children.

That high-spending consumer society that the previous generation had known only from American movies and which Scott, Crombie, Dankworth and the others had seen and marvelled at in New York, seemed finally to have arrived on the doorstep. Commercial television had arrived, too, and amidst much controversy, to advertise it all. Children had been given high expectations in the 1950s. George Melly, sharing the bill with Tommy Steele at a South London gig in the mid-fifties heard those expectations cut loose after an audience mostly comprising sixteen year olds had listened to the opening set by the Mick Mulligan band in virtual silence. During the interval, Melly wrote in *Owning Up*: 'A low continuous hum began to rise from the auditorium. It was like a swarm of bees getting ready to swarm . . . the moment the curtain went up a high-pitched squeaking and shrieking started. I was absolutely amazed.'

Rock 'n' roll swept the nation. Not appreciating its import, Ronnie Scott and Harry Klein went to what they thought was just another recording session to be sidemen with Tommy Steele's band at the Decca Studios in West Hampstead. It was, as professional musicians went, something to be sniffed at. Nobody had prepared any arrangements, and Scott and Klein had to figure something appropriate out for themselves. Not long afterwards, Steele's records were dominating the charts.

But Tony Crombie was one jazz musician who had tried to get in on the act, eventually turning his touring band into a rock 'n' roll group called Tony Crombie's Rockets, and persisting with it until 1957, when it became obvious that what really made a hit rock band was a personality at the microphone who was a good ten years younger than most of the Rockets could claim to be. It didn't, however, stop them conducting themselves the way rock stars of a decade later became notorious for. After a nationwide tour by the band, it became legendary as the outfit that no hotel would welcome twice. Crombie, an ingenious operator, took to booking his outfit's accommodation under implausible alibis like 'Professor Cromberg and a party of students'.

A TV show *Six-Five Special* went out on Saturdays to cater for the new craze. Amplified music did inspire a kind of an antidote in skiffle, which was a do-it-yourself idiom based on country-and-western music and black folk art like Huddie Ledbetter's, performed on home-made instruments like washboards and basses made of broom handles and string. But for modern jazz, there continued to be an audience of informed enthusiasts, the days in which its practitioners could make a respectable or more than respectable living by playing a hybrid version of it somewhere between bebop and pop music had all but gone until 'fusion' music made its appearance in the late 1960s. Pop music had simply moved on, though some jazz musicians made an attempt to cross the divide. Benny Green recalled the story of the saxophonist Wally Bishop, who in discussing his credentials to join a rock 'n' roll band was asked: 'Can you play a 12 bar blues lying on your back?' Bishop, a man with an enthusiasm for the occasional drink, observed: 'Yes, but who's going to pick me up again?'

Shortly after his thirtieth birthday, in February 1957, Ronnie Scott got a chance to return to the States, and an unexpected opportunity to experience the rock boom at closer range than he might have liked. Harold Davison was handling a tour by the Eddie Condon Sextet (a further sign of relaxation of the old union clampdown) and an exchange group was necessary to keep the arrangement above board. Ronnie Scott set about assembling a suitable touring group, with some trepidation since it seemed to him that America needed a tour by British musicians playing American music like, as he put it, a synagogue in Damascus. In the event he booked Phil Seamen, Derek Humble, Jimmy Deuchar, Victor Feldman and Lennie Bush to accompany him on the trip.

The job looked difficult enough as it was, but on top of that there was always Seamen to worry about. The drummer was an unmatchable performer at the top of his form but his off-stand habits were a perpetual wild card. 'For Christ's sake don't try to take anything over with you,' Scott warned Seamen. 'Don't worry,' Seamen assured him, as he always did. When the departure time arrived, Ronnie Scott travelled late to Southampton through visa delays. When he got to Customs things immediately looked ominous. 'You Mr Scott?' the officer enquired. 'Come this way please.' He found Phil Seamen in the company of two Customs men. 'Mr Seamen is one of your party I understand,' the officer continued. 'We have discovered narcotics in his drum kit.' It was a desperate situation for a bandleader contemplating a tour that already seemed unnecessary and happening purely for reasons of music business politics. 'Look, it's vital he comes to the States for this tour. Couldn't you nick him on the way back?' Scott enquired of the customs officers. They looked at him with as much pity as resentment.

Ronnie Scott rang Harold Davison and asked for Allan Ganley, a young drummer with a tasteful and elegant grasp of bop, if not of Seamen's audacious waywardness with the idiom, to be flown out to join the band for the start of the tour. It was the start of a series of surprises. A dock strike in New York diverted the *Queen Elizabeth*; it sailed for Halifax, Nova Scotia instead, so that the performers had to fly down to New York from there. The plane trip prevented them from continuing with their luggage, so the Englishmen inauspiciously began the journey wearing as many of their clothes simultaneously as they could manage and still stand upright. They felt they were about to become a part of the hippest musical community on earth, and feeling as unhip as they conceivably could.

But this was to be no jazz tour. The Scott band was booked into an all-black rock 'n' roll show. On the bill were Chuck Berry, Fats Domino, Lavern Baker, Bill Doggett (the jazz organist who moved successfully over to pop) men who would have made the show a huge hit in the rhythm and blues boom of only a few years later but who even in 1957 represented a package of considerable prestige. Six Englishmen careering their way through a handful of choruses of the single bebop tune that constituted their contribution to an all-black package before escaping gratefully into the wings was a bizarre enough event in itself but the Scott band was made more uneasy by the fact that it had never performed before audiences of such a size before – 20,000 or so was the average attendance on the gigs.

It was on that tour that Ronnie Scott came to hear at first hand two of the saxophonists that he would unreservedly admire throughout the coming years. One was the thirty-three-year-old Edward 'Sonny' Stitt, a Boston-born musician of immense technique and awesome musical literacy who was increasingly regarded in the States as the true inheritor of the message of Charlie Parker. Stitt's father was a professor of music and his mother a teacher of piano and organ, in which respect the saxophonist was a striking example of the kind of sophistication increasingly common among the second wave of bebop artists, bringing orthodox Western theory to bear on the harmonic labyrinths of bop. Ronnie Scott heard Stitt on a stopover in Buffalo and when the band returned to New York to discover that Stitt was playing in a club across the river in Newark, a return visit was compulsory. Benny Green and another London saxophonist, Jack Sharpe, were staying at the President Hotel in New York on a busman's holiday to keep the Scott band company. Scott burst into Green's room with the exultant words: 'I'm going to take you to hear the greatest saxophonist in the world.' Stitt, a tall, rangy figure with awesome energy and a relentless, competitive drive, played stupendous music, cascades of eighth note runs pouring from his horn. He played tenor and baritone as well as alto that night, part of his strategy to escape the 'new Bird' tag which he felt might stay on his back for life.

The other event to make a lasting impact on Ronnie Scott during that tour was hearing Stan Getz in the flesh. Getz was almost exactly the Englishman's own age, a swing-derived performer whose work was attractively inflected with bebop. Getz was a longtime admirer of Lester Young rather than Charlie Parker. He had a lighter, more delicate tone than most of the beboppers and a lyrical imagination that gave much of his work a fragile, porcelain-like quality rare in jazz.

The journey back to England was principally memorable for Tatiesque farce. Because of the row over the luckless Seamen in Southampton, the band had panicked and hidden its small supply of cannabis in a lavatory cistern on the *Queen Elizabeth*, none of the members having the courage after such bad omens at the outset to risk taking it off at the other end. The indecisiveness wasted most of such relaxation they might have got out of the journey back. All six musicians spent the entire trip looking for that lost stash. They split into pairs, combed the ship, met at prearranged rendezvous to compare notes, reconsidered, started all over again. The *Queen Elizabeth* had too many decks, too many lavatories and too many cisterns for any of them ever to be sure that somebody else hadn't got there first.

When Ronnie Scott and the band returned, the seeds of an old dream were revitalized. As they had realized during the Flood Relief concert, the British public was being deprived by the ban on imported players of some of the most vital and living music of the century – and a music that, by virtue of residing principally in the heads of great improvisors rather than captured in written composition, was changing all the time. Scott knew that there would be a sizeable audience for the likes of Stitt and Getz as long as they could be persuaded to come to England. And the nature of their gifts was such that it would be preferable to present them in the intimate atmosphere of a club rather than a concert hall.

Some years previously, on a guest appearance with a local rhythm section at a south London gig, Ronnie Scott had been approached by a chubby teenager who had shyly asked him, 'Do you mind if I play?' Scott had greeted the prospect with the same mixture of weariness and sympathy that soloists out on one night stands had grown accustomed to exhibiting. There was always someone out there whose ambitions exceeded their capabilities to the point where you would have to accommodate their desires as best you could. But when the chubby kid played the horn it was immediately obvious that something special was happening. He had everything – stunning dexterity of a calibre to rival the superfast American hard boppers like Johnny Griffin, rich imagination, sensitivity to what the other players were doing, and astonishing wind and stamina.

His name was Edward Brian 'Tubby' Hayes. In a succession of bands that Hayes was to lead in the 1950s, he demonstrated himself to be an improvisor of a confidence and attack almost unheard of in the faintly apologetic world of British jazz. His father had been a violinist and he had himself played the instrument for some years before switching to the saxophone at the age of twelve. His entire musical background was altogether more rigorous, sophisticated and considered than the hit-and-miss manner in which so many of the Archer Street players of the previous generation had served their apprenticeship, and that greater fund of knowledge had led him to want to compose and arrange as well. It was these talents that Ronnie Scott had a special admiration for, as he had for Tony Crombie and Jimmy Deuchar in the days of the nine-piece. 'Beats me how they do it,' Scott would muse. 'I can't arrange a vase of flowers.'

After the American tour, Ronnie Scott and Tubby Hayes seriously began to consider the prospects for forming a band. There was already a cult for the two-tenor front line since Sonny Stitt and the powerful, furiously rhythmic Gene Ammons had been partners in such an outfit throughout the fifties. Since Hayes also wanted an outlet for his writing, the ensemble would work with a good deal of his own material, laced with the prominent jazz tunes of the time. The name – the Jazz Couriers – was a close approximation to that of one of the perenially popular American hard bop groups, drummer Blakey's Jazz Messengers. In addition to Hayes and Scott, and a regular pianist, Terry Shannon, it featured a variety of drummers and bassists.

And from its first performance on 7 April 1957 at Wardour Street's Flamingo Club, making its own debut as a jazz venue, the band looked a winner. It didn't get the euphoria in the music press that the nine-piece had done at the beginning of its life, because times had changed and a jazz story wasn't the big deal it used to be, but the opening show – with Joe Harriott playing opposite in a band led by drummer Tony Kinsey – demonstrated just how formidable the combined powers of the country's two strongest tenor modernists actually was. Bookings followed thick and fast. Pete King continued to take care of the business. He also got married at Caxton Hall only a month after the band took wing. Scott, though he wouldn't contemplate the institution himself, was delighted for King, and was present at the service along with other musicians and friends. The registrar had changed quite unselfconsciously from an entirely conventional mode of speech whilst dealing with the bureaucracy to a bizarre tone of ecclesiastical piety as if he were doing impressions once the ceremony began. This curious turn of events crippled Scott, Benny Green and the photographer Harry Morris, who snorted into their handkerchiefs throughout, much to the new bride, Stella Ferguson's discomfort. In the event the newlyweds couldn't afford to buy the official prints that appeared in the music press. They bought, and still proudly possess, photographs of their wedding with the word 'PROOF' stamped across them in large letters.

Plaudits began to flow the Couriers' way. Even Ronnie Scott, not given to overstatement, was convinced that the critics and the public were not deluded when the band soon began to win readers' polls and inspired observations that this was the most assured and exciting outfit in the history of British modern jazz. The Couriers began to tour and record. Although the times had changed, there was a large enough jazz public – notably of the better educated, more sophisticated and gently rebellious post Beatnik citizenry much of Hayes' own age – to ensure that the band became something of a cult.

Hayes was fitfully a cause for worry because he could not control either his drinking or his habits with narcotics. Unlike the drummer Phil Seamen, who was sometimes incapable of performance, Hayes was rarely inhibited from playing at least acceptably, and often brilliantly, certainly in his early twenties. The effect of heroin use, when it finally took toll of him, was to undermine his health before his willpower, in a manner that was first crippling and then fatal. But the Tubby Hayes of the late 1950s was a man at the height of his powers.

To be co-leader of the foremost jazz group of its day was diversion enough for Ronnie Scott. Though he felt that his partner's playing was streets ahead of his own, this diffident opinion wasn't always shared by observers who appreciated his more thoughtful, mischievous and gentler style. And the younger man's drive had re-energized Scott; playing with the Couriers gave him a new lease of playing life.

The band toured the country with an American blues package at one point, under the guidance of Dougie Tobutt, a dapper, humorous road manager from Davison's office. Heading for a gig in Glasgow, the band bus arrived at a transport café on the Scottish border. Tobutt hauled the vehicle up some distance from the establishment and informed his charges, many of them veterans, but strangers to Britain: 'We're approaching the Scots customs now. If you're carrying anything you shouldn't be, now's the time to lose it.' The bluesmen frantically took to clearing their luggage of drugs. Tobutt then got all the travellers to line up outside the coach. 'I want you to hold your passports in your left hand and raise your right' he informed them gravely. 'Now say after me, "I pledge allegiance to Her Majesty the Queen during my stay in Scotland and undertake to be of good behaviour throughout".' Tobutt then collected the passports and took them inside the 'border post'. He hadn't cracked a face muscle throughout the exercise. It was a stunt worthy of the Sculthorpe Letter.

The honeymoon was punctured from the most unimaginable quarter. News came that Jock Scott was ill. Ronnie met him in an Archer Street café and found him thinner, and seriously worried about his health. 'Maybe you need a holiday,' Ronnie Scott suggested. 'Maybe I do,' Jock agreed. 'I was thinking of going to Switzerland. Would you come with me?' At the time, there seemed many other things to do.

Not long afterwards, it was clear that what was troubling Jock wouldn't be solved by fresh air. Since the *Caronia* tour, both men had lived their own lives and been active enough, despite their admiration for each other, not to pursue the connection with particular urgency.

Suddenly time seemed telescoped. Jock was worse, by all accounts. Ronnie Scott got a call that he was in Hammersmith Hospital. He drove there one day in the summer of 1958. All the past crossed his mind on that journey; all the bewilderment that might have stemmed from pondering the unimaginable trail from the elegant night-spots of wartime London to this unforeseen moment, all the memories of his father's occupation of the mantle of an irrepressible entertainer rolled up into one deafening discord before the opening bars of that coda were even complete.

Because the gatekeeper at the hospital was the glamorous saxophone hero of Princes and the Potomac, minstrel to the wartime wealthy, Reggie Dare.

The change in Jock was hard to believe. Haggard and yellowing, he had lost a great deal of weight and his old bravura and bounce were gone. He still didn't know how bad things were, and neither did his son, but it was obvious to both men that something was seriously wrong. The encounter was tense, awkward, but full of affirmations of what the future might hold. There had been so many obstacles to their getting along, which a conversation in a hospital ward couldn't blow away as if they had never been. There had been the episode over the *Caronia*, which Jock had always resented. There had been his son's headstrong nature, swept along by the modernist movement and by the wild life of clubland, which

(*Above and below left*) Jock Scott, Ronnie's alto-playing father, in his prime. He 'played the boats' for much of his career

(*Below right*) Ronnie's mother Sylvia, better known as 'Cissie'. Also in the picture, Solomon 'Sol' Berger, her second husband and the man who helped the young saxophonist through the foothills of his career

Ronnie considering a dance hall edict with actor and jazz fan Mario Fabrizi

Rehearsing the nine-piece in the spring of 1953. The bandleader runs through the part, with Benny Green, Pete King and Derek Humble in hot pursuit

The nine-piece assembling for business in Archer Street. Benny
Green is holding up the band bus

Faces of the 1950s. Trumpeter Jimmy Deuchar (left) and altoist
Derek Humble trying to get a reaction from the sauce bottle at the Harmony Inn

Ken Wray's wedding – the trombonist (left) is with his bride Peggy. Jimmy Deuchar is behind his head, then Jeff Ellison, Derek Humble, Keith Christie, Lennie Metcalf, Lennie Bush, Fred Perry, Dave Usden, Pete King. Scott is proudly at the wheel of his Jaguar XK120, the revolutionary British sports car of the early 50s (*Melody Maker*)

Ronnie Scott on baritone with Tubby Hayes and the Couriers at the Savoy, Catford in April 1959. They could only concentrate if they didn't look at the backdrop (*Melody Maker*)

Dexter Gordon's introduction to the West End on the celebrated visit to Ronnie Scott's in 1962. Gordon and Lucky Thompson were the first black Americans to play there (*Val Wilmer*)

Ronnie Scott jamming with Sonny Stitt at Gerrard Street in 1964. Stitt was one of the Americans Scott remained in awe of from the first time he heard him in Newark in 1957. Gene Wright, then with Dave Brubeck, guests on bass (*Val Wilmer*)

Ronnie Scott with Sonny Rollins, one of the most prolific and idiosyncratic of all jazz improvisors (*David Redfern*)

The proprietor at Frith Street, in early days (*Val Wilmer*)

The twilight world of Frith Street's 'office' – night and day, it always looks the same. The profile is unmistakeable. The opponent is Dizzy Gillespie (*Val Wilmer*)

Becky, Ronnie and Mary, Christmas
1973

Becky and Ronnie at the Village G
in New York, 1985

Twenty-five years and
counting. Pete King ('if we
were shrewd businessmen
we wouldn't be here') and
Ronnie Scott ('not keeping
you up, am I sir?') at the
club's celebration in 1984.
Bassist Ron Mathewson is
in the background
(*David Redfern*)

Jock had always felt to be a distraction from the pursuit of true professionalism. He hadn't been able to restrain himself from lecturing his son as to how he thought a life in the music business ought to be properly conducted. Neither of them had taken much opportunity to get to know each other better during the 1950s when they were both highly regarded in the same business, were sharing the same market place of Archer Street, and could have met frequently.

After that visit, Jock saw the specialist. He had been stalled a number of times and didn't want to hear any more variations on the theme. 'You can tell me,' Jock insisted. 'All right. You have cancer of the pancreas,' the consultant informed Jock Scott. 'What are the prospects?' 'Not good, I'm afraid.' 'I don't mind what it costs,' Jock insisted to her. 'If it's a question of money.' The doctor gently informed the patient that it wasn't.

He couldn't believe the news. And he received relatively few visits whilst in hospital, apart from the constant attentions of some of the musicians of his own age who had worked with him and loved him. Nissel Lakin, the drummer from the *Caronia* trip came with parcels of sweets and cigarettes for Jock. Scott told Lakin, 'I'm fed up with this. I'm going home.' Ted Hughes, the saxophone player who took over running the band at Hatchett's Restaurant in Piccadilly in his absence, was offered the dying man's golf clubs. 'I play golf about once every fifty years,' Jock said to Hughes. 'I don't suppose I'll be needing them now.' Hughes wasn't a golfer but accepted the clubs and became obsessed with the game. Jock Scott discharged himself from hospital and went back to his flat in Marble Arch.

One afternoon a few weeks later, at the Alexandra Park races, Ronnie Scott saw his ailing father again. Standing at the back of the grandstand, the young saxophonist suddenly glimpsed Jock through the binoculars, standing close to the railings, a shadow of himself, of the practical joker, the optimist, the gambler, the balladeer, the *kletzmorim*, the admirer of women, of elegant music, of fancy clothes. Ronnie Scott pushed his way through the crowds in search of his father, past the punters in pursuit of that last flutter that would change everything, past the small and the big-time, the high-rollers and the amateurs, the resigned and the euphoric and the indifferent, and when he got to the track his father was gone.

It was the last time Ronnie Scott saw his father alive. The news came on 28 May that they had had to break down the door of the flat and found Jock dead, following an overdose of sedatives. Ronnie tried to comfort his mother, who was deeply distressed and confided to him then that she had always loved Jock. The man who had played such a part in both their lives, but in such different and difficult ways, was no longer an encounter to be savoured through some chance meeting in Archer Street, a voice on the end of a telephone after a long silence. Jock Scott was gone. He was fifty-five.

6 / The Late Late Late Late Show

'Wail!' yelled Tubby Hayes, as his partner launched his solo on 'Some of My Best Friends Are Blues', a mid-tempo 12-bar that constituted one of Ronnie Scott's only contributions to the art of jazz composition. The tenor was harder and more gravelly now, but zigzagging gracefully over the chords like a skier. A packed house at London's Dominion Theatre on that night in 1958 had already warmly greeted the band's breakneck opening version of Cole Porter's 'What Is This Thing Called Love?', even though the band they had really paid to hear was still to come – the American Dave Brubeck Quartet, then at the beginning of its boom years.

Hayes and Scott cut distinctly contrasting figures in the footlights. Though both were immaculately attired in suits – something that the sartorially-preoccupied older man had always insisted on for bands he was in – clothes always looked as if they fitted him to the last fraction of an inch, while Hayes couldn't help resembling a schoolboy who had borrowed his father's Sunday best. As with most British modern jazz ensembles, nobody did anything particularly demonstrative on stage. Scott would stand virtually motionless at the microphone, the horn held slightly to one side, his eyes often closed. He was restrained in the presentations on that night, slightly nervous but still registering his old familiar trademark.

'Thank you very much,' he said to the audience's applause for 'Some of My Best Friends Are Blues'. 'And now from a brand new LP which you may have seen in the shops, entitled *Elvis Presley sings Thelonious Monk . . .*'

The furious delivery of the Cole Porter tune had been virtually a definition of their style, preceding the melody with wild, nervy riffing like the sound of frantic footsteps on a staircase, Porter's original notes suddenly materializing as if the perpetrator had suddenly burst through a door.

Most of what the Couriers did had that crazed momentum about it, it was sealed, hermetic, impervious, unsuitable to expression of human frailties of the kind that were being poignantly articulated at the time by Ronnie Scott's old playing partner, the West Indian Joe Harriott, or by the Scottish player Bobby Wellins. But it had an infectious drive about it. On the Dominion gig, they closed an equally tumbling version of 'Guys and Dolls' with a call-and-response section that turned into a headlong unison coda ending on a blipping high note as if someone had abruptly planted a full stop in the music. It brought the house down. The finale was a rendition of 'Cheek To Cheek' so fast that only dancing partners bound at the neck could possibly have sustained Irving Berlin's original sentiments.

Though Brubeck himself, highly impressed with Scott and Hayes, was to say at the end of the tour 'they sound more like an American band than we do', there was an unintentional irony in his remark. Brubeck didn't really sound much like an American at all, being preoccupied with European conservatoire music and a kind of ornate, theoretical jazz. But American modernist outfits like those of Art Blakey and Hank Mobley in reality sounded quite different to the Couriers.

Much of the difference lay in the attack of the rhythm sections – Blakey's cymbal beat was restless and probing, the momentum sporadically lifted by huge, breaker-like rolls and admonishing tappings and clatterings. With underpinnings so strong, the soloists could afford to play less, and avoid the hysterical, fill-every-chink manner frequently adopted by their admirers abroad. Deep-rooted insecurities about their quality by comparison with the Americans also led British bebop bands to a kind of over-compensatory pyrotechnics as well, like teenagers driving cars too fast to prove that they were men. The palais-band tradition was even audible in the Couriers' work too, in expert but fussy arrangements that sounded very close to the repertoire of a miniature dance orchestra. But the Brubeck tour of Britain was a golden opportunity for the band, and the Dominion gig – recorded for EMI as 'The Jazz Couriers In Concert' – was a high spot of it.

Though the band represented as much as he'd ever wanted from playing, Ronnie Scott revealed later that year, in a passing remark in an interview, that he had not forgotten that old 52nd Street dream. He was featured in *Melody Maker* in the autumn of 1958, where he was described as 'one of the post-war angry young men of jazz.' It was a routine enough story. Scott reiterated his dislike of critics, a point he made whenever he got the opportunity. He was asked if he wanted to be a session player and replied that nothing would please him more, except that 'the only sessions I've done recently have been rock 'n' roll, where I have to play out of tune.' The payoff of the interview showed the way his mind was turning. What were his hopes for the local jazz scene? 'I'd like to see a new type of jazz club in London,' Scott replied. 'A well-appointed place which was licensed, and catered for people of all ages and not merely for youngsters.'

By the summer of 1959, the steam was going out of the Jazz Couriers. Tubby Hayes had never really stopped relishing the idea of a larger band, one that could handle the increasing ambition in his writing and arranging. The last date was 30 August at the City Hall in Cork. And after the demise of the Couriers, which was a band that for once Ronnie Scott would have continued with if the choice had been entirely his, there seemed little enough to get excited about in the jazz world. The only versions of the music that seemed likely to attract a substantial following were the Dave Brubeck group and the Modern Jazz Quartet. Neither ensemble was particularly prone to the creation of either original improvization or that infectious creative tension audible in Stitt's band, or Miles Davis', or the Couriers themselves on a good night. After the first tidal wave of rock 'n' roll had subsided, you could demonstrate a touch of class by having a recording of one of Brubeck's fussy explorations of fancy rhythms and hybrid classicism in your collection, or the hushed, cut-glass chamber-jazz of the MJQ. They were a massive hit with the public.

Benny Green had by this time virtually stopped playing and was working increasingly as a jazz critic for the *Observer*, a new career offered to him by that newspaper's most influential jazz fan, Kenneth Tynan. Green was a fluent and witty writer, one of the few jazz musicians who was comfortably capable of turning the offhanded, oblique, observant and frequently macabre humour of the music business into prose. He hated the hyping of Brubeck and the MJQ and frequently laid into them in print. 'The British jazz fan is highly conscious of his own insularity' Green began an article on Brubeck during the pianist's 1959 visit to the Royal Festival Hall, making clear in the process the assumptions as to gender that characterized the period, and the music. 'He yearns to be in the swim, so our promoters cater most thoughtfully for this desire by sticking topical labels on their American touring shows.' Green went on to describe Brubeck's popularity 'as one of the peculiar aberrations of current taste,' much to the chagrin of Brubeck.

The Modern Jazz Quartet fared little better, Green concluded resignedly that: 'For the last five years four men have sought with painful eagerness to transform the racy art of jazz into something aspiring towards cultural respectability.' It was all true. The MJQ took pains to dress like a classical chamber group, perform everything with a measured deliberation – despite the suppressed ingenuity of vibra-harpist Milt Jackson – and generally carry on as if the life and hard times of a man like Charlie Parker had only served to get the music a bad name.

While on holiday in Majorca with Green that year, Scott met the proprietor of a jazz establishment called the Indigo Club, a bop fan and drummer who reminded him that running a club could be simply fun, which was all he'd ever really asked for, and an opportunity to make a little money, present musicians he admired, and have somewhere amenable to put on bands of his own.

The drummer, whose name was Ramon Farran, and who was the son of a Catalan bandleader himself, had married Robert Graves' daughter Lucia. Through Farran, Scott came to meet the old man at Canellun, the house that Graves had built at Deja in 1929. The poet's first query of the saxophonist was simply, 'What's the pot situation like in London now?' He turned out to be fascinated by jazz, and loved drummers in particular. Scott was fascinated by Graves and a little discomfited by his circle too. They had all read so much, and they were so humorous, but with a humour so impenetrably rooted in education, not the wisecracking, fatalistic, self-defensive shield against fate that came from a childhood on the streets of the East End. Graves showed Scott around his den, lined with books. 'I've tried writing,' Scott began tentatively, 'but I find it the hardest thing in the world.' 'Of course you will,' Graves replied somewhat brusquely. 'Unless you're God.' They got on well. Scott spent a good deal of time walking and swimming with Graves, perpetually astonished by the old man's boundless energy, springing up the steep slope from the sea to the house like a gazelle.

By 1961 Ronnie Scott was visiting Palma regularly, often performing with Farran's Wynton Kelly-like trio at the Indigo, and he was to continue his visits until the early 1970s. Graves would periodically visit London, too, in the days after Ronnie Scott had become promoter as well as a performer of jazz. 'Bobby's in the club,' Scott would ring Benny Green to say. 'Do you want to come down?'

The big chance was an accident, as usual. Jack Fordham, the Soho entrepreneur had lost interest in the Gerrard Street premises that Scott and King had occasionally used for their own jazz presentations in the past. Fordham's principal living came from the hamburger joint – one of the first – he ran in Berwick Street. Eventually he offered 39 Gerrard Street to Scott for a knock-down rent. It became Ronnie Scott's first club.

Pete King – who like Benny Green had by now realized that to pursue a playing career was unlikely to take him any further – was now virtually entirely involved with promotion, partly on his own account, and partly in association with Harold Davison and worked out of his own Soho office. He caught Ronnie Scott's conviction that this was the moment. Then Scott went to his parents to ask for help and got a loan of £1,000 from his stepfather to get the ball rolling. Sol Berger was by this time a successful partner in a textiles company, and he bought a stake in his son's club in exchange for a partnership in a very different kind of enterprise.

Number 39 Gerrard Street had nothing but space and not very much of that. The two would-be jazz club proprietors went to the East End in search of cheap furniture and bought a job lot of chairs which they arranged in austere lines in front of the bandstand. Pete King's father-in-law, a Manchester carpenter, came down to help build a few rudimentary tables. Then there wouldn't be room for dancing, so it was going to have to be a venue for fans who really wanted to come and listen. It would also have to be for visitors who could pass a few hours without the need for alcohol, since there was no liquor licence and the best the establishment was likely to be able to provide was tea, a staple of the Archer Street metabolism for years (the two men had established what they called a 'tea bag connection' with a Chiswick wholesaler who stayed with them forever after), coffee, and maybe a hamburger.

From the start, it was an unspoken agreement that the front man would be Ronnie Scott and that the club would bear his name, even though King was crucial to the graft of administration even then, and would become the difference between survival and collapse in later years. It was not that he was on the case less regularly than his partner – from the outset it seemed inevitable that Stella would bring up their children herself because of the hours her husband would put in at the club. To King, Scott was the star. Someone had to *be* the club in the eyes of the jazz public. Scott was the most highly regarded modern jazz musician in Britain, apart from Tubby Hayes, and his reputation was the beginning and end of the argument.

The London modern jazz world of the late 1950s was a limited market and for the new contenders in it, the lie of the land was not so difficult to gauge. In Wardour Street, a stone's throw away, was the Flamingo, already in existence for two years. The old Studio 51, which opened after the Club Eleven's demise had started life with a modern jazz policy but by 1959 was presenting revivalist and traditional music. As for the amount of music you could reasonably expect to present and still come out ahead, Saturday night audiences were good and Sundays passable, but weekdays were graveyards.

Scott and King thought the entrance prices charged by the other jazz clubs were too low to ever be able to finance really unusual acts. They never considered Americans, and any way

the embargo was still firm. They would gradually improve
their modest premises so that one day it would be the kind
of place where people wouldn't mind paying a little more to
be in a *real* club. And they would build towards making jazz
a part of London life.

And after scratching together the basis of an establishment,
they went about developing a marketing policy. What this
amounted to was a weekly pooling of gags by the musicians
that could be deployed in small ads in *Melody Maker*. Scott
had never seen any reason why you shouldn't present any
enterprise to your customers as if the whole thing were a
joke, as long as you didn't treat it as one when you were
actually executing it. He therefore placed an entry in the
columns of *Melody Maker* of 31 October 1959 which declared
the following:

RONNIE SCOTT'S CLUB
39 Gerrard Street, W1
OPENING TONIGHT!
  Friday 7.30pm. Tubby Hayes Quartet; the trio with
  Eddie Thompson, Stan Roberts, Spike Heatley,
  A young alto saxophonist, Peter King, and an old tenor
  saxophonist, Ronnie Scott
  The first appearance in a jazz club since the relief of
  Mafeking by Jack Parnell
  Membership 10/- until January 1961. Admission 1/6 (to
  members) 2/6 (non members)

The entry concluded boldly: 'The best jazz in the best
club in town,' Ronnie Scott having learnt from the American
example that you didn't lose anything by extravagance. If the
punters didn't agree they could always assert their side of
the transaction by simply not coming back. It was a gamble.
Jock would have expected nothing less.

Scott and King had opened the proceedings with a shrewd
mixture of attractions, a blend of the new and the familiar
intended to cut across as many of the modern jazz persuasions
as possible. Hayes was a sure-fire cert, of course, and would
be appearing with the Couriers' old pianist Terry Shannon,
and with Phil Seamen on drums and a brilliant new bassist,
Jeff Clyne, who had played on the streets of Edgware with
Ronnie Scott's step-sister Marlene and who had revered the

local heroes, the Feldman brothers, on those same streets. The reference to the 'young alto saxophonist Peter King' was not a gag at his partner's expense but a description of a sensational new arrival on the scene, a thin anxious-looking nineteen-year-old from Tolworth in Surrey, who had been playing for just a little over two years and already demonstrated his intense admiration for the work of Charlie Parker – King's speed of thought and richness of resources were close to rivalling Tubby Hayes even then. The newcomer's preoccupation with Parker extended, as Benny Green observed, to his small-talk consisting almost entirely of analyses of the structure of various Parker solos.

Peter King was modest about his achievements in conversations with the press at the time. He said he was 'limited, both technically and musically. But I can feel something coming.' In fact, as the more discriminating of local observers immediately realized, King was one of the few British inheritors of the Charlie Parker style to execute the complexities of bop with an air of ease and relaxation. This was not so much discernible in the young man's demeanour – his eyes would be downcast as he played, his legs splayed and knees bending with the beat like a man who had spent a long time on horseback, and he perpetually looked nervous – but in the fluency with which streams of melodic invention tumbled from his horn and the momentum of his rhythmic attack. King had never served an apprenticeship in one idiom and then switched to another. He was a modernist through and through. King's very existence was a testament to the value of the players of Scott's generation having made those pilgrimages to New York, spent those long hours in Carlo Krahmer's studio listening to imported 78s. They had built a springboard for new players that would make possible a conclusive rejection of the inferiority complex that British players had about their jazz.

The first gig also featured Eddie Thompson, a pianist whose ideas absorbed swing music, bop, the majestic 'orchestral' jazz pianists like Art Tatum and Duke Ellington and a good deal of classical music too. In featuring Thompson, the club was opening with one of the finest keyboard artists in the land.

It was an evening of magic. Scott and King had already set

themselves several dates that they had eventually missed and the club wasn't really ready for business even on that memorable occasion of 30 October 1959. It became an exhausting weekend for both the proprietors, since Ronnie Scott's Club began with shows every night of that weekend; in the daytime furious efforts were made to improve the ambiance. The club was packed with musicians and friends. Ray Nance, Duke Ellington's trumpeter who was returning to the States after the band's European tour, dropped in on the Friday night to wish Ronnie Scott luck. It became obvious that the all-nighters were such a magnet for after-hours players looking for somewhere to blow that the club began to charge them 2/- for the privilege, a state of affairs that caused a good deal of hurt surprise. Many in the business, who thought they knew only too well not only the prospects for modern jazz in London, but the temporary nature of some of Ronnie Scott's enthusiasms as well, gave the place no more than a couple of weeks. But in the event it was just what the London jazz public needed. It was informal, it didn't charge night-club prices, the music was consistently good and it was devoted to a no-messing policy of presentation of the best practitioners of jazz in Britain. *Melody Maker* ran a spread on the club the week after it opened, with photographs of Scott, Thompson, Tubby Hayes and others, and the copy declared:

'In addition to presenting the top names of British modern jazz, Ronnie intends to feature promising young musicians at the club and Friday's guest stars included the new alto sensation, Peter King.' In its pre-Christmas edition, its correspondent Bob Dawbarn also commented on the new arrival as 'a highly optimistic note for British jazz. There are still too few places for the modern musician to ply his trade, but the players themselves took matters into their own hands.'

Word of mouth was the publicity machine for the most part, apart from those little ads in *Melody Maker*. Scott devoted himself to making a miniature art-form out of them in the hope that people would seek them out, promising anything he could think of to establish an identity for his premises that would be an instantaneous trademark. He would maintain steadfastly that the club would be featuring an unexpected joint appearance by Sir Thomas Beecham,

Somerset Maugham and Little Richard. He would promise food untouched by human hand due to having a gorilla for a chef. The place caught on. Visiting musicians from abroad, increasingly prevalent in Britain as Harold Davison and others staged more and more concerts that would tie into existing European tours, were to be seen in Ronnie Scott's, which added to the glamour of being there. There were, after all, few enough places in any town where such a rare bird as a jazz musician could truly feel at home. Shelly Manne the drummer, in London with one of Norman Granz's 'Jazz At The Philharmonic' packages, even returned to the States to open a club of his own having spent some time absorbing the atmosphere at Gerrard Street. The fact that the place was run by musicians was already promising to be an enormous benefit. Even though Scott and King were not in a position to pay big money, they were in the same business as the professionals they were hiring, and they were straight. The crippling paranoia, fleecing and all-round disrespect that characterised relationships between jazz musicians and promoters – especially in the States – wasn't much associated with the establishment.

Two problems were soon apparent. The first was that there was a law of diminishing returns about presenting British jazz players – even the very best – night after night. The jazz public would lose its sense of urgency about such a promotion. Scott and King soon felt the draught of this difficulty. They ran the establishment on a simple principle, based on a consultation with the rudimentary books at the end of each week. If there was a serious prospect of there being enough in the kitty to pay the artists and the rent for another week's work, then they were in business.

The second snag was the absence of a bar, more easily fixed though it seemed like a monumental performance at the time. Scott and King looked into the formalities of legalizing the latter. The regulations were complicated. If you were going to serve alcohol, you needed a 'wine committee' to take responsibility for such a subversive pursuit. Ronnie Scott and Pete King formed two-thirds of the wine committee the due process of law required. They asked Benny Green to be the third, being a literary man and a correspondent for a high-class newspaper. Green duly travelled to Wembley

Police Station to make a statement as to why Ronnie Scott's Club wanted to make a public nuisance of itself in this way. 'What is the purpose of this club?' asked the station sergeant wearily. 'It's to try to get rhythm sections to play in time,' intoned Green, straight-faced. The sergeant dutifully took it down word for word. The club's liquor licence was also dependent on providing some form of emergency exit in the case of fire. It was rudimentary enough, and fortunately never had to be tested, being simply a metal ladder that extended upstairs into the hallway of the Jewish garment manufacturer above. Relationships with that establishment were mixed during Ronnie Scott's tenure in Gerrard Street.

Early on it became apparent that Scott and King were going to be no orthodox club-owners. Scott's philosophy, as it had been back in the days of the nine-piece, continued to be that if you could get a laugh out of it, it couldn't be all bad. The word soon got around. Here was a place where all of the misfits and square pegs of a square mile of London dedicated to the entertainment of the normals by the aliens could relax in congenial company – like writer Colin MacInnes, a deep devotee of jazz and friend of Denis Rose, like actor and playwright Harold Pinter. A man called Fred Twigg attached himself to the enterprise to become the club's odd-job man and cleaner. He took to sleeping on the premises, which worsened a chronic condition that Twigg lived with – apparitions. He often complained to the proprietors of flying creatures and gorillas that frequented the establishment at night. And in those early days, the club unexpectedly became an actors' studio as well.

Ronnie Scott had known the actress Georgia Brown from the East End, and she suggested to him that the Gerrard Street cellar would be perfect in the daytime for rehearsals for an actors' company. The company turned out to involve, in the end, the likes of Maggie Smith, George Devine of the Royal Court Theatre, Michael Caine and Lindsay Anderson. Ronnie Scott fell unrequitedly in love with an actress called Ann Lynne and visited the Royal Court night after night to watch her in performance with Albert Finney. Scott and Benny Green found the rehearsals irresistible. They both took to standing behind the tea bar for hours, hypnotized by the display, making lemon tea for the labouring thespians, and eventually found their own communications with others helplessly enmeshed in fake stage-speak. 'What dost thou fancy in the 4.30?' Scott would enquire of Green.

One of the rehearsals involved George Devine donning an elaborate mask, and demanding that the actors guess the emotion expressed by his body without the clues of physiognomy. Devine went up to the street to begin his descent in to the auditorium bearing the testing message, and promptly vanished. The luckless artiste had, it turned out, been mobbed by the passing citizenry of Soho, demanding to know if his get-up meant that the establishment was trading in some hitherto unexploited form of fetishism. Devine eventually tore himself away from this unwelcome new public for his work and fled gracelessly down the steps. 'Fear' promptly supplied the members of the actors' company on the appearance of the master, still holding loyally to the original brief.

Throughout 1960, the difficulty of sustaining an audience for the local musicians continued to nag at Scott and King. The Musicians' Union ban had stopped being unconditional two years previously and international artists regularly came and went. But residencies, the maintaining of an imported star in a British venue night after night for a week, or a month, had not been considered. King, who still worked with the now highly successful impresario Harold Davison, knew that the latter would not be keen that his protégés impinge on what he regarded as his own territory of international jazz promotion.

Pete King then got his act underway to forge the first links since things could not go on as they were. He began at the British Musicians' Union, with the assistant secretary, Harry Francis, who was amenable to the idea of a new arrangement that would suit the requirements of a specialist nightclub. If the exchange of artists would be one for one, Francis was convinced that the request would go through on the British side.

King turned his attention to the real nub of the problem. Since the 1930s, James C. Petrillo of the American Federation of Musicians had effectively battened down any form of trade in musical resources likely to cause any loss of earnings to his own members. Petrillo (nicknamed 'Little Caesar' because of his stocky, pugnacious, Edward G. Robinson-like demeanour) was a man with a straight-shooting style of debate that made him a formidable opponent. The American Federation's policy had grown out of far leaner years than the 1950s and King made no secret of his sympathy for the union's original position. Its obstinacy from the mid-50s onwards was principally fuelled by the attitude of the British Musicians' Union, which was convinced that American members would receive far more attractive invitations to Britain than the other way around. King reasoned that if jazz musicians were the Cinderellas of the profession already, it was short-sighted now that times were not so hard to turn down a policy that might further the public's interest in the music generally.

Scott and King needed to pick their first guest, then worry about the bureaucracy once they had an American jazz star in the bag. They chose Zoot Sims, a one-time partner of Stan Getz's in the Woody Herman band and a player with much the same lyricism and raffish elegance as Getz but with a more robust and muscular delivery. Sims was popular at the Half Note Club in New York, run as a family business by the Cantorino brothers, an Italian family business with a reputation similar to that of the Scott club in London for presenting good music to audiences that cared about it in an atmosphere conducive to relaxation and inventiveness. Sims, having accepted the London offer, knew that he had to help prepare the ground if he was ever to get over to England and take up his residency. King went to New York to try to sew it up. He told the music press that Tubby Hayes was taking a holiday in America at the same time, and it was only reasonable that he, as Hayes' manager, should make an attempt to arrange some work for his client. King met Sims for a beer to chew it over. They played Tubby Hayes' records to the Cantorinos, and from distrusting a project they felt they didn't really need – an English jazz soloist on a residency in the heart of New York's jazzland for a month – the Italians came around to the idea, and wanted to help Zoot, an old friend. The matter went backwards and forwards inside the American Federation officials' headquarters for what seemed like an age to King. But the news finally came through that Petrillo had accepted the deal. King rang Scott in London and told him they were in business. Scott rang Harry Francis at the Musicians' Union and the swap was on. Finally they called Sims. The laconic Californian simply asked, 'When do I come?'

The exchange was arranged for November 1961. Ronnie Scott's Club was about to become an international jazz venue.

7 / California Cool, East Coast Ecstasy

'Don't ever shrink from the belief that you have to prove yourself every minute, because you do.' (Sonny Rollins to Kitty Grime, *Jazz at Ronnie Scott's*, 1979.)

Zoot Sims was a delight.

After his first show, the proprietors of London's new international jazz club sat bemused in their locked-up premises, counting the hours until they could hear him play again. For Scott, who had probably already subconsciously decided that a policy of booking practitioners on his own chosen instrument was going to be one of the early ways he would enjoy himself as a promoter, Sims was virtually a definition of the modern jazz musician who was still functioning wholeheartedly and pragmatically in the world. He had a lot in common with Ronnie. He had been a teenage saxophone star in a showy jazz orchestra, the Woody Herman band. He was an unpretentious, unaffected, music-loving enthusiast. He knew jazz history. And he always played the music as if he enjoyed it. Sims was the kind of player who could have thrived in just about any kind of jazz band of the previous forty-odd years.

Sims delivered his easy-going swing and gentle rhapsodizing throughout the month of November 1961 to devoted audiences at the club. A casual, fresh-faced man, Sims would play without demonstrativeness, holding the instrument still. His opening bars would establish the tune with the directness and confidence of a man completely at ease with his raw materials, and much of his appeal was founded on the manner in which his sound exhibited both confidence and a heady lightness, as if he were performing a graceful juggling act in slow motion. King arranged a short tour of out-of-town venues for Sims, and the proprietors presented him with a silver brandy flask after his last performance. Other local musicians donated such peculiarly British gifts as copies of the 'Goon Show' records. Sims was the first American to experience the off-beam goings-on that would become legendary behind-the-scenes features of Ronnie Scott's establishments in the years to come. Somebody threw a smoke-bomb into the room on 5 November which cleared the premises, but the Californian did little more than raise an eyebrow. Fred Twigg, the club's vision-prone cleaner, was deeply suspicious of the quiet, unassuming visitor. 'Russian spy,' he warned Scott ominously. 'He's a Russian spy.'

In an interview, the normally unforthcoming Sims declared himself delighted with the experience of playing in London, since the intimacy of a club gave him the opportunity to relax. 'It reminds me of the Half Note,' Sims said. 'The atmosphere is warm and it's an easygoing place. Musicians like it. It has the same kind of management.' Sims added that he'd like to see Ronnie Scott play in the States. 'It depends on his confidence,' the American opined. For Scott's part, he was sad to see Sims go. 'My God,' he mused. 'What an anti-climax next week's going to be.' The Sims season proved that the problem of the European rhythm section was soluble. This issue dominated conversations in local jazz circles. Though Ronnie Scott, Johnny Dankworth, Tubby Hayes, and a handful of other performers had demonstrated at least a modicum of confidence in their skills as front-line performers, European rhythm sections were on the whole not popular with visiting Americans, considered to be insensitive to the essence of jazz timekeeping or incapable of relaxed swing. On top of that, the club proprietor faced the choice between accompanying musicians whose independence was such that they might try to strongarm the honoured guest into playing something they didn't want to play, or patsies whose very inertia would so lower the tone and drive of the entire proceedings and it would be difficult even for the most sensational soloists in the business to sound good.

The solution to many of these problems was Stan Tracey.

Tracey had a considerable musical pedigree by 1961. He had begun at Gerrard Street within months of the opening and was a quietly truculent figure whose playing style was loosely derived from the robust and percussive keyboard style of Thelonious Monk. Like Monk he was a confirmed admirer of both the composition and piano playing of Duke Ellington. Tracey had been a teenage accordion player in the forces entertainment network ENSA, had performed in the RAF Gang Show directed by the late Tony Hancock. He had first come across Ronnie Scott when the saxophonist was playing a guest spot at the Paramount in Tottenham Court Road, a venue predominantly for London's male black population of the early 1950s. Tracey performed there on a piano with a bass player who doubled on hi-hat, an ignominious role occasioned by the absence of a drummer, so the bassist was obliged to deliver beats one and three on the bass and two and four on the hi-hat.

When Laurie Morgan had formed a band called Elevated Music, after his departure from the Club Eleven circle, Tracey left the Paramount to be in it. Thereafter Tracey had played on the boats – on one occasion in 1953 on the *Caronia* with Jock Scott as his bandleader – and eventually toured the United States with the Ted Heath band. He had a vigorous, muscular way of playing, possessed a receptive and forceful improvisor's intelligence and swung furiously. By the time he became involved with Ronnie Scott's Club, when many piano players of Tracey's age wanted to adopt the smooth and elegant style of an accompanist like Wynton Kelly or the piquant classicism of Bill Evans, Tracey was determined to tread a different path.

Zoot Sims and Tracey made an album while the saxophonist was in England, on which Ronnie Scott and the trumpeter Jimmy Deuchar also appeared. Recordings of British modernists with their American counterparts were virtually unheard of at the time. It was also a kind of defiance of the sort of jazz that could make you money. Dave Brubeck's 'Take Five', a catchy melody in one of the pianist's gimmicky time signatures was in the pop hit parade that week. Bandleaders were complaining that they were having to disappoint their customers because the sheet music for Brubeck's record was so hard to get hold of.

The Gerrard Street premises began to build a reputation.

It was already a strong competitor with Wardour Street's Flamingo as the leading establishment of its kind in London, and it had an atmosphere all of its own, something of that risqué mystery of both the 52nd Street places and the wartime bottle-party joints, the definition of a below-stairs dive in which people who had never known what conformity meant, people who were trying to slough it off, and people who were taking a night off from it would listen to a music that seemed itself to be an antidote to much of the schmaltz that still overwhelmed Tin Pan Alley and pop music.

Down a rickety stairway into a basement, beckoned into the depths by the loudspeaker on the stairs that would relay some of the atmosphere of what was going on inside (some poorer fans would simply prop themselves up outside and listen to the stars over the sound-system), getting a chance to get close to these legendary figures, even snatch a conversation with them at the bar because the place was so small they couldn't get away from you anyway. At the beginning, in that cramped rectangular basement, the bandstand had been placed at the far-end of the room, the coffee bar at the other. As times improved, so too did life for the long-suffering punters (even at bursting point the place wouldn't hold much more than 150, one reason for the precarious nature of its economics). A tier of seats on one long wall was built, with the bandstand facing them halfway along the other.

An evening there was something to look forward to, waiting for players like Sims or Getz to be brought by Scott or King from what the club ironically termed its 'office' (a cubby-hole under the thoroughfare of Gerrard Street itself) through the crowd, enthusiastically parting to let them by, up to the tiny stage to wait for one of Tracey's quirky, sidelong introductions before filling the room with that rich, rounded, heart-quickening sound of the saxophone.

But getting a laugh out of life wasn't always unimpeded. For a young man like Ronnie Scott, waited on hand and foot by two women during all of his life at home, the only male offspring in a Jewish household dedicated to the encouragement of overnight success that might ward off the hardships and setbacks of generations of wandering, reverses were hard to cope with and in those years of the early 1960s seemed to be coming in battalions.

It had begun with the death of Jock, and followed with the death of Nana Becky in a Hendon hospice in 1960. She had gone on to a great age, and she had been as close to Ronnie Scott as Cissie had been, and for all the world was his second mother. Cissie had died unexpectedly two years later, pouring tea for the women who used to come to the Edgware-bury house weekly to play cards with her. Sol had been in the back room, reading, and Ronnie was upstairs in the tiny bedroom that had been kept for him, looking just the way it always had, in anticipation of his regular visits. He remembered the doctor's words to the ambulancemen, 'I won't be needing you now,' that moment of hope that she might have recovered, then the realization of what the doctor actually meant and that Cissie was gone, and with no warning, nothing to help him prepare.

He felt that the deaths of Nana Becky and Cissie had changed him. It was as if it was impossible to be quite the same freewheeler again. It brought him to the front line in his family. When they were alive, they stood between him and age, maturity, seriousness. They were the nurturing forces in his life; now he was exposed.

Gerrard Street was making a name for itself. There was another new night-haunt close by, in Greek Street, that was similarly on the way to cult status. The Establishment Club was opened by two young graduates, Peter Cook and Nicholas Luard, to represent the growing fashion for satirical humour – a byproduct of the expansion of higher education in the post-war years, its target exactly the complacent and self-congratulatory British society whose boom time had fuelled it.

The Establishment invited the savage American genius Lenny Bruce to perform on its premises. Bruce was drawn to Gerrard Street as much as the jazz club's patrons and staff were drawn to him. Lenny Bruce and Scott talked jazz, and the American gave him a pass to the Establishment to watch the act. Also on the bill were the Alberts, a British ensemble led by the performance artist Bruce Lacey who wore Edwardian suits and National Health glasses and performed a kind of impassive slapstick. Scott would for years dissolve at the memory of their version of a quiz show. Quizmaster: 'Are you ready for the sixty-four-thousand-dollar question?' 'Yes' (Bucket of whitewash on contestant's head). Pause. Contestant: 'I'm sorry, could you repeat the question?'

Kenneth Tynan had described Bruce's work as 'outspoken harangues in an idiom I can only describe as jazz-Jewish.' It might have been a phrase tailor-made for Scott and his playing companions, but they soon learned that Bruce's muse came from a darker and more relentless compulsion than theirs. Scott loved Bruce's flailing vulgarity – the comic believing then that sexual and physical repression was at the root of many of the ills he directed his spleen against. It was this kind of material that got Bruce's act labelled 'sick and lavatory humour' by the then Home Secretary Henry Brooke, and a ban from the country for a return trip. But Bruce's real clout was as a trenchant social critic. He revealed in routines like the Madison Avenue plot to increase cigarette sales by making cancer a status symbol, an act that would sound almost like a social service today.

Ronnie Scott's Club gathered steam, and London seemed to be becoming an interesting town once again. A succession of illustrious visitors came and went, and Stan Tracey went on adding to his encyclopaedic knowledge – material that would shortly surface in some remarkable compositions by the pianist, including his 'Under Milk Wood' suite, which became famous not only for some memorable melodies but notably the yearning, atmospheric tenor playing of the Scots musician Bobby Wellins. Scott and King, at that time ever enthusiastic for ways of branching out, organized a jazz package for an all-in price of 110 guineas covering hotel bills and club admissions in that period, for some of the London fans newly-nurtured on live appearances by their heroes and heroines to catch the music on its home turf in New York. It was a once-only attempt. Scott claimed that King couldn't count in guineas. None of the partners' efforts at diversification ever came to much. They lacked the will to follow it up, to make a business out of it. All either of them really wanted to do was run a jazz club.

In the summer of 1962 there was an unexpected hitch in the proceedings. The gown-manufacturer who owned the premises upstairs was furious about noise from the basement. The offending circumstances seemed to be the rehearsals that took place in the club in the afternoons, and which brought the place some much-needed extra revenue. The argument, which passed through polite requests, irritability and finally fury, ended up in the courts. The plaintiffs eventually produced a single witness in the secretary who worked in the room above the bandstand and who insisted that she couldn't receive 'important telephone calls' because of the noise. The judge remarked to her at one point 'some people like jazz. They might consider you lucky to have it while you work, without paying for it.'

The witness continued to recount the import of two principal complaints. On the first, she said she had discovered a group of buglers downstairs, at their devilish work on the bandstand, she said. 'I told the conductor he was too noisy, but he told me he didn't want to know' – a contention that astonished the defendants, who couldn't lay hands on a bugle between them. On the second, the noise had similarly been so intense as to provoke a personal visit, but when she arrived in the basement, she had found it empty. The defence enquired as to where the noise could thus have been emanating from, and answer came there none. Scott and Benny Green had already spent much time hovering in the upstairs passage in the presence of a young man with a sound level meter while Ella Fitzgerald was using the establishment for rehearsal. The machine had hardly registered more than, as Green recalled, 'our own heavy breathing.'

The insubstantiality of the gown-manufacturer's witness led to an out of court settlement in the end. Scott's lawyer demanded life membership of the club in part payment. 'Whose life, yours or mine?' the proprietor asked him pointedly.

Lucky Thompson was the first black American to visit Gerrard Street. And then, in September 1962, the mighty Dexter Gordon followed. Gordon was a jazz giant in all senses. He was six foot five, with a deceptively gentle and courteous manner, and his own version of showmanship was a kind of studiously careful demeanour with his audiences which would take the form of elaborately fastidious announcements of tunes, as if the punters were all deaf or incapable of understanding the language. 'Society Red' Gordon would announce as his next tune, the kind of funky mid-tempo blues that he was famous for extemporizing endlessly on. 'So-cie-ty Red' he would repeat with sibilant emphasis, as if the repetition of the title would make everything crystal clear.

Dexter Gordon virtually defined what was hip to the modern jazz fans of the day. He sang a good deal on his opening visit to the Scott Club, not one of his greatest attributes, but one that he would be moved to explore if in sufficiently convivial mood. Gordon and Ronnie Scott recognized that they were kindred spirits and as the run progressed they took to exchanging impromptu comedy routines during the shows. Scott would stare up at Gordon's elm-like proportions from the floor, and inform him gravely that there was no money to pay the wages that week. Gordon would elaborately act hurt.

He was a spectacular sight at full cry. His massive feet flapped enthusiastically as huge, gravelly expositions rolled unquenchably from his horn. Sweat would form rivulets down his face that would fall in an explosion on to the raised bandstand, close to the glowing faces of his admirers. As the evening wore on, Gordon's huge collar would detach itself and fly out around his enormous neck like a sail. And at the end of the performance he would hold the tenor, which seemed hardly bigger than a toy in his hands, out toward the audience as if it were a gift or he were inviting them to share with him a tribute to the instrument.

It was the appearance of Roland Kirk in 1963 that was as big a landmark in the history of the club as that first booking of Zoot Sims had been. Kirk was the best public relations exercise any jazz club could conceivably embark on. He was a blind multi-instrumentalist from Columbus, Ohio, who had become one of the most remarkable phenomena in the music by 1963. He had been a powerful improvisor from his days in the Charlie Mingus band, but had developed techniques for not only playing several reed instruments at the same time and performing simultaneous vocal and instrumental lines on the flute (that owed a little to his predecessor in the Mingus group, Yusef Lateef) but also for sustaining an improvization over lengthy periods without interruption, by the technique known as circular breathing – whereby the musician would be capable of breathing in through the nose and out through the mouth at the same time. The late Mal Dean, a trumpeter and a cartoonist for *Melody Maker*, even represented Kirk with an array of oxygen bottles behind him connected to his head by a tube.

Kirk also gave the club its first taste of what the new black militancy would sound like. 'Black classical music' was the saxophonist's category for his work. Unlike many of the visitors, whose loquacity in their music would be matched only by their indifference to speech, Kirk was persistently garrulous as a presenter of his own repertoire, and introduced pieces with lengthy preambles peppered with anecdotes of black American history. Kirk was only interested in producing a music that drew crowds. Many came to watch what seemed like a sophisticated freak show – since the ingenuity that went into being able to simultaneously perform a three-part harmony on a trio of saxophones would sometimes take on a sideshow bravura – but it was obvious on his debut performance at Gerrard Street that he could play a straight-ahead bebop tenor solo as seriously and inventively as anyone in the business. He proved to be that rare thing – an all-round entertainer who could play first-class jazz, and remain true to his first principles. As such, he had little time for critics who dismissed him as a circus act. He even hauled one of his detractors, the critic Steve Race, on to the stand one night. Knowing that Race was a pianist of some accomplishment, Kirk insisted that they play together; it was not a dignified experience for the Englishman.

Kirk was suspicious and difficult with Scott and King at first. 'Blind and black,' King thought – he rarely minced words. 'How many times has he been ripped off?' The American wanted his money in cash at the end of each night's work on those first days, a precaution born out of bitter experience. It was one of the more striking instances of a jazz club run by musicians helping to solve a potentially difficult diplomatic impasse. But within days Kirk's mind was at rest.

Rock players were fascinated by Kirk, who was both a

passionate artist and a showman. And because the rock boom already breaking at the time was fuelled by black rhythm 'n' blues, Kirk's earthy approach to, and the accessibility of, his work made him virtually a guru to the young white rock players, who in desperation for authenticity sought out many major black artists. The Beatles came to Gerrard Street in the foothills of their success to hear the great multi-instrumentalist, in 1963, the year of their real impact on the music business and the British public – twelve months in which they had five chart hits. Kirk was never truly a member of the avant-garde and the label was only attached to him because he was *weird* and would occasionally launch into odd effects such as endlessly sustained exit notes, wild off-the-register top notes or dissonant wails with three horns played together. A number of English rock artists – including the drummer Jon Hiseman, at that time making the transition from avant garde jazz – made a short film with Roland Kirk on that tour.

Kirk's force as a performer made him a man whose opinion you respected. On his first visit he was introduced by the locals to the playing of Tubby Hayes, a man who on the face of it was as American as you could get in his confidence and the speed and agility of his playing. 'He's very fast,' Kirk agreed. 'But the best player I've heard here is Ronnie Scott.'

8 / Royal Procession

'I love this club, it's just like home. Filthy and full of strangers. Last night vandals broke in and redecorated it.' (Scott
routine)

'Certain neuroses, cultivated by a pogrom-orientated mother
and a father leaning toward Utopian socialism, inevitably
inclined me to a humorous point of view.' (Cecil 'Flash'
Winston's memoirs (so far unpublished).)

The proprietor was urinating into the washbasin of the club's
'office' as Flash Winston came in. Winston coughed. Scott
looked up in mock alarm. 'You haven't just washed in this
bowl, have you?' he greeted Winston with elaborate fastidi-
ousness. The stocky, bird-like man was still attempting to
pursue a career as a stand up comic despite a decade of
reverses and an attempt to improve his image with a nose-
job that he swore had led his mother to wail disconsolately
'you won't be able to be buried in a Jewish cemetery'. 'That
reminds me,' Winston came back without a pause 'I said to
the man in my garage "I gotta leak in my radiator". He said
"it's your radiator, go ahead".' Scott returned 'you got a ready
wit, Flash. Maybe it isn't ready yet.' Winston believed it was
the chance of a lifetime.
   'As a matter of fact, it is,' he said urgently. 'Put me on
tonight, Ron. I won't let you down.' Scott went into brief
consultation with Pete King. He finally said 'OK. You're on
in fifteen minutes.'
   Scott then set about introducing Winston to the Gerrard
Street audience. 'It's a great pressure, er, pleasure,' he
began, 'to introduce a young man who has just finished
cabaret in the north, and is now here to finish it in the south.

How about a nice round of applause for Flash Winston.' Following that introduction, Winston excelled himself, and even the normally unforthcoming Scott was complimentary. Winston was invited back the following night. He couldn't sleep with the excitement of the opportunity, his second show was a shadow of the first, and Ronnie Scott – a friend from the days when the public had never heard the names of either of them, but whose life had taken a very different path out of the East End – was forced to cancel him for a third.

But it wasn't just old loyalties that had inclined Scott to giving Winston a chance in the first place. Life seemed to him a matter of snap decisions made on gut feelings. He and Winston had had a conversation like one of his old tenor exchanges with Tubby Hayes that first night, so the chances were it might lead somewhere. When it didn't, you could always, maybe regrettably, start over. It would be a long time before Ronnie Scott would consider that this philosophy didn't always work.

In 1963 Ronnie Scott got a new opportunity for an American trip, this time with a band of his own. It involved returning to the Half Note in New York where Tubby Hayes had triumphed to make Zoot Sims' journey possible two years before. Scott went to the States with Jimmy Deuchar and saxophonist Ronnie Ross to work with a band featuring the Massachusetts pianist Roger Kellaway, who had made a reputation for himself in both modern classical music and jazz. But despite the fact that the Cantorino brothers welcomed the Englishmen and the club was comfortable and pleasant to play in, Ronnie Scott still felt like an interloper, bringing American music on to its home soil. He blotted out most memories of the trip, but the return journey etched itself on his mind since his taxiing aeroplane caught fire at Idlewild and the recollection of the chutes and the firemen in asbestos suits returns to him every time he has boarded an aircraft since.

Deuchar and Ross found it easier to forget since they had both been drunk when the trip began. 'My saxophone, my saxophone,' Ross had wailed to Scott as he stumbled down the aisle to the exits. 'Fuck your saxophone,' Scott replied, pushing him out of the door. Since his professional life was geared to travel, and increasingly so in the years to come, the experience at Idlewild became a lasting problem.

But if that journey to the States had been memorable to Ronnie Scott principally as a reminder of the potential treachery of fate, there was also a nuance to it that would not become apparent to Scott and to Pete King for another year at least. 1963 was the year of the Beatles. The Liverpudlian group, itself steeped in exactly the sort of music that had formed the repertoire of the black rock package on Scott's previous visit in 1957, was now not only an inspiration to aspiring British pop musicians – who were by now emerging so ubiquitously that almost every school in the land would have at least one band of young hopefuls trying to follow in their footsteps – but to young white Americans as well. The Beatles, and the dozens of British bands that came in their wake, were soon to make such an impact in America, that the quota system applying to the transatlantic exchange would shortly become irrelevant. It was perfect timing. The expansion of Ronnie Scott's Club through the 1960s would have been much harder without it.

At thirty-six Ronnie Scott was becoming the representative of the British modern jazz scene most widely known outside his home beat. The growing reputation of the club enhanced it. As a player, his style was taking on a firmer, grittier stance. He had found two new inspirations, in Sonny Rollins and Hank Mobley. The latter was a model that seemed to reveal a meeting-place between his own background (palais-band work, and that peculiarly Jewish mix of pragmatism and romance that he had found a voice for by borrowing the cool elegance of Getz) and the more imperious, independent and soulful world of black American jazz.

Mobley was a Georgia-born musician three years younger than Ronnie Scott, a 'musician's musician' who had worked in Blakey's Jazz Messengers, who possessed an original musical intelligence, poise, restraint and softer sound that appealed to the more introverted Europeans, and an ability to construct his solos through highly original suspensions and manipulations of the basic pulse. This came at a time when men like Sonny Rollins and John Coltrane were producing music that would frighten their mothers by (in Rollins' case) the use of a bleak tone, oblique musical jokes, unpredictable stutterings and stumblings between loquacity and impenetrable pauses, and (in Coltrane's) a tendency toward stark and unnerving off-the-register harmonics and drenching super-development of bop harmony to generate a seamless, trance-like effect. Ronnie Scott was fascinated by both of them, but they were unswerving experimenters, and he was not. It was Mobley who seemed to retain the grace that Scott's deepest sympathies inclined to, one that seemed to retain a little of Jock's values, that 'good sound'. He regularly bought the American's albums as soon as they hit the shops.

Ronnie Scott was by now going out with a German girl, Ilsa Fox, who had been first a member at Gerrard Street, and then a waitress there as its growing popularity obliged an expansion of the staff.

Ilsa was intelligent, strong, loved music and was able to share the eccentric life he led. Though they spent a lot of time in each other's company, they didn't live together, and Ilsa continued to occupy her bedsitter. Toward the end of the year, she discovered that she was pregnant. Ronnie was no nearer wanting to be a family man now than he had been in the 1950s with Joan. It was partly that he doubted that the life of a practising jazz musician could easily be squared with it – what had happened to Jock and Cissie was proof enough of that. Ronnie would sometimes simply make it seem as if he found children a drag. But it wasn't simply that, as the women who were close to him quickly realized. He was afraid of the responsibility. Though his life was founded on gambles, this was one that you couldn't just write off if it turned sour.

Initially they considered abortion, but Ilsa wasn't really keen. Ronnie considered that if this baby was born, it would be his responsibility to contribute to its maintenance. Ilsa enjoyed her pregnancy, and was happy to go ahead, with or without him. The child would be born the following midsummer.

In the club, life wound on its erratic, sometimes surreal course. A landmark of the year in its gallery of holy fools was the arrival of Gypsy Larry. Scott and King had decided that the place needed a facelift. They had improved the food by the simple expedient of sending out the orders to the local restaurants. They also wanted to smarten the place up and in the course of one period of redecoration an imposing, grey-haired, weather-beaten old man in a bandana entered the premises, requested a paintbrush and stayed for twelve years until his death. His name was Gypsy Larry. Nobody knew another.

Larry was unquestionably a man with a past. Some Soho regulars knew him from the beginning of the 1950s in his old association with a legendary bohemian of the area, Iron Foot Jack. Jack was a man who held court to audiences of entranced children in Old Compton Street; he had white flowing hair, a cloak and a swag bag, sold old jewellery and bric-à-brac. His efforts to do the best he could extended to founding a religion all of his own, into which it was alleged that a sizeable number of impressionable and underage girls were recruited as worshippers. The stories found their way into the Sunday papers of the day.

On 6 March 1964, Stan Getz arrived to play in Gerrard Street. It was a major coup for Scott and King, since the virtuoso saxophonist had got into a drugs problem on his way into Britain four years previously. It was assumed that after such an event, getting a work permit for Getz would be a proposition not worth attempting. On top of that, both men assumed that Getz's fee – particularly now that he was enjoying unprecedented success in the bossa nova boom thanks to the album he had made with guitarist Charlie Byrd and singer Astrud Gilberto the previous year – would break the bank anyway. *Jazz Samba* had featured famous tunes of the Latin American idiom – like 'Desafinado' and 'Girl From Ipanema' – and with the coming of the record Getz helped reveal to the world the talents of two remarkable composers, Antonio Carlos Jobim and Joao Gilberto. At the time the two Londoners tried to haul Getz into the net, he was bigger than he had ever been, a stature that they were sure would be reflected in attendances at the club.

King was by now getting to know the ropes of immigration department. He began to drop some hints to people he knew raising the issue of a permit for Getz. Astonishingly, it came through. King promptly flew to New York to see if he could set up what he figured would be the coup of the club's life so far. 'If I *could* fix a work permit,' King reasoned, 'would you do a month at the club at $300 a week?' Getz, accustomed to three times as much, was sure that King would never get the permission and was just blowing smoke rings. He therefore let it ride, agreeing to come for the $300. He wasn't overjoyed to discover that there would be no problem, but stuck to his promise in the end.

That was just the start of the uphill struggle to get this exquisite performer to unfurl his remarkable gifts for the benefit of a club audience in London. Everything about Getz was difficult. He had been in trouble with hard drugs for years and was temperamental, unpredictable, and easily thrown off balance. He took firmly against King after the episode of the original booking, and fell out with him on the first day of rehearsals with the Stan Tracey group because noisy running repairs were going on in the room at the same time.

But he couldn't miss with the public, whatever the difficulties of actually getting him to stand in front of it. The club raised its admission fee to cover the American's season, but 'House Full' notices were displayed outside throughout the month. The lucky ones inside weren't disappointed. Getz was at the peak of his form. His lovely tone, his fastidious distaste at the playing of anything that orthodox musical standards would consider ugly, the tireless facility with which he would embroider and add flourishes to the fundamentals of a song, and the gentle acknowledgements of his discreet quotation from past Lester Young triumphs like 'Lester Leaps In' and 'Dickie's Dream' all combined to make his performance a *tour de force*. Getz would also ensure that he chose the best songs for his rhapsodies, and some of his finest playing was to be heard on a neglected Jerome Kern tune 'Why Was I Born', held by those present to rival the version recorded by Billie Holiday in its poignancy.

For Ronnie Scott, the Getz season was a personal delight, soured only slightly by the difficulties he and King experienced with their new guest off the bandstand. Scott had been devoted to Getz's work since the American's period with the Woody Herman band in the 1940s. But it also brought a woman into Scott's life who was to become as close to him as Joan Crewe had been.

Early in the Getz run, a young Welsh nurse, who had

come to London from a hospital in the Midlands, went to the club with a French girlfriend. Mary Hulin was a jazz-lover, her mother a music teacher, and she had learned the violin from childhood. As a student nurse in Burton-on-Trent she had explored what there was of the local jazz scene, but she knew there were better things to be heard in the south. The arrival of Getz in town was a high point for her, as it was for most of those packed into the tiny basement. As it was, she and Ronnie Scott very nearly missed each other. Both girls were leaving after Getz had played, but ran into a friend arriving in a cab in Gerrard Street, and changed their minds about leaving.

Late in the evening Ronnie Scott spotted Mary and offered to buy her a drink. He was on top form, wisecracking with that complete absence of his old inhibitions that would always come when he felt comfortable and in congenial company. He could be sensitive and attentive as well, and Mary, who had no idea who he was at first, was nonetheless immediately attracted to him. She was surprised by how self-effacing he was once she got behind the smooth operator of the bandstand.

He was hardly domesticated, but nevertheless he had a colony of cats in the flat, newly arrived kittens in a drawer. She watched him roll up the silver paper from the packets of Senior Service that he constantly smoked, roll them across the floor and get the cats to bring them back to him.

Ronnie found Mary not only strikingly pretty, with the willowy elegance of a mannequin, but possessed of great relaxation and gentleness. She hadn't found nursing work in London, and had a job as a waitress at a French restaurant nearby. When he learned of this, Scott said, 'If you're going to do that kind of work, why not do it here?' Mary Hulin came to the club to work as a waitress. The new affair helped Scott to relax in the face of the substantial strain that the presence of Getz was imposing on his patience, and on Pete King's. Getz was determined to be patronizing about his appearances in such a far flung outpost of the jazz world and was casual about his appearances on the stage. Dexter Gordon had often been late, but this was different. Getz took so long getting from the bandroom to the stand that the crowd would become distinctly restive. Stan Getz was determinedly sulking by this time and took longer and longer to make his appearances. Eventually his hosts cracked. King had said to his partner, 'Listen, I've got to keep out of his way, or I don't know what will happen.' Scott and King got into a furious row with the saxophonist, at the end of which the virtuoso grew very distressed, even apologised. The two men had considered replacing Getz with Zoot Sims.

For other musicians Getz continually made music a competition rather than a pleasure. Stan Tracey, who was really too spikey an operator to be likely to find common ground with a performer as classically balletic as Getz, had serious problems with the American. Tracey, whose efforts to keep up with the demands of such a varied succession of powerful artists six nights a week, month in, month out, had turned him increasingly toward stimulants, was becoming as volatile as some of those he was there to support. When Getz publically criticized the rhythm section one night during the run, Tracey simply shouted, 'Bollocks' at the American and left it at that. Getz, when seriously challenged, frequently backed off.

Getz and King were left to each other for the latter part of the saxophonist's season. Scott had slipped a disc getting into his car the day after the row, and was in traction for more than a week. The event formed a staple of Ronnie Scott's repertoire. 'I slipped a disc bending over backwards to please Stan Getz,' Scott said in a BBC interview.

The middle-sixties was to be later viewed with hindsight as a golden age for the establishment musically. Following Getz into Gerrard Street in May 1964 was Sonny Stitt, the man who had made such an impression on Scott and Benny Green on the American tour seven years before. Stitt was still his old terrifying, competitive, eat-you-alive self, difficult to cope with too, but principally on the stand. Scott jammed with Stitt in Gerrard Street one night, with the Jamaican guitarist Ernest Ranglin, in the company of Brubeck-bassist Gene Wright, and trumpeters Oliver Beener and Roy Burroughs from the Ray Charles band. Stitt tried to throw Scott by playing a fast blues and changing the key each chorus, but by coincidence the Londoner had been practising exactly the same device and stayed with him.

The fans who were there that night knew that they had witnessed in action exactly the kind of musical electricity that the Kansas City clubs of the 1930s, or the 52nd Street clubs of the 1940s were famous for, but this time with a twist that had a particular appeal for a London audience. Ronnie Scott's real inventiveness as an improvisor was probed and exploited by the ferocious competitiveness of Stitt, exhibiting characteristics almost unknown on the local scene. Not a sound was audible in the basement save for the music as the dogfight soared on and on. And after it, Ronnie Scott, though he clearly felt that a distinctly unusual adventure had happened to him, was phlegmatic in his discussion with Mary about it later. He was convinced that all jazz musicians felt like him – that they could have done it better.

As for Stitt, his relationship with Stan Tracey had less sublime moments. The American even publically lectured Tracey on the stand one night, and stopping the show to grab the pianist's hands and place them where he wanted them on the keyboard. Tracey restrained himself.

Ronnie Scott was later to confess that of all the American saxophonists capable of unnerving him musically, Stitt was the most formidable. What made it so difficult to handle was that – unlike Charlie Parker or John Coltrane – Stitt was clearly not inspired by the kind of genius that motivated those musicians to find ways of turning the accepted practices inside out. But the fact that he was not a true original only made it worse. It meant that an ordinary mortal could learn to play like that, given enough practice. Though Ronnie knew his dedication didn't stretch that far.

On 21 June 1964, Ilsa Fox gave birth to a son, who she called Nicholas. Ronnie Scott was, to Ilsa's surprise, fascinated by the boy. Friends said that it was Jewish pride in the male issue. She was intrigued and delighted to be a mother, even though she was alone, living in a bedsitter, and discovered within weeks of leaving hospital that her child had a hole in the heart. The health visitor was astonished by the woman's exuberance given the circumstances, and informed Ilsa that she was the happiest mother she had ever come across. For her part, Ilsa concluded that the difference between her and Ronnie was greater than could be explained simply by his distrust of the notion of parenthood. She had carried this child for nine months, and however she was feeling, and whether Nicholas was happy, or sad, or sick or well, the bond between them was something unimaginable until it actually happened to her. She knew that it was not the same for Ronnie. Nor could it be slowly fostered, since he would see relatively little of the child. But he immediately began to pay for the upkeep of his unexpected family. This was a gambling debt that couldn't be welshed on.

But Ronnie's attempts to play down his relationship with Ilsa to Mary were impossible to sustain, and soon the two of them were frequently visiting the young mother in her bedsitter. Ronnie had, as it turned out, visited Ilsa and Nicholas every day while they were in hospital. Nicholas' illness made it harder for Mary to resent the woman or the child, and the experience of nursing helped her to anticipate what a struggle their life would become – years of uncertainty at the slightest sign of sickness, constant visits to hospitals, so many of the pleasures of childhood containing a threat as well as a promise. Ilsa's determination, spirited independence and her devotion to Nicholas impressed Mary despite herself. It continued to impress Ronnie too, who was not as detached from the mother of his child as Mary thought.

But nonetheless the relationship blossomed. Mary left the house she was sharing in Chelsea, and they moved to a flat at Chesham Street, in Belgravia. But if they had regularised matters, they had not established a routine. Ronnie was unpredictable. He could be moody and withdrawn, though sometimes he would career off into outrageous public clowning – in restaurants, in the street, anywhere – that would reduce the young woman, and eventually both of them, to helpless hysterics.

But life did follow a pattern in that part of the day they both so intimately shared through their work – the early hours. When they got home from the club, Mary would make tea (he was determined that she should avoid, as he had done for most of his life, any enthusiasm for alcohol) and they would sit in the two big wing chairs in the living room, and talk. They found there was a lot to share. Mary was adopted, was obsessed with finding her real parents, and the preoccupation struck a chord with Ronnie, recalling the tensions he felt between the fascinating, absent Jock and the staid, reliable Sol. But one night, Ronnie Scott made an observation of an entirely unexpected kind.

'Mary' he began. 'Maybe you and I should consider not seeing each other any more'.

The girl was astonished.

'Why's that?' she quietly asked him.

'Well, I don't think I'll ever be able to marry you. I just don't believe in being that tied down.'

Mary let it ride. But at twenty-one, in the midst of an affair with a charismatic and unpredictable man sixteen years older, she felt that she was going to have to grow up fast.

At the end of the year, Scott and King booked into the premises one of jazz music's best-loved artists, a man who virtually defined the image of the art in the public mind – Ben Webster. Webster was fifty-four when he came to play his first season, and had been one of the handful of jazz musicians to have helped put the tenor saxophone on the map in the 1920s. As Benny Green was later to acknowledge in the *Observer*, men like Webster and Coleman Hawkins had virtually made it possible for players like himself and Ronnie Scott to exist at all. Webster was by now already playing unevenly and passing into a period of his life in which he was frequently drunk onstage. When Scott and King went to collect Webster from Southampton (he refused to fly), the saxophonist was incapable of independent locomotion from the moment he left the boat and had to be shoe-horned into the back of King's mini, where he slept resolutely throughout the journey, only waking to shout 'Give 'em what they want – as long as they don't want too much!' to the mystification of his chauffeurs. Webster's behaviour at this first encounter did make the two Englishmen ponder on just what they were getting themselves into.

On his first appearance at the club, his music was mostly as romantic, breathy and full of silky sensuality – particularly on ballads – as it had ever been. And though he was less secure on uptempo numbers by this stage of his career, and had never overly relished them, he would deliver a grainier,

more gravelly and laconic series of monologues, splashed over
by frequent broad, palette-knife flourishes that characterized
the self-confident, expansive jazz of the swing era. Midway
between ballad tempo and a brisk trot, Webster would place
one of his favourite tunes, Gershwin's 'Our Love Is Here To
Stay', on which he would blow smoke rings of sound that
both maximized the effect of his rich, shimmering tone and
simultaneously highlighted the ingenuity of the composer.
Roland Kirk, in the audience during Webster's season,
remarked that such a sound ought to be impossible to produce
on a saxophone.

The significance of having a legend like Webster on the
premises was most moving of all to Scott himself. One night
toward the end of Webster's visit, Mary Hulin witnessed a
cameo that caught in flight what jazz meant to an old travelling poet like Webster and to her new partner. On the rickety
wooden steps of the club, the massive American stood
embracing the young man who had brought him to London.
'It's marvellous that I can come to a place like this in London,'
Webster enthused. 'A place where I can settle down, play
for a month, relax.' It was much the same insight that Zoot
Sims had made. Scott said enthusiastically, 'It's great to have
someone I've admired so long working here.' Mary remembered a lesson she had heard Ronnie Scott deliver to all the
incoming staff of the club. 'The artists are the most important
people who come here. Always treat them with the greatest
of respect.'

The arrival of Theodore Walter 'Sonny' Rollins at the beginning of 1965 provided the sharpest and most formidable illus-
tration of what the music of an artist entirely dedicated to
the pursuit of the oblique, the subversive and the unexpected
could sound like night after night in an atmosphere tailor
made for the avoidance of the easy option. Rollins made an
impact on London musical life, in that year and 1966 that
shook the predominantly cool and restrained demeanour of
jazz style in the capital. He was in his prime when he arrived,
and his musical curiosity was boundless. Such audacity and
cliff-hanging inventiveness in performance forged an
immediate bond with his audiences. Some fans visited the

club three or four times during the season to hear how Rollins would twist and tangle, bludgeon and illuminate the popular song forms that he would use as what seemed impossibly flimsy triggers for elaborate spontaneous concertos.

Rollins was thirty-four at the time of his first visit to Ronnie Scott's Club, a one-time alto player who had been fascinated by the riff-dominated 'jump bands' of the immediate postwar years, forerunners of rhythm 'n' blues. He concentrated on the horn playing of Coleman Hawkins to begin with, intrigued by that big, assured tone and the deliberate, measured tread of Hawkins' methods of extemporization. A neighbourhood friend, Thelonious Monk, introduced Rollins to the playing of Charlie Parker, which he then attempted to graft on to the swing band saxophone style that gave his playing a quirkiness even at that early stage.

His individuality quickly endeared him to Miles Davis, who employed him in 1951, and six years later Rollins released a record on the prestigious Blue Note label called 'Saxophone Colossus' that secured his reputation once and for all. The album was a virtual definition of that development of the methods of Charlie Parker and Dizzy Gillespie that came to be known as 'hard bop'. The style was notable for a deliberate eschewing of romanticism and sentiment and a preference for rugged, vibrato-less tone, the development of themes in very long solos that would frequently run into a dozen or more choruses. It was also characterized by a perfunctory indifference to over-elaborate themes, preferring the functional and the skeletal that could be simply used as a springboard to blowing. Whitney Balliett, reviewing 'Saxophone Colossus' for *The New Yorker* at the time, wrote that Rollins' solos 'often resemble endless harangues' but that the younger man's melodic imagination probably rivalled that of Charlie Parker.

At Gerrard Street Rollins got the ball rolling in a rehearsal with the Stan Tracey group that included bassist Rick Laird and drummer Ronnie Stephenson. But it was no ordinary rehearsal. Rollins began by restlessly pacing the room, bouncing booming sounds off the walls, examining the saxophone as if encountering it for the first time, adjusting the mouthpiece endlessly. Tracey and his partners waited patiently, aware that something unusual was happening.

Eventually the saxophonist made up his mind. He asked for 'Prelude To A Kiss'. Rollins then took the tune and played it fast and furiously, slow and with passion, with shrugging indifference as if trying to freeze the last remnants of it from the bell of his horn, with braying, spine-tingling laughter and generally performed, as he frequently did, the act of the taking the tune and shaking it so vigorously that every last coin, matchstick and fragment of long-lost memorabilia fell out of its pockets. The musicians began to realise just what it was they were rehearsing. This was the rehearsal of an understanding of the American's *attitude* toward playing, and to absorb the spirit that underpinned it, rather than a series of party-pieces.

That this was the intention behind the American's eccentric way of introducing himself was borne out by the events of the next four weeks. Rollins never referred to 'Prelude To A Kiss' again, and the band – after, as Tracey was to describe it later, 'playing the arse out of it all afternoon' – was never asked to play it. Rollins was a law all to himself. Dedicated to his work, and to preserving the mechanism he had culti- vated over the years that made it possible (immense self- discipline enabled him to overcome heroin addiction by simply taking leave of the music business and getting labouring jobs for as long as it took him to get straight) Rollins rarely socialized with the musical community, rarely kept later nights than were obliged by the booking and was much given to exercise, mysticism, and the sometimes off-putting pursuit of facial isometrics. The bassist Rick Laird encoun- tered Rollins alone in the bandroom one night, wearing a beret, gesticulating before the mirror and announcing in a Clouseauesque stage whisper, 'I am Pierre the Frenchman.'

Simply standing at a microphone with a horn was unimagin- able tedium to him then. He arrived one night at the club in a taxi, playing the tenor as he stepped out of it and went down the staircase. He would frequently begin playing whilst still in the tiny office under the stairs and move throughout the crowd with thunderous noises tumbling from the bell. He would sometimes leave the bandstand while the perform- ance ran on and lead the crowd, Pied Piper-like out into Gerrard Street, Tracey's men still furiously pumping away and just audible in the subterranean depths.

It was also Rollins' shaven-headed period, and a time of wayward experimentation with dress. Hats were a particular preoccupation with the American – sometimes the famous beret, sometimes a Stetson. He wore a mackintosh throughout one performance at Gerrard Street, and displayed an occasional fondness for more elaborate embroidery, like a row of tambourines tied to a belt around his waist.

Ronnie Scott was fascinated by Rollins and watched him night after night, as attentive as in those early days in the wartime clubs, relishing the privilege of hearing an improvisor in the prime of his inspiration. He got to know the American well during that period and on later visits, and on their work on the soundtrack of the movie *Alfie*, which was made at Shepperton studios, and which involved Scott, Phil Seamen, Stan Tracey and trombonist Keith Christie among others.

Rollins had been invited over to write the music – the director's son was a lifelong Rollins fan. The American was staying at the Royal Garden Hotel in Kensington and Christie and Scott began the project by visiting him there to get the lie of the land. Rollins' sense of occasion didn't let him down. The saxophone was on a sofa with spotlight shining on it. If Rollins was trying to say that's where the music is, he couldn't have put it any better. All three men got very stoned in the course of the discussion and eventually the two Englishmen asked to see Rollins' ideas for the score. He brought out a sheaf of manuscript paper and laid it before them. Every sheet was blank – except one. A fragment of phrasing was notated there, in a childlike hand. 'How should we treat the music?' Scott asked, puzzled by the American's apparently cavalier disregard for the responsibilities of the job. 'Treat it lightly,' Rollins advised. In the circumstances, there wasn't much choice.

In the event the *Alfie* score could only have been performed by jazz musicians. There was hardly anything to go on, which was exactly what Rollins wanted. The director would put the key scenes on the screen, tell the musicians they had 16 seconds to fill, and leave them to it. Whether they took a long time over the job, or hurried it, Rollins' reactions would be equally unpredictable. After a long morning of preparation with an unusual degree of attention to detail, Scott took the American down to the river in his MGB for lunch. The dessert was a large joint. When they got back, Rollins said, 'All that stuff we did this morning, forget it.' They started again. He even made the job an opportunity to indulge a kind of sartorial English identity, wearing a hacking jacket, cavalry twill trousers and an English country squire's hat.

Rollins' anarchic presence hovered over the movie to the end. At the London premiere of *Alfie* Scott and the other musicians were present to play its big themes They were supposed to begin the *Alfie* theme on the signal of a green light and stop on a red light, due to appear a couple of minutes later and which would signify the platform they were playing on being lowered out of sight and the curtains opening. The green light came right on cue and the band eased into Rollins' playful, jaunty opening bars. The red light was nowhere to be seen. They played the theme over and over, with all the variations they could think of for over twenty minutes while technicians sweated in the projection room to locate the hitch. It was just the way the composer would have wanted it.

9 / Not on Our Piano You Don't

'The person who sees furthest into the future is likely to be the person who sees furthest into the past.' Bill Evans, *Jazz and Pop*, 1965.

Ronnie Scott's relationship with Sonny Rollins continued through the years, with some golden – and grasped – opportunities and some missed ones. Scott would forever regretfully recall the occasion in a New York hotel room in the small hours of the morning when he turned down Rollins' out-of-the-blue telephone call asking him if he wanted to come over and practise out in the country. And for Rollins' part, the experience had been a pleasure as well. He threw everything he had into those performances – improvization of a quality and style rarely represented on his records except possibly *Our Man in Jazz* – and he enjoyed working with Tracey, who he later publically applauded in the music press with the words that brought such a glow to the hearts of British jazz fans unaccustomed to much acknowledgement of the home-grown version. 'Does anybody here know how good he really is?' Rollins enquired of Tracey's playing. Some did, but not enough.

Sonny Rollins was a hard act to follow, but the arrival of players of the highest calibre was becoming a routine occurrence. This in itself contained the seeds of insecurities to come. Booking the international stars was what Scott and King had always wanted to offer to the British jazz scene, though the cost of air fares, hotels, competitive fees and incidental expenses were not going to be sustained week in and week out in an establishment that could only contain 150 people. As long as they remained in Gerrard Street, the success of Ronnie Scott's Club would continue being a rod for the backs of its inventors.

In March 1965, Ronnie Scott's Club was able to announce proudly the arrival of the first all-American group to play on its premises. Bill Evans was indeed something to be proud of. He was that rare breed, a jazz performer with a strongly European bias toward reflection rather than explicit emotion who could still convey all of the orthodox jazz virtues of swing, profound understanding of the blues and a strong sense of spontaneity. A bespectacled, studious-looking performer from New Jersey, he had learned the piano and violin as a child, and grown interested in the swing pianists at the tail-end of the boom in popularity of that music, unaware except by rumour – as most white players were – of what was really going on in the New York clubs where bebop was being forged. College and the army further kept Evans from the new developments, but eventually the clarinettist Tony Scott brought him into the 52nd Street clubs and he was noticed by Orrin Keepnews of Riverside Records.

The pianist's growing reputation through the recordings made with Riverside led, as many young performers of imagination and originality found, to the Miles Davis band of the day. (Though legendary for his ego, Miles Davis has never allowed his temperament to impede his openness to the work of newcomers, a flexibility which has paid off in the trumpeter's sustained ability to remain contemporary – and fashionable.) Evans stayed with Davis for only eight months and was exhausted by the experience, but the period produced one of Davis' greatest records – the modal 'Kind of Blue', a variation of the structure of improvization such that solos would be based on cycles of scales rather than on chords. It imparted to the music a mysterious, displaced and ambiguous quality more reminiscent of Indian music, that was generally unavailable to jazz through the more explicit and predestined quality of the song form on which even the wild flights of bebop had been founded. Bill Evans' ruminative piano style was perfect for it, and Davis later acknowledged that the pianist had been a considerable influence on his thinking about the new idiom.

It was the perfectionist quality of Evans' approach to

playing and the immense subtlety of his thinking about it that made Scott and King realise that they would have to improve the facilities a little for a player so dependent on an instrument capable of expressing musical minutiae. The club's piano was a battered grand that had been in use there since the establishment opened, its eccentricities and weird ways being by now instinctively grasped by Tracey, who knew every treacherous habit it had. But there was no question of expecting Evans to play on it. So the two club proprietors performed the long-postponed ritual of selling the upright the weekend before Evans was due to arrive. They then set about hiring a grand piano. What seemed like a simple enterprise on the face of it, as long as you had the cash, turned out to be a nightmare.

The representative of the hire company arrived at the club on the Monday of Evans' arrival to examine the premises. When he discovered it was a jazz club he was immediately appalled. 'What's the problem?' Scott and King enquired in alarm. The salesman protested that jazz pianists would have no idea of how to take care of an instrument of the class that he was expected to furnish them with, and in any event they would never be able to get a grand piano down the steps of the establishment. 'Anyway,' he complained, 'it will simply get damaged. There'll be drinks spilled all over it. Girls sitting on it . . .' His vision of what a jazz club was like had clearly been drawn from George Raft movies. Scott and King tried offering everything they could think of, the value of the instrument as a deposit, money they didn't have but thought they could rustle up if the worst came to the worst. None of it made any difference. The man stonewalled for an hour.

King eventually looked as if he'd had an idea. Conspiratorially, he beckoned the piano man close. Scott wondered if his partner may have hit on a deal. There was a pause. 'FUCK OFF,' King eventually yelled in the ear of the attentive listener. All bets were clearly off.

The two men began a frantic round of the central London hire companies. They found a German manageress at Steinway's in the Edgware Road, who had no grands available but some beautiful uprights. 'Do you know how good this pianist is?' they pleaded with her in despair. 'We can't ask him to play on an upright.' 'He's a jazz musician isn't he?' the woman continued, trying to be helpful. 'He vill be able to see the rest of the boys over the top of it.' The whole exercise was a reminder of just what a backwater jazz still was in the respectable world outside of number 39 Gerrard Street, a state of affairs that in the euphoria of the previous three years of presenting fine musicians to enthusiastic audiences they had tended to forget. Eventually a friend and sympathizer with the club's objectives, the jazz pianist and composer Alan Clare, was able to arrange for the loan of a grand piano for Evans' opening show. It came at the eleventh hour.

When Evans began to play, all that anguish was instantly forgotten. Like Rollins, he had distinct mannerisms in performance, though where Rollins' were explosive and centrifugal. Evans' seemed part and parcel of what appeared to be his desire to escape more and more comprehensively into a fascinating landscape inside his own head. A thin, intense-looking figure, he sat at the instrument with his head bowed over it, his nose at times virtually touching the keyboard, hands floating ethereally through a mixture of evaporating arpeggios, crisp, sinewy single-line figures that would erupt and vanish in an instant, and an ever-present rhythmic urgency that continually prodded at the otherwise speculative and other-worldly quality of his work.

Unlike many of the bebop pianists, Evans did not merely concentrate on chorus after chorus of melodic variations on the harmony – the latter usually expressed in bald, percussive chords designed to emphasize the beat – but sought to develop a solo as a complete entity with a fundamental logic and shape, his left hand developing and enriching the harmony. Like the composer Gil Evans, like Art Pepper, like Getz, Bill Evans – as the *Village Voice* writer Gary Giddins remarked – exhibited the white jazz players' gift of 'swinging with melancholy'. Evans became another regular visitor to the Ronnie Scott Club over the years, and with a succession of drummers and bassists.

The illustrious procession wound on in and out of Gerrard Street through 1965. One of the greatest guitarists in all jazz, Wes Montgomery, followed Evans on to the premises performing with Stan Tracey, and astonished his listeners with the amiable, easy-going manner in which he spun fresh melodies from the instrument. Montgomery never read music, had taught himself to pick the strings with his thumb instead of a plectrum – because he didn't want to disturb his neighbours and because nobody had told him any different – and was, like Evans, brought to the recording studio by Orrin Keepnews of Riverside on the recommendation of Cannonball Adderley.

By the time he arrived at the club, Montgomery was already on the way towards being a big star. Not because he was a jazz player – the skills of an improvisor never led to big record sales – but because his artless way of learning the instrument had given him a rich and resonant tone unusual in a music where guitars were usually played in a spindly, single-note fashion as if they were pretending to be saxophones. He had developed a way of playing solos in octaves that was original and exciting in the context of an improvising group stretching for variation of texture, but which could just as easily be adapted to wall-to-wall music for the MOR market. When the Riverside record label went under in the year before Montgomery came to London, the guitarist went to Verve records and was induced by a producer there, Creed Taylor, to develop those soft, plush sounds for the commercial market and cut down on the slashing, slalom-like runs and prodigious facility for melodic improvisation that could take an audience's breath away in a club. Montgomery never lost that facility in informal surroundings, but the experience with the record business – though he went along with it, and not least for the sake of being the breadwinner for a family of six children – distressed him increasingly as the years passed.

His season at Ronnie Scott's was the old Montgomery, the cavalierly casual, effortlessly musical artist who would smile broadly at his audience throughout his set, hardly looking at the guitar, notes flying and tumbling from the strings. Montgomery, whose early playing circumstances had obliged him to meet the demands of both a day job and performance in the evenings, was to make only one visit to Ronnie Scott's. Three years later, having barely enjoyed the fruits of the success that he had felt so confused about securing, Montgomery died of a heart attack at the age of forty-three.

The last link in the intimate circle of Ronnie Scott's family life was finally snapped in 1965. Sol Berger, Ronnie's quiet, bookish, hardworking stepfather was found dead in bed by Rachel, his wife of less than eighteen months, and Ronnie, who had been the apple of the old man's eye almost as much as he had been of Cissie's and Nana Becky's, was immediately summoned to the house. Sol's world had been turned inside out by the events of the previous two years. Cissie's sudden death after a quarter of a century of marriage had left him lonely and confused. He had met Rachel, a lively divorcee in her sixties at an engagement party at the end of 1962, the year of Cissie's death, and at the end of the evening intently sought her out. 'I must see you again' the old man had insisted. 'I know we've got things in common.'

Ray, the nickname by which she was known, though surprised by his determination, thought him interesting and flattering, and sensed his loneliness. She was keen for a change in her own life, liked Sol, and knew she could feel comfortable in the quiet Edgware back street. They had married in January 1963 and Ronnie Scott had come to the party, though surprised and a little discomfited at first by the alacrity with which Sol had started afresh. But it was to be a short interlude. Thrombosis undermined Sol's health, he had to walk with a stick, and he was disheartened by the discomfort after an active life. It was difficult even to fulfil his duties to the local British Legion, to which he had given a lifetime of service.

When he died, the household at Edgwarebury Gardens went into the traditional seven days of Jewish mourning. Ronnie Scott came to the house every night to take part, for which Ray was grateful, describing him to friends as 'a wonderful boy. There was nothing he wouldn't do.' But Ronnie had good cause to be grateful to Sol. From the suits he had made for Ronnie's first band, to the investment he made in the first Ronnie Scott Club, Sol Berger had never failed his wayward but gifted stepson when he had needed him. For Ronnie Scott's part, he wanted to make up for the missed chances that death brought so relentlessly into focus, his absences during Jock's last weeks, that rare row with the mild-mannered Sol when the boy had impulsively shouted 'you're not my real father anyway'. Much of what he had done with his life would never have been without Sol, and he knew it. Scott's gold disc, a *New Musical Express* pollwinner's trophy, still remains in the front room where Cissie died, and Ray still lives.

As the year passed, some old favourites made a return visit, and some newcomers arrived. The emphasis remained on saxophonists, but the public kept coming. The pressing problem was, that it was getting harder and harder to accommodate all those who wanted to come.

In the summer of 1965 Scott and King found what they thought were ideal premises at 47 Frith Street. But if they were trying to get into a different league with their public, they were also getting into a different league as businessmen. This was not the kind of establishment you could put on the road with a lick of paint and a loan of £1000 from your stepfather. Scott and King did the rounds in the effort to raise cash for the big leap. They even went to the Arts Council, at that time hardly involved in subsidizing jazz at all.

It wasn't a happy meeting. The two men felt ill at ease in any event, in a land of modulated voices, discretion, cut glass chandeliers, softly ticking clocks, oak tables. They were kept waiting for what seemed an age, until an earnest looking assistant finally arrived, rubbing his hands together in what appeared to signify both bonhomie and a vigour about getting down to real business. But it just wasn't real. 'Now then, about this Bonny Scott's Club. How can we help you gentlemen?' Scott and King looked resignedly at each other. 'In the circumstances, you can't help us at all,' they informed him and left the premises without so much as opening a briefcase. In the event, it was Harold Davison who came through with the means for the second incarnation to get under way.

Davison was by now involved in big-time promotion, frequently bringing the most illustrious names in jazz music to Britain for large-scale concerts and tours. His business had become part of the giant MAM agency. But if Davison was a businessman first, he was a jazz fan a very close second and he had admired Ronnie Scott since the days of the nine-piece. He agreed to come up with £35,000 to finance the refurbishing and launch of the club in Frith Street. The transaction tied up the fortunes of Scott and King with the MAM operation. The money was repayable on reasonable terms and Davison remained in the background, not attempting to influence the views of the two proprietors to protect his company's cash.

Benny Golson, an eloquent and elegant improvisor on the tenor (and later to be a composer for Peggy Lee, Nancy Wilson and Sammy Davis Jnr) was the last American to be formally presented under the portals of number 39 Gerrard Street. But though it closed on 27 November 1965, the lease still had eighteen months to run and Scott, bearing in mind the catalyst the old Club Eleven had been, intended to keep it on as a jamming centre for local players.

10 / The Air's Thin Up Here

'You sit there and you learn. You open your mind. You absorb. But you have to be quiet, you have to be still to do all of this.' John Coltrane to Frank Kofsky, *Black Nationalism and the Revolution in Music*, 1970.

'I have decided to break off my engagement with W. She doesn't understand my writing, and last night said that my "Critique of Metaphysical Reality" reminded her of "Airport".' Woody Allen, *Without Feathers*, 1972.

The Scott establishment had by now secured its status as a purveyor of very high-class entertainment indeed, for those who stood on the other side of the cash-desk and the spot-lights it was frequently a source of as much diversion in its regular behind-the-scenes rituals as for the goings-on that the public parted with money for. There had always been a house-style at Ronnie's, even in the old days. Friends of the enterprise would edge into the band-room under the feet of the oblivious pedestrians of Gerrard Street to find Sonny Rollins performing contortions with his jaws, pallid acquaint-ances looking like minicab drivers sitting on upturned instru-ment cases reading the racing pages or telling deadpan jokes, Pete King sitting expansively behind a desk like an up-and-coming boxing promoter, greeting the unwary with those East End street-wise blandishments that sound like a threat to shoot your dog. "*Allo* boy, still creepin' about?' There might have been Ronnie, performing his elaborate silent mime of an astronaut attempting to masturbate at zero gravity. At Frith Street it was the same only more so, because there was more room for manoeuvre and a bigger cast.

One house-rule, an unspoken one, remained. Neither Scott

nor King could stand either their customers or their guests on the bandstand pulling rank – through money, class, bloody-mindedness, or any other reason. Jock's old partners from the boats and hotel bands would continue to be welcome, get a drink on the house, sometimes a permanent loan if times were hard. Musicians who had been contemporaries of Scott and King in Archer Street but who by 1965 were finding the phone ringing less and less found that they could treat the place as home, and some got jobs on the premises. Jeff Ellison, a drummer and long-time friend (who had been in Club Eleven on the night of the drugs raid and accidentally spared from arrest because Scott, who he was due to follow on to that exposed position on the stand, played one more number than he should) took up a responsibility for the door, often a punishing job in a nightclub. 'Stick with me and you'll make a fortune,' Scott had said to him.

The composition of the audience changed with the move. At Gerrard Street, the proportion of diehard modern jazz enthusiasts was massive compared to the passing trade. Going upmarket altered the percentages. It also meant that the club would have to deal with more punters whose remittance of the entrance fee led them to believe that they owned the place. People who were arrogant, aggressive or loudly drunk wouldn't get the time of day from Scott, who developed a repertoire of gags to deal with the problem ('Good evening sir, sorry to hear you've been drinking on an empty head'), nor did he ever learn to butter up wealthy customers in the way that most West End nightclub proprietors would have considered second nature. A rich hooray arrived in the foyer one night with two women in furs, for the latter's benefit noisily enquiring of the nearby proprietor 'Hello Ronnie, what have you got for us tonight?' Scott looked down his considerable nose. 'Excuse me, do I know you?' he said in a tone that insisted that the conversation had no possible future.

Ronnie Scott was in good spirits. The death of Sol Berger had upset him, but life was running fast again. He was now working regularly with the all-star line-up of the multinational big band led by American veteran bebop drummer Kenny Clarke and the Belgian composer Francy Boland – and though the old nervousness still gripped him in the presence of

American saxophone heroes like Johnny Griffin, the band was exciting and new, travelled widely and the diversion of its exotic gigs was comfortably enough to offset the agony of being obliged to fly to them, for which he still had to douse himself in whisky and tranquillisers. His affair with Mary, who had moved with him to the new premises and become the club's cashier, convinced him temporarily that his self-image as a freewheeling loner maybe didn't have to follow him into middle age.

And his love of play-acting flourished. He would without warning lurch into a lugubrious Herbert Marshall impression, even for the benefit of the younger waitresses who hadn't the least idea who the ancient actor was, and then when the phone rang with an enquiry from a prospective customer would charge unswervingly on in the same vein – 'Have we got a table? Certainly sir, would you like it here, or take it away?' He would also continue to slip round the corner to the betting shop whenever a likely runner presented itself, or had a name he liked. 'I can stop a runaway horse just by putting money on it,' became one of the proprietor's favourite observations about his hobby.

The only unforgivable sin was to be boring, which meant not being able to think on your feet, not being able to see the funny side of Sod's Law, self-importance, and priggishness. Scott was free to pursue his playing career and principally find the club a source of pleasure and entertainment, because the relationship between himself and King was by now so secure that very little of what it consisted of ever needed to be articulated, and the latter would take most of the responsibility for making sure the figures added up. As the club's repertoire broadened out – notably to include more singers opposite pure jazz acts to sugar the pill for the new clientele – King expanded his role as the anchorman. He took charge of an increasing proportion of the booking. Many of the club's visitors – like Roland Kirk, Ben Webster, Zoot Sims, Sonny Rollins – had naturally become firm favourites. Scott was content to leave it with him, yet his role in the expanding club never became purely that of a figurehead. Scott had a talent for taking risks, it was the legacy of much of his family life.

* * *

But out front, everything had changed. Benny Green pointed out at the time the unerring accuracy with which you could usually estimate the musical virtues of a nightclub just from a computation of the weekly expenses. Regular visitors to Gerrard Street could be in no doubt that many things had changed for good. On a bad night now, Scott's and King's new staff could comfortably outnumber the customers. There were waitresses, barmaids, doormen, ushers. There was comfortable furniture, soft lights. It was, at last, the place that Scott had been describing from his imagination and his memories of New York in that 1958 interview in *Melody Maker*.

London itself had changed. The bohemian Soho where artists and eccentrics of all kinds could feel they were for once in a world that ran according to their own clocks, was running out of room to move. Rents were rising. The pornography industry was gathering such steam as censorship was relaxed that the money it was making could outbid almost any other line of business. Scott and King were to find that when the lease for 39 Gerrard Street came up for renewal the rent had tripled. The days when Soho premises would stand idle while their owners scratched their heads over what use to make of them were long gone.

There was rock music. Central London had played host to skiffle a few years before – Terry Nelhams, later to become Adam Faith, was discovered by producer Jack Good playing skiffle in the Two I's coffee bar, and Gypsy Larry had passed through a phase in which the coffee houses and modest night-clubs would give him work as a skiffle bassist – but the rhythm 'n' blues boom that was ushered in by the success of the Beatles at home and abroad had had strong roots in London clubs, notably the Flamingo, and the Marquee in Wardour Street. The 1960s decade was a period of prosperity, the mannerisms of classlessness, and a redoubled interest in the arts in the 'new meritocracy' of Harold Wilson's Britain. Scott found his club doing tolerably well, he was hiring musicians whose work he loved, he was taking the odd glam-orous session job – playing on occasion on Beatles records like 'Lady Madonna' when the composition called for horns – and everything was there but the wild and raucous atmos-phere of the Archer Street days. Ronnie Scott was thirty-eight when the Frith Street club opened for business, in an atmosphere in which anybody who had taken a more commercial route toward rock music could probably have cleaned up.

From the mid-1950s in the States, a massive change was underway in the hands of the descendants of Charlie Parker and the first-wave modernists. It was not wholly the inheritance as exemplified by experimenters with bop like Rollins, Charles Mingus or the composer George Russell (who announced the campaign as the 'war on chords') who attempted to loosen the format from inside. Two men of much the same age as Rollins (Ornette Coleman and John Coltrane) and one six years younger (Albert Ayler) were about to launch an assault on the raw material of jazz that would rebound around the world.

The problem, in its way, was hard bop. Rollins, of course, was capable of undermining the formalism in anything, but lesser players were bogged down in a game of harmonic puzzles, struggling ever harder to fire denser and denser fusillades of semiquavers into ever more complicated structures played at faster and faster tempos. It was as if a pinball game were being portrayed on a film played at double speed. It was hard to imagine where such an obsessive – and impassive – pursuit of technical expertise might lead except into the kind of inertia and self-regard that would in the long run be death to any vibrancy in the music. But the public was used to it. The mixture of competitiveness and cool symbolized by late bop was popular, particularly with whites. It became the evidence of a certain kind of cultural arrival.

Coleman, Ayler and the prodigiously resourceful pianist Cecil Taylor were the most notable guerillas to finally launch a counter-attack on these increasingly muscle-bound developments. Coltrane initially explored a ground that owed at least some inspiration to Rollins. But they all went about their work in different ways. Coleman, a Texan, had been a blues player around Fort Worth from his teens but fell out with many of the local musicians who claimed that he couldn't play in tune. He had actually reverted to some of the earliest principles in jazz – the vocalized tone, the exultant abandonment of concert pitch – and mixed them with an improvisational method that retained a close approximation to regular melody of a kind, but with random or absent harmony.

By the mid-1960s Ornette Coleman had laid most of his cards on the table. His recordings with the Atlantic label revealed his music to be as down-to-earth as a Texan barndance in some incarnations, and as bluesy as anything in the black tradition in others.

Albert Ayler, six years Coleman's junior, had also come up through the r & b bands, and was demonstrating by the mid 1960s that there was mileage in a return to the New Orleans tradition but with the fierce and uncompromising vocabulary of a new black consciousness expressed through it. Cecil Taylor was a pianist with a profound grasp of both European and black American traditions (he would insist that both had African origins) and a technique capable of impressing even classical enthusiasts who disliked his ideas. He also exhibited an inhuman stamina that would permit him to improvise at feverish pitch for long periods, and expressed impatience with the black condition in his music and in his public conduct. As for John Coltrane, he was the avantist who most successfully trod a path between experiment and popularity for much of his later musical life. He influenced not simply the generation of musicians just entering the scene, but even astonished and inspired performers older than him.

As the sixties culture of dope, self-examination and a preoccupation with the East gained strength, so the inspirational influence of Coltrane widened. The saxophonist's journey became so single-minded in his last years that some of his former close associates refused to play with him. It was obvious that Coltrane was prepared to make considerable sacrifices to propel his music on to the plane of sublime suspended animation that he seemed to hear in his head. When he died of liver disease in 1967, much of that work remained undone. Many musicians, black and white, took it upon themselves to carry on.

It was against this background that the developments in contemporary jazz in Britain in the 1960s had to be heard. Everywhere in the jazz-playing world, the personal prospects for a life devoted to the sharp end of the music were not good, but in Britain some music of real originality had been generated at the beginning of the decade and once again the power behind it – in this case the Jamaican altoist Joe Harriott who had performed that brief and unsettled stint with the Ronnie Scott Orchestra in 1956 – had been allowed to run downhill.

After his stretch with the Scott orchestra, Joe Harriott's work began to be increasingly adventurous. Working with the bassist Coleridge Goode, a Jamaican who had come to England as an engineering student in the 1930s, he formed his own band in 1957 that included pianist Harry South and trumpeter Hank Shaw.

Harriott's working life was to be dogged by illness. He got the first intimations of tuberculosis and spent some time in hospital at the end of the 1950s recovering from it. During that period he began to write music and form his ideas. When he recovered, the band got a job in Frankfurt for a month, developed methods of working together that had previously never been attempted in British modern jazz, and in 1960 he recorded his first 'free form' album, ostensibly conceived without reference to anything that Ornette Coleman was doing across the Atlantic.

The band had occasionally appeared at Gerrard Street, and many of the more conventional players had little time for it. Harriott was finding the going increasingly hard temperamentally, but with the albums *Free Form* and *Abstract* he won recognition from the source that British musicians still most valued – America. The prestigious West Coast jazz magazine *Downbeat* gave the albums five-star ratings in their polls. It meant a great deal then. But though his original inspiration had been Parker, Harriott's music was not by any means exclusively American. Tunes like 'Calypso Sketches' were drawn from his background in the Carribbean, using local rhythms hitched to jazz.

The band was endlessly inventive. Fellow West Indian Shake Keane would use a tumbler over the bell of his trumpet to give a muffled, trombone-like tone. Players would randomly begin riffing energetically behind solos and then drop out as abruptly as they arrived. Harriott would suddenly zigzag across jaunty, dancing tempos with wild, bleary howls.

'Modal' on the *Abstract* album had been entirely improvised in the studio, taken up while the band was packing away its kit and inspired simply by vibrations on a cowbell and a drinking glass. Harriott claimed his interest was to add 'colour' in jazz – loosening improvisation to 'paint freely in sound'.

Other artists in London then wanted that freedom too. Young poets like Mike Horowitz and Pete Brown were finding in collaboration with musicians an opportunity to bring poetry to audiences previously shut out by it. Poetry and jazz combined to express the resentment that many younger citizens felt at what they regarded as the cosy materialism of the British boom of the 50s. The poetry was frequently political and sexual. The music, some of it adopting the more impressionistic methods of Harriott and what local performers were already hearing in the work of Ornette Coleman and John Coltrane across the Atlantic, was increasingly fragmentary, atmospheric and self-questioning. The rhythm section at Gerrard Street, often composed of Stan Tracey and bassist Jeff Clyne with a variety of drummers, would periodically be invited by Horowitz and Brown to perform collaborations, invitations they enthusiastically accepted.

Eventually a group came out of it, the New Departures Quartet, which featured Bobby Wellins on tenor – a man who could conjure up the blue and misty contours of the Scottish highlands with a saxophone style that had some distant similarities to that of Stan Getz. Wellins wrote a brooding jazz suite for the group called 'Culloden Moor', which was then developed by Stan Tracey into a larger work for a full jazz orchestra. It was this ensemble that performed 'Culloden Moor' at its only full-scale public outing at the St Pancras Town Hall in 1960. The New Departures pioneers asked Ronnie Scott to be the MC for the night, and the saxophonist obliged by promptly querying Wellins' desire to commemorate such a resounding defeat for his home side in the course of his introduction. The performance was memorable for the sheer dimensions of its commitment to a use of contemporary jazz for a truly home-grown purpose – and with considerable flexibility for improvisors within it. It was also memorable for the return of Denis Rose to the public arena for the first time in ten years. Rose repeated the habit he had been prone to even in the days of working in the gangsters' clubs – he was an hour and a half late, principally through nerves but delivered one slightly unsteady but typically oblique trumpet solo at the close despite the management unceremoniously dropping a curtain on his head.

Involved with the presentation of the New Departures concert was a young jazz writer called Victor Schonfield, brother of the economist Andrew Schonfield and a jazz enthusiast from Oxford college days. Schonfield was a comparative rarity in the field of jazz criticism, since his overriding interest was good improvisation, rather than an undue concern over how much an artist seemed to accord with some handed down principles as to what constituted the art of jazz. He was thus one of the most open minded observers of the scene then operating, particularly since Benny Green's occupancy of the jazz critic's chair at the *Observer* and Philip Larkin's at the *Daily Telegraph* were increasingly tending to present a line that perceived the experimental jazz of the period as destructive to the music, ignorant of its traditions, and professionally incompetent.

The German critic Joachim Berendt decided to help bring Ornette Coleman to Europe, and the saxophonist financed the rest. Coleman already knew of Schonfield as one of his most committed supporters in Britain, and decided that the writer would be his promoter here. Schonfield put Coleman's trio on for a concert at the Fairfield Hall in Croydon in the autumn of 1965, in a curious billing in which the other half of the show was a non-improvised performance by a classical wind quintet playing a Coleman composition. This odd state of affairs was occasioned by the last vestiges of the Musicians' Union difficulties. Schonfield had brought Coleman in as a classical musician which he thought would avoid difficulties with the union. That organization responded by preventing him from being able to present a Stan Tracey group as the complement to Coleman on the billing. Schonfield therefore had to organize classical players to appear, and those that did eventually had to defy the union's discouragement to make the concerts.

Coleman then went to Europe, making a pair of excellent live albums at the Golden Circle Club in Stockholm at the end of the year. He returned to England in 1966 to play a season at Ronnie Scott's Club. It was here, in a venue so previously dedicated to the traditional virtues of jazz that the enfant terrible really lifted the lid.

Coleman would break up the performance in completely unexpected ways. He would play a flurry of abrasive saxophone sounds, end it on a foghorn-like honk, then silence. Then he would edge gently in with a playful, folksy melody, drummer Charles Moffett padding softly behind him, then silence again and another flurry, or a sudden snap on Moffett's snare. He would then even mischievously slip in the occasional quote from a standard, then reel mockingly away from it. Coleman's high sustained alto notes were a heartfelt cry. Oddly, considering the reaction he was getting, many of his performances at the time were actually quiet. Moffett frequently used brushes, or gentle rolls with mallets. On fast pieces Coleman would vary the dynamics – playful, squawky melodies interrupted by honks, themes that would get swing-style treatment but in a sidelong, disrupted kind of a way.

Schonfield wrote in the sleevenotes to 'Ornette Coleman in Europe' 'his lovely tone is essentially the sound of jazz, like those of Johnny Dodds, Bubber Miley, Lester Young and Charlie Parker.' Charles Fox, the *New Statesman's* correspondent, believed that the improvising he heard on the last of six visits he made to hear Coleman in that season, was the best he had ever heard anyone deliver in the flesh. Not so Benny Green, nor particularly Ronnie Scott or Pete King. The men who had learned their craft in Archer Street circles were difficult to persuade. Their fundamental suspicion about the defenders of 'high art' and the richness of their experience of charlatans of every kind made it difficult for them to hear Coleman's ideas for what they were. They thought it was not jazz as they knew and loved it.

Green was distinctly unforgiving of Coleman's work at Ronnie Scott's. He referred to Coleman's trumpet playing as his 'Trumpet Involuntary' and concluded: 'He is not, however, without shrewdness. By mastering the useful trick of playing the entire chromatic scale at any given moment, he had absolved himself from the charge of continuously playing wrong notes. Like a stopped clock, Coleman is right at least twice a day.'

Scott took some comfort from the opinion of Thelonious Monk, who came to the club one night during Coleman's run and publically ridiculed the newcomer's performance from the floor. 'Why don't you get yourself a fiddle player?' Monk enquired of Coleman's efforts with the instrument. For Scott, the whole business was incomprehensible. But Coleman had unquestionably attracted attention and interest. It was a fore-taste of the club proprietor's lack of the kind of energetic bigotry that actively inhibits progress. Scott disliked Coleman's music and couldn't see how it was going to take jazz anywhere. Like Green, he felt that the traditions from which jazz had emerged were being casually thrown aside by such methods.

It wasn't as if he hated all of the heroes of the New Thing. Scott had profoundly admired Coltrane, despite the latter's inclination in his later years to propel the music into ever more mystical and other worldly territory, because Coltrane was obsessed with harmony and with trying to manipulate the saxophone into sound effects that no-one had previously believed it to be capable of. Even the old-timers from the dance-bands could admire him, whether they liked his music or not. It was different with Ornette. Ornette didn't seem to care one way or another about the respect of his peers.

The visit of Albert Ayler in 1966 made it even harder. Ayler's music seemed more unfinished and ill-conceived even than Ornette Coleman's. One night at Gerrard Street several of the musicians had tried to make sense of an Ayler album, even trying the record player on different speeds. Many of the London players, including Scott, went to hear Ayler's concert at the London School of Economics, recorded for BBC-2; it was once again indirectly the work of Berendt, who was then running the Berlin Jazz Festival and gently blackmailing mainstream impresario George Wein by threat-ening not to take his conventional package unless he included an avantist of Berendt's choice as well. There was no ambi-guity about the blackness of Ayler's music. He did not flirt with Western techniques of construction, or seek to further develop harmonic principles as Coltrane did, or to find ways round them as Coleman did. His horn was simple, emotional, wild and loud.

In September 1966, Ronnie Scott and Pete King offered

Gerrard Street to the up-and-coming local youngsters. The impact on the British scene was as critical as the opportunity to hear American players of the calibre that Scott and King were presenting. The band of the young Plymouth art student Mike Westbrook appeared at what came to be known as the 'Old Place' on a long series of spectacular Saturday all-nighters, and with it were the new young soloists like John Surman and Mike Osborne who had absorbed the work of the American avantists like John Coltrane and Eric Dolphy. The expatriates of the South African Chris McGregor group played there, as did the bassist and composer Graham Collier. Scott had originally attempted to entrust the running of the establishment to John Stevens, a young drummer who had been running a gig at the Little Theatre Club in St Martin's Lane on a virtually exclusive policy of free-jazz. Stevens was unsure of the long-term prospects given the condition of the lease, and preferred to hang on to the Little Theatre which continued to be a meeting place for the most adventurous and least commercial improvizors in London for many years afterwards. The Old Place, however, became the focus of the local jazz scene. A good many of the Little Theatre's visitors – musicians and fans – drifted over to it. It became the most dynamic venue for the presentation of home-grown modern jazz talent that London had known since the days of the Club Eleven. It was a forcible reminder of how unlike New York London was (and how unlike itself in the years of the Second World War) that the presence of two such venues in one of the world's great capital cities should seem like any kind of a luxury.

11 / They're Playing Our Tune

'I go up in a rocket ship, don't know where I'm gonna go but you can all come with me, every one of you if you want. Join me on my ship.' (Jimi Hendrix to *Melody Maker*'s Roy Hollingsworth.)

'Do you know this feller?'

The driver was pointing to a huge figure slumped in the back of his cab, apparently almost unconscious with drink. The figure stirred briefly to recognize Jeff Ellison, now regular doorman at Ronnie Scott's establishment; he had grown his hair long acknowledging the dominance of the hippy era. 'Jeff, what the hell have you done to yourself?' it growled at him in anguish, before passing out and having to be extracted from the cab by a process somewhat like trying to get a cork out of a bottle with a toothpick. The figure was eventually drawn over the threshold of the club, where it finally formed an immovable obstacle in the doorway through which the club's clientele were obliged to gingerly step.

It was par for the course of Ben Webster's later years. Travelling always brought it out in him, as Scott and King knew from the first encounter with Webster at Southampton. He once had to be collected from an empty train at Victoria Station, having fallen out of the carriage and wedged himself between the vehicle and the platform, from which impasse he was eventually wheeled away on a luggage trolley. He had also been heard to enquire of two policemen who were staggering under his weight, 'Listen, this is important. What do *you* think of Art Tatum?' Webster was the stuff of many after-hours tales like that. Nor was it ever seriously suggested that the price the saxophonist might have paid for his own affability and gentleness in the face of the society he was obliged to inhabit was chronic alcoholism.

But at least it was familiar. In a world that to the Archer Street men seemed to be going off the rails musically, there was always the comforting madness of Frith Street, and the club began to gain a reputation for the enactment of Pinteresque curiosities. Living hard but laughing about it, being uncomplaining about reverses, taking responsibility for yourself and not making a performance out of your own opinion of what was your due, this was what made sense to the pragmatic East End war-children who made up so much of its inner circle. So men like Ornette Coleman and Albert Ayler were hard to figure out personally as well as musically. They were a different kind of black musician to easy going freewheelers like Webster, to self-contained poets like Sonny Rollins, or even to wired-up, competitive gunslingers of the business like Lucky Thompson and Sonny Stitt.

Roland Kirk was halfway between, a man with a profound awareness of the black traditions (far more so than was appreciated by some of his early critics, who seized on what was taken to be the 'gimmickry' of his street-busker image and multi-instrumentalism) but also comfortable with the demands of showmanship and audience involvement. He came back to the club for his second visit in October 1966. By this time he was now familiar with Scott and King and trusted them as employers. He had become a powerful draw at Frith Street, the act that even non-jazz punters would recall long afterwards, a showman who put everything into his work. His desire to draw his audiences in had an odd twist on that second tour.

He had in his repertoire by this time a tune called 'Here Comes the Whistle Man', for which he passed tin whistles out to the crowd and invited them to blow the daylights out of the instruments at strategic points in the music. One night Kirk charged into the theme, enthusiastically blew the first choruses and gave his fans the nod to blow everything at much the same moment as the officer in charge gave a similar order to the assembled throng of police officers assembled outside in Frith Street. As the crowd tootled gaily inside, the

Metropolitan Police, sounding their own whistles for all they were worth came charging through the front door. It was an exquisitely-timed raid by the constabulary, zealously enforcing a technicality of the licensing laws which said that non-members couldn't buy a drink in the establishment. The police had visited the club incognito on previous nights to confirm that legislation wasn't rigidly observed by the staff.

Kirk had no idea what was going on. Neither had the police, who eventually started pulling at the saxophonist's clothes to get him to stop. Kirk was used to the over-enthusiastic in the front rows doing this to him and carried on regardless. 'Tell that man to stop playing' the officer told Scott and King. 'You tell him to stop,' they replied. An eager subordinate leapt into the breach with the words 'I'll stop him, sir,' but the experience of seniority convinced the man in charge that this was an area in which they risked being seriously out of their depth. 'Let Mr King deal with it,' he conceded. Roland Kirk was finally brought, puffing like a runway steam engine, to a standstill. It became one of the many legendary anecdotes of the club.

1967 was a good year for the club. Membership had gone up, and business was consistently flourishing. For Ronnie Scott's part, the improvement was sometimes a means to a not wholly musical end. He was in these years a keener gambler than usual, often out of boredom. He would spend hours in the *spieler* across the road from the club, playing cards in the company of highly unmusical gentry whose principal understanding of time was the kind you did as a guest of Her Majesty. Sometimes he would call Mary when the game was going against him, get her over to the gambling den to stand behind his shoulder and maybe change his luck. Like his father, who had gone racing with one of Soho's old godfathers, Albert Dimes (the man who had given Scott and King a magnum of champagne to drink when they got rich, and which lies unopened in the office to this day) Ronnie didn't dislike gangsters on sight, and in any case thought it was healthier to make friends of them rather than enemies. In pursuit of this, he would sometimes invite them into his premises as guests. On occasions the place seemed so full of menacing-looking customers and their girl-friends that more conventional visitors to the club would get up and leave in alarm.

The old gamble – how to get through the next week without losing your shirt – was still just about paying off. Increasingly ambitious projects were possible. Buddy Rich brought a big band in in the spring of that year, and established just what a powerful impact a really large outfit could have in those intimate surroundings, where the front row could shake hands with the front line. A charismatic, wisecracking, businesslike performer who resembled a diminutive James Coburn, Rich became in his own way one of the club's major draws – not so much because of the jazz content of his shows, which tended to be rehearsed to the last detail and often featured precise but unimaginative sidemen fresh out of music college, but because of the leader's own extraordinary drumming.

By the autumn of that year, it was time to make another attempt with an avantist, this time with Archie Shepp, one of the most uncompromising defenders of the 'New Thing'. Shepp was a curious mixture. An intellectual, and one of the new breed of black musicians with a developed perception of their social position in America, he had involved himself with drama and poetry as well as music. He wanted his work to be articulate about black consciousness, and in as many ways, as possible. Shepp's music in the 1960s was popular with both white intellectuals and with blacks from the ghettos, not always the case with the most unbending forms of the new free jazz.

Shepp's visit laid to rest at least one myth that tended to follow iconoclasts like him around. Waitresses at the club in those days found him to be one of the most considerate and polite of the guests. His music at the time was nonetheless quite the reverse. It featured two trombones in Grachan Moncur and Roswell Rudd and involved a good deal of fierce and dissonant squalling. Shepp was preoccupied with expressing impatience and rebellion in his work. Ornette Coleman's inventions, once the passage of the years defused the hysteria that had sprung from its departures from convention, came to be recognized even by the saxophonist's former detractors, as being as lyrical and shaped as anything in the jazz of earlier decades. But Shepp's most experimental phase wasn't like that.

It mystified and provoked audiences and musicians alike. Jazz has had a short history. One lifetime could still span the progress from the archaic, marching-band jazz of Bunk Johnson, through 1920s classicism (elegance and balance through unquestioning concern for form in the collaborations between Louis Armstrong and King Oliver) and then the fragmentation, sparked off by Armstrong's irrepressible individual genius into a spray of separate trajectories – swing, orchestral jazz, bebop and beyond. At 47 Frith Street, on and off the stand, the legendary figures of all those diverse persuasions would meet, play, talk it over, argue about it. Coleman Hawkins and Stan Getz were at a table one night during Shepp's season. Hawkins is rumoured to have remarked to Getz at a particularly storm-tossed moment, 'Hey, they're playing our tune.'

And it was Hawkins, sixty three years old at the time, who followed Shepp into the club that year. He was not growing old gracefully except in his playing. For years he had ostensibly been living on a diet of Rémy Martin brandy and cigarettes and was hardly known to eat. When he arrived at the club, the proprietors did their best to introduce Hawkins to food, but even a bowl of soup was mostly beyond him. Mary would try to slip an egg into the brandy, but he would always spit it out, protesting furiously. Vitamin B shots had to suffice.

Clearly, Hawkins was past his prime. Music taken at any sort of lively tempo would unsettle him, and the effort to keep up would distract him from the flow and miraculous sense of form for which he had grown famous. His tone had become querulous, the gaps in the flow of his ideas were obvious and couldn't be explained as interpretation. Yet his old admirers were not uncharitable, particularly Benny Green in his published commentaries, who was astonished by Hawkins' courage. The old man did not let himself off lightly, even playing the slow Kurt Weill tune 'September Song' without any accompaniment to cover up his difficulties.

Ben Webster was in town at the same time. Webster was in effect dependent on much the same lifestyle that was killing Hawkins. The younger saxophonist had by this time struck up something of a familiarity with the regulars of

Ronnie Scott's Club and was frequently attended by the doorman and sometime-drummer Jeff Ellison.

Late one night, Webster ran out of alcohol. Ellison was perplexed – it being the early hours of the morning – as to where he could fix Webster up with a drink. The American knew that his old mentor and Svengali, Coleman Hawkins was in town, in residence at the Piccadilly Hotel. 'Bean'll have a drink,' Webster triumphantly decided. 'Let's go and see Bean.' Somehow they passed the foyer of the hotel in the small hours of the morning, the bear-like figure of Webster unconcealable, not least because he would let out an ear-splitting '*my man!*' to everybody he could see. When they got to Hawkins' room, he indeed had his bottle of Rémy Martin and the ice water. But he kept Webster talking, tantalized, knowing what he wanted, and never offered him the drink. Webster, for his part, was always in thrall to Hawk. It was like Stitt and Byas. Webster didn't enquire about the drink.

Pete King had arranged for Webster to go on a short tour of Britain at the time, and the presence of Hawkins in town meant that at least one attempt to get them to play together on one of the dates was inevitable. But Hawkins' health seemed too far gone to risk it. The old man, however, wouldn't miss his chance to play with Webster. He made the gig, performed three tunes with the younger man after a shaky start, and recaptured much of his old élan even though struggling for breath before he went on stage. A local doctor concluded that Hawkins was suffering from pneumonia, a diagnosis confirmed by the Club's own doctor in London. Hawkins was due to leave for Stockholm to begin a European tour, and the medical advice was he should stay right where he was. Hawkins ignored it all, checked out of his hotel and flew to Stockholm anyway. He was to die in May 1969.

Ronnie Scott and Pete King knew that their role was changing. Neither of them had had grandiose ambitions when the club began, a little place to play in and meet like-minded people was all it was ever supposed to be. It was a line of work not generally commercial, that ran to distinctly unsocial hours, and that put immense strains on domestic life. The two men were powerfully bonded (though they would have thought it sentimental to discuss it) by both a highly traditional *esprit de corps* about professionalism and the still-surviving rebelliousness of their youth. Pete King had now formed a booking agency, still using Ronnie as the front man just like the old days, called Ronnie Scott Directions, which would sometimes use artists who had visited the club for a season on packages that would tour the country. They had done this with Ben Webster and in 1967 sent out tours that featured the singers Dakota Staton and Blossom Dearie.

And if their business commitments were broadening, the club's clientele had changed just the way that Benny Green had forecast on the move to Frith Street. (Once again with Davison's help, they were able to expand the premises by buying the next door lease as well, using its upstairs room initially for local jazz talent and then for pop and soul. The impresario Norman Granz also lent money for improvements.) The identity of the establishment had changed from a jazz club to a supper club that specialized in jazz and the old audience had to rub shoulders with the new. The dedicated followers of jazz mingled increasingly with tourists, expense-account business customers, passing trade. It was the only way to make the books balance. But it was going to make Scott and King think harder about acts like Shepp's in the coming years.

Sonny Rollins revisited in 1967, not with quite the same élan with which he had taken Gerrard Street by storm, and playing more frequently with Gordon Beck, an excellent British pianist who was nonetheless not so quirky as Tracey and less provocative of Rollins' wayward muse. The year also saw the longest residency by a single artist in the establishment – and, unexpectedly, for a woman instrumentalist. Elvira 'Vi' Redd, a Los Angeles saxophonist, had abandoned the temptation to consider singing the only feasible outlet in jazz for her sex; she came from a musical family with a drummer for a father and an amateur saxophonist for a mother. Redd's great-aunt, Alma Hightower, persuaded Vi Redd to play the saxophone as a child. She developed a powerful and hard-hitting alto style modelled on Charlie Parker and was soon displaying talents that should have earned her a soloist's career as prominent as Johnny Griffin's or Hank Mobley's but which, as the critic Leonard Feather had pointed out five years before, was simply invisible because she was a woman. Feather wrote that Redd was thought of 'not as an available saxophonist who plays and reads well and can hold down a chair in any man's reed section, but rather as a novelty who can't really be that good.' Redd herself remarked on the number of times that men in horn sections walked offstage as she came on. She said, without rancour, 'I often tell people the fact that I'm a female is an act of God.'

She did however get a chance to put the record straight in her season at Frith Street, on a tour of Europe that followed a successful appearance at the Monterey Jazz Festival. She worked at the club for a ten-week stretch, and demonstrated her own brand of dismissive running commentary with awkward audiences. One night, finding herself playing to an indifferent but largely silent crowd, Vi Redd upbraided them with the words, 'I go to church on *Sundays*'. She came to Europe again the following year – this time with Count Basie. She left music in the 70s to raise a family but returned to it in 1976.

1968. London's music business had boomed in the previous five years. An odd convolution had happened to the way that the industry bought and sold its property. As long as Ronnie Scott could remember, every square inch of the music world he knew had been mapped out by an American first. American popular culture was so dominant that players from across the Atlantic would have swamped the local music profession. Now it was all different. Or was it? British pop music appeared to have taken the world by storm, but founded on the precepts of black rhythm 'n' blues. The Rolling Stones and the Beatles never disguised their indebtedness to the very artists that Ronnie Scott, Stan Tracey and the others had nervously toured the States with back in 1957. Some cynics argued that since American hard cash dominated the British record industry anyway, hadn't the names simply been changed to protect the guilty?

But whatever was pulling the levers, rock was big. So was marijuana, hitherto in limited use and up until then strongly associated with the modern jazz community. The two phenomena affected each other. Forms of rock music power-fully influenced by drugs encouraged more prolonged and preoccupied instrumental explorations rather than the wham-bam style of the older rock and r & b tradition (cult bands of the time like the Grateful Dead mingled electronics, country rock and long, jazz-like instrumental jams). John Coltrane's later odysseys, mystical and semi-religious as they were, also had a strong influence on rock players – not always for the good, since musicians who weren't necessarily good improvisors in the first place were not improved by thrashing around in what they assumed to be a Coltrane-like manner. Coltrane never toyed with electric music himself, but his influence on it was heightened by the tragedy of his prema-ture death in 1967.

Some jazz artists did attempt – for a mixture of artistic and pragmatic reasons – to absorb the more fashionable devices into their own work. Miles Davis, a dictator of musical fashions for years, was prominent in the move – persuaded via his own adventurous tendency to hire young sidemen into hearing music by Sly Stone and Jimi Hendrix. This new musical development appealed more to Scott and King's generation. Some of it was tuneful, it was possible for good soloists to make a mark on it, and it swung.

But if some jazz musicians were listening with increasing interest to the new rock, for many others it was simply the old temptation to ditch improvisation and play 'hot licks' instead. The single-minded journeys of Coltrane, Cecil Taylor, Ornette Coleman and others were affecting the younger generation of British jazz players in different ways. Some had turned their back on any kind of commercial status and were exploring 'free' music with ascetic rigour, mostly in back rooms to tiny audiences – though the atmosphere for experimental art of all kinds in the London of the late 1960s, particularly in establishments like the Arts Lab, meant that the climate was more encouraging than it had been or would be not so very much later on. Others were deploying the less fierce instrumental innovations – particularly of Coltrane's earlier period during his stint with Miles Davis, to produce what was more like a contemporary version of hard bop with 'free' excursions thrown in more as sound effects than a real musical philosophy.

* * *

Ronnie Scott passed his fortieth summer in the midst of these upheavals. The music business of his youth had changed out of all recognition. The reign of Archer Street was over. It wouldn't be long before he could say that he had been a club proprietor for a decade, and the duration of his commitment to any single pursuit in his life had generally been a great deal shorter than that.

He took to walking the streets of the city in the early hours of the morning with Mary after the club had closed. Normally he drove everywhere, but virtually gave it up. The saxophone was played less and less. He had never been able to share the confidence of his admirers about his horn playing, and would repeat to Mary over and over during those long walks 'What am I doing with my life?' It was partly exasperation at his own contrariness. He loved music, loved those who made it, and could be an inspired exponent of it himself. But he was also a prisoner of his own sporadic lassitude, and found himself becoming prone to depressions. He believed he was being trapped by the obligations to be the club's trademark, its downbeat front-man. Mary heard the rhetorical questions go on and on.

'It's ridiculous,' he would say. 'What am I doing but spending my life repeating a lot of stupid jokes?' 'Why do it?' she would say. 'Because they expect it,' Ronnie would come back. 'It's what I'm supposed to do.' It was a sense of obligation as old as performance itself. The punters were the customers. The customers paid the artists, and the rent. If a man asks a tailor for pin-stripes, it's not the tailor's business to tell him he ought to have cavalry twills. He was in a pincer of being a Jewish boy with a small-business background, devoted to a musical culture that was often anarchic and subversive. The thesis in his life that contained the mysterious and long-gone showbiz glamour of Jock was pitched against the antithesis of Cissie's protective love, his grandmother, Sol's textile business, the security of Edgware-bury Gardens. The same tension existed between his affection for women who were creative, witty, enterprising – music-lovers, painters, designers – and that old deep-rooted Jewish perception of womankind as the creators of chicken stew, cinnamon balls and clean shirts, cherishers and nurturers, the protectors of homes that you would from time to time go back to.

And in Ronnie's professional life, there was turmoil too. He was glad that the club existed, but the procession of legends that had entered it were a disturbance to his equilibrium as well as a delight. At least the business could provide work and a congenial environment for so many players he had admired from a distance, and he and Pete King even did what they could to help old professional friends out whether they were playing on the premises or not. There were the calls that would come through to Elm Park Mansions, like the one that came one morning from Ronnie's old hero, Hank Mobley, stranded at Heathrow Airport with just enough money to ring through to the flat.

Mobley was sick, broke, and physically worn out, and had come to London to seek help from people that he believed appreciated him and his work. Mary recalled how Ronnie had pulled his clothes over his pyjamas, driven to the airport to pick up the saxophonist, made sure that the club took care of the American's accommodation and care until he got back on his feet. Frith Street was at least an oasis in which the practitioners of a generally neglected art could find support. But as a saxophonist, Ronnie Scott was constantly plagued by doubts. He thought of trying to change his career, but did not know how to. He felt he had reached a hurdle in his own playing. It was a period of marking time.

In the late summer of 1968 Ronnie Scott, impressed with the work of some of the young players he had begun to make contact with as the Gerrard Street 'Old Place' continued to play host to local talent, decided to form a band that would marry their own uninhibited ideas with his own more formal approach. He included some of the musicians of the New Wave in Britain – including John Surman, a Coltrane-influenced saxophonist from the West Country, who had made a considerable reputation for himself in the Mike Westbrook band and was noticeable especially for his unconventional decision to use the unwieldy baritone saxophone as a fleet, front-line soloing instrument in the way that Coltrane was using the tenor and soprano.

The band also included Gordon Beck on piano, Tony Oxley on drums and Kenny Wheeler on trumpet, a shy Canadian expatriate of cool eloquence as a soloist who had worked in a succession of John Dankworth orchestras. It also included an excellent altoist, Ray Warleigh, trombonist Chris Pyne and the remarkable double-bassist Ron Mathewson. Mathewson was part of the club's house team, another musician with a prodigious capacity for alcohol whose playing seemed mysteriously unaffected by it. They were just called The Band.

Tony Oxley, who for a brief period in the new band's short life was the drummer alongside Tony Crombie, was also by now a regular accompanist for visitors at the club. He performed in a manner quite unusual for British players. He was not in the respectful mould of following the innovations of the American gurus to the letter. Nor was he in the Phil Seamen mould of possessing that relaxed, sensual swing, subtle shading and reserve about extremes that won the older man such acclaim as the English drummer who sounded 'black'. Oxley learned every trick in the book, invented several of his own, and then set about playing in such a way that nobody could be in any doubt about it, a rodeo horse of a drummer on which only the most flexible and experienced of performers could ride. Jokers would compare Oxley's cymbal beat with the onomatopoeia for the sound of a bebop ride cymbal sound ('ten-to-ten ten-to-ten ten-to-ten') and describe him as being closer to 'around about a quarter past eleven' because he would embroider the basic time in clusters of jostling beats but still remember, in some metronomic circuit in the depths of his brain, exactly where the beat was and come back to it at intervals with an emphatic crash that seemed to say 'told you so.'

He would frequently unsettle soloists or lose them altogether. Just as Stan Tracey had been, Oxley was a house player of a completely unorthodox type who revealed that perverse, let's-see-what-happens streak in Scott. Where he could have made a point of always hiring high-class metronomes who wouldn't push the guests, he chose to make two of his most prominent house sidemen the most intractable, challenging, unpredictable and sometimes bloody-minded performers he could find. Some visitors disliked such quirks. Some – like

Johnny Griffin – deliberately sought out Oxley, just as Rollins had been delighted by the opportunity to play with Stan Tracey.

The new band didn't last. The personalities of the younger players were too strong to be restrained by the kind of arrangements that Scott and Crombie liked. Scott took to calling the outfit his 'all-star aggravation'. And there were about to be other things on his mind. The expansion of the club through the acquisition of the next-door lease was just about to begin. The gritty, Rollins-like American saxophonist Joe Henderson played the last stint in the old room before the place was closed to knock the two downstairs rooms together to form the layout as it is today.

The opening of the expanded club brought conflicting memories back to Ronnie Scott. Ted Heath, his old employer, the man who had helped him to become a teenage star, came to Frith Street for the opening night by Buddy Rich's band. But Heath had had a stroke by this time and couldn't enter the premises unaided. He was helped in by another man who had made it possible – Harold Davison – and by Tito Burns. Rich's band was forced to open for business while some of the work was still in hand. 'First time I've ever worked in a building site,' Rich maintained from the stage.

But if Ronnie Scott's attempt to draw the new generation of players into his own musical sphere was unlikely to succeed, neither were men like Surman and Oxley in the long run likely to see eye to eye with each other. The new players divided into those who derived their inspiration from jazz and those who derived it from elsewhere. The problem of a home for young British players had reached a crisis point. Scott and King had been forced to close the Old Place when the lease finally ran out; they maintained they had lost over £100 a week on keeping it open and had ended up £3,000 in debt on its account. An effort to use the upstairs part of the new Frith Street premises hadn't worked. The musicians themselves had then grouped together to form the Jazz Centre Society, an organization dedicated to the long-term objective of establishing a building in which jazz could be played, taught, read about and listened to by its devoted practitioners and fans. But there was an irony. The avant garde players were convinced that the music they were pursuing was of little interest to the organizers of the Jazz Centre Society. The twist was that although the Jazz Centre's policy was almost certainly one that was more attractive to Scott and King (and which would be attempting to fulfil the role they no longer felt able to for local players) it was they who found themselves offering shelter to musicians whose work at times made Shepp's performances the previous year seem like a Palm Court Orchestra.

It was partly the association which Oxley, a musician for whom they had the utmost respect, that forged this ironic link. Oxley was a player who could do anything that Ronnie Scott himself could require of an accompanist. If Oxley thought there was something in a music in which people scraped sheets of metal, banged gongs, performed strato-spheric ear-splitting whistles way over the upper register of saxophones and listened to Stockhausen and Pierre Boulez, then that was fair enough to at least give it a try.

In 1970, the London Musicians' Cooperative was formed. It was the logical outcome of the parallel line of jazz that had been going on at the Little Theatre Club and elsewhere. It called its opening press conference at 47 Frith Street, and it staged Sunday night concerts there for some months. Ronnie Scott and Pete King lent their premises to the Musicians' Cooperative for nothing. Members of the Co-op recalled the gesture years later. It would have been very easy for a West End club proprietor to discourage anything that might adversely affect business, and on some of those Sunday nights outraged visitors were heard to leave the premises complaining that if this was the place where you could hear the best of the world's jazz then they didn't know what the world was coming to.

The club's tenth anniversary came and went, the BBC using the premises for a series of filmed concerts – including the only appearance in the club of Miles Davis, performing with an electric band – and the Kenny Clarke-Francy Boland big band, with which Scott had enjoyed a fruitful association throughout the 1960s, put in a convincing appearance.

In September 1970 Jimi Hendrix died, a young legend on the rock scene who was one of its most inventive and passionate guitar virtuosi. He had been performing in the club on the night before his death, jamming with War, Eric Burdon's rugged rhythm 'n' blues band. Burdon had been a long-time fan and friend of the guitarist, had asked Hendrix to come to the club, and sensed from the uncertainties of their guest's performance on the first set that something was wrong. Hendrix hadn't wanted to go back on after the interval, but eventually did return and played like something close to his old self on 'Tobacco Road', demonstrating that melodic sense and the suppleness of long, B. B. King-influenced lines that lay beneath the performer of wild, squalling sound effects. 'He was a genius' the anguished Burdon said to *Melody Maker*. 'But I knew there was something bad in his mind that night.' The public were shaken by the news of Hendrix. He was one of several casualties of a romantic pop culture that pretended that hang-ups were things of the past.

Another once-only appearance by a legend was the arrival of the formidable Charles Mingus in 1971. It was a show that started out with a distinctly curious overture.

When he arrived in London he found a tax demand for work he had done in Britain on the movie *All Night Long* years previously. He strode on to the stage on his opening night roaring, 'I've just had a letter from your Queen,' and then proceeding to beat the living daylights out of the bass.

If Mingus was the repository of old values and the directness of the earliest jazz, Weather Report – the electronic band that came to London the following year – was a powerful example of the best that could emerge from the now headlong drive to fuse jazz and rock. The whole idea was paradise to the music business, which had never really had much idea what to do about jazz anyway and was forever chiding its practitioners for indifference to public opinion. Jazz-rock. It was perfect. All the mannerisms of pop were there – heavy backbeats, electric guitars or keyboards that sounded like guitars, dominant bass sounds. But Weather Report wasn't so easily put in its place. The band featured two excellent performers who had worked extensively with Miles Davis in pianist Joe Zawinul and saxophonist Wayne Shorter, the man who had finally replaced Coltrane in Davis' band. Weather Report's season was a milestone, but Zawinul and Shorter were fine soloists who would only later become cramped by the idiom.

And as the climate grew warmer for a certain kind of jazz playing, it grew as cold as it would ever get for some of the British scene's most creative artists. In 1972 both Joe Harriott and Phil Seamen died. Harriott was still plagued with the tuberculosis. To be a West Indian playing adventurous jazz music would put intolerable strains on the most robust of temperaments and physiques and Harriott was not strong in either area. Seamen eventually died of his heroin habit at forty-six, making a record (*The Phil Seamen Story*) in his last months that catalogued in music and speech his chequered history in the music business.

Tubby Hayes departed the following year, in June 1973, at the age of thirty-eight. His health had been bad for years, and his heart was not strong enough to enable him to play with his old careening power, but he had adopted a slower, more lyrical approach, as well as concentrating on his other love, the vibraharp that gave his work a new reflectiveness that had been camouflaged by its pyrotechnics. Ronnie had visited him the night before he died, and they had talked over all the things they had in common. Tubby's father was a highly respected musician, so was Ronnie's. The parents of both men had separated when they were small children.

Ronnie Scott was forty-five. He had been living for nearly eight years with Mary Hulin and it was the most committed relationship he had been involved in since his long on-off affair with Joan Crewe. They had moved from Knightsbridge to Fulham, to Elm Park Mansions, a rambling redbrick block built around a secluded courtyard just off the Fulham Road. It was easy for Ronnie Scott's old fears about domesticity to be kept under control in that partnership. Mary worked in the club and kept the same hours as him. She was popular among the musicians and was comfortable in any company. And she looked after Ronnie.

1971 had been a year that brought many changes for them both. In March, Nicholas had been operated on for a repair to his heart valves. Though he was a quiet and reserved child, his doctors had been astonished by his will to survive – when he was ready to cope alone after the surgery, he had even pulled out the drips himself. The experience had profoundly disturbed the boy's father who had paced the flat all night before the operation was due, not having seriously considered, until he heard it from the mouths of the doctors themselves, that Nicholas might not come out of the operating theatre alive.

In the Christmas of that year Ronnie Scott – who liked the opportunity to play Santa Claus even if he didn't regard himself as the world's most natural father – went shopping with Ilsa to buy presents for the boy whose future they were now celebrating more gratefully than on any of his seven Christmasses past. Nicholas was recovering well and growing more robust – he was even the only boy in the ballet class of the bilingual German/English school that Ilsa had taken him to in Petersham, one achievement that she kept from his father. Ronnie bought Nicholas a train set. Ilsa bought him a Lego kitchen and bathroom kit to put into the miniature house she had built for him at home.

'Isn't that a bit cissy for him?' Ronnie asked dubiously. 'You'll be telling me he goes to ballet classes next.' Ilsa didn't have the heart to say how right he was.

And at that time too, Mary told Ronnie that she was pregnant. She had already decided that she would have a baby by the time she was thirty and had already miscarried once, though in all the conversations to secure Ronnie's consent to fatherhood, he had always unequivocally refused. He never really visualized it as a source of more pleasure than anxiety. He tried to talk Mary round to the idea of not going ahead. It was soon clear that she would not be diverted, despite Ilsa's warning. 'If you're going to have a baby, Ronnie won't be able to cope with it,' Ilsa had said.

For Mary, doubts about Ronnie were unconvincing. She liked children, and her partner's concern about Nicholas's health had helped to convince her that things could really change. Mary's mother, who had sufficient of a traditional view of men and women to understand Ronnie well, was more cautious. 'Make the most of your stay in hospital,' she had said. 'You'll need to pay equal attention to Ronnie as well as the baby when you come out.'

Ronnie Scott had other fears about it all, those deep-rooted anxieties about accident and physical decline that represented the mirror image of his anarchic self, fears enhanced by the memory of Jock's appearance at the end, the decline of Sol, the sudden departure of his mother. He convinced himself that he was too old for fatherhood, that middle-age might have increased the risk of his child being born unhealthy. He wanted Mary to have every test she could, visited doctors with her, listened intently to advice. And when he was assured that it would be all right, he relaxed and began to look forward to it. They took Mary into hospital in the final weeks of her pregnancy, and the medical assessment was that she still had a while to go on the night before their child arrived. Ronnie Scott went home to Elm Park mansions. Mary gave birth to a daughter on the morning of 5 September 1972. The child's father, by this stage of his life with a profound loathing of life before lunchtime and not anticipating developments, couldn't be contacted. Three hours after the birth, he arrived at the ward, grinning broadly. 'My God, Mary, she looks just like my grandmother,' Scott exclaimed in astonishment as he looked into the cot. So they called her Rebecca, in memory of a woman who had given the baby's father so much cause to welcome life and enjoy its opportunities. For eighteen months Rebecca shared the flat in Elm Park Mansions with them, and the child's discoveries of the world that had become so familiar to her father were unexpected invitations to rediscover it himself.

Some of the discoveries were devoted to grasping old fantasies. Already, in the summer of that year, Ronnie Scott had gone motor racing for the first time in his life – an old dream since that romantic image of his ex-boss, Johnny Claes, in that big, brutal Grand Prix racer back in the 1940s – taking part in the 'celebrity races' that were run at Brands Hatch and driving in formula saloon car competitions. (He mused that in a short career at the wheel, winning two races, doing well in two others and bending two cars he had, on percentages, come out ahead of Jackie Stewart.) Pete King and Ronnie Scott, both long-time motoring fans, both made concerted efforts to rerun their childhoods in their forties.

In 1973 Ronnie Scott began an affair with a new waitress at the club. Linda Poulton was a young would-be singer looking for opportunities, was fascinated by the world Scott moved in. She played the guitar, enjoyed painting and sculpture, even thought she would be a useful addition to the personnel of Scott's own band. Little Rebecca was not much younger than Ronnie himself had been when Cissie forced Jock to face exactly the same problem forty-three years before and Mary was no more prepared to accept that it would go away than Cissie had been. She knew Linda well from the club, had had many intimate conversations with her, and found out about the affair through the hints of another member of the floor staff who advised her not to go on confiding in the younger woman. Mary soon confronted the new arrival with the implications of what she and Ronnie were doing. Ronnie Scott alternated between agonizing about it, considering ending it, and trying to believe that Mary's displeasure wasn't really happening. After all, Cissie and Nana Becky, the first women he had known in his life, had never complained about anything he had wanted to do, had always been there when he wanted them. Why was it all so different now?

It was about as different as it could be. Linda Poulton went to America during 1973, to begin what turned out to be an unsuccessful engagement with the Mel Lewis band. Ronnie Scott went to France to play some concerts around that time and sent a message to Mary in London saying that he had been invited to take a temporary assignment in a French big band whose tenorist was sick. Since they were going to be playing some upmarket shows, would she send a tuxedo out to him? It was all an implausible stab at an alibi. Mary sent the tuxedo, but soon learned that Ronnie had actually gone to the States in pursuit of Linda. She knew then that Ronnie had become obsessed. Though she still loved him, she could see no way out. All of her friends were Ronnie's friends. Her life was in the club, where everyone knew Linda too. This couldn't be any ordinary separation. In February 1974, Mary left for New York with Rebecca.

Ronnie Scott knew of old that he was nothing like the cool, phlegmatic deflator of the Big Deal that constituted the public face illuminated night after night by his own footlights. His impulsiveness surfaced in bursts, hand in hand with the romanticism that was the flipside to Jewish pragmatism, the survivor's compulsion to dream. It had shown itself in the first journey to New York in 1947, the trip for the Holy Grail. It had gripped him helplessly in the drop-everything trip to America in the mid-fifties to follow Joan Crewe and Spencer Sinatra. It betrayed him all over again by never letting on that there would be women in the world who would have their own lives to live.

Midway through 1974, it was all going downhill fast. Mary and Rebecca were gone. Linda Poulton had come close to being a singer with the hard-swinging trio that Scott had formed with the organist Mike Carr and drummer Bobby Gien, but Mary had furiously objected. Linda left America for Australia and then New Zealand, where her parents lived.

Ronnie Scott was getting into bad shape. Finding himself plagued by anxieties about Mary and Rebecca, and unable to stop thinking about Linda either, he was becoming dependent on sleeping pills and whisky to get any sleep. He had only ever been a moderate consumer of alcohol in the past. This time, all the unanswered questions of his life rose up and nearly drowned him. He rang Linda twice, three times a week. He pleaded with her to come back.

But there was good work to be done, if he could hold himself together. For the autumn of 1974, Scott's trio was booked on to a long tour of Australia and the United States with the irrepressible Parisian violinist Stephane Grappelli, who had performed at the club the previous year, and the tour was to culminate in a Carnegie Hall concert in New York. Grappelli was popular everywhere he went, playing a jaunty, dancing, raffish kind of swing like an elegant conjuring act. Scott's band, built around the deep, reverberating tones of Carr's organ (Carr would add the role of the missing bassist by performing bass lines on footpedals) was equally rhythmic, though the leader was by this point inclining toward adding the packed and tumbling melodic constructions of early John Coltrane on top of the Mobley grace.

Linda came to see him play in Sydney, and they spent a week together. The tour went on to the USA, where ABC-TV recorded Scott's week of performances in Rochester, New York State, and he and Grappelli played Carnegie Hall. The concert wasn't all that it might have been. The band discovered in rehearsal that the specifications of American electricity fouled up the mechanism through which Carr's bass pedals got their proper effect. They eventually had to hire another instrument, which wasn't set up to replicate a real bass as Carr's was, with the result that the organist's dancing feet produced a brisk, jovial, unsustained and distinctly unhip sound like a low-pitched xylophone.

Scott was still in a bad way, barely able to get through the work, always performing with a jug of iced water on stage because the sedatives were drying his mouth. He spent much of the time in New York with Mary and Rebecca, still drinking heavily and taking anti-depressants and sleeping drugs. In his depression, and veering wildly between the impossible choices he had set himself, he found it hard to deal with Rebecca and could only cope with it by reserve and distance. But they visited the children's clothing department of Macy's one day to buy presents for the little girl. Confused and still badly strung out, Ronnie Scott sat on the floor, propped against a display stand, people seeming to float around him like ghosts. He fell asleep there, with Macy's customers going impassively about their business all around. Eventually the presence of the exhausted, dishevelled looking man on the floor attracted a crowd. When he woke up, Mary was anxiously slapping his face to bring him around, while Rebecca looked on.

It was the fall of 1974. Ronnie Scott knew that it was time to come home.

By Christmas Pete King was seriously worried for Ronnie as a friend and for what seemed like a lynchpin of the business, but was uncertain how to help. As the year came to a close, on what seemed like just another night's work, there was a sharper twist to the knife. Scott was by now barely functioning except by reflex. A drunk in the club got argumentative, Scott tried to throw him out, frog-marched him through the aisles toward the door in a rage. The drunk twisted and knocked the proprietor's glasses flying into the twilit room. Scott hit him in the back of the head and broke his little finger. The drunk came out of it intact, but for Scott it was clearly going to be impossible to play the saxophone until the fracture healed, a pursuit that had become the last refuge. He rang Linda Poulton in Auckland one more time. 'I feel completely useless,' Scott told her. 'I can't play. I can't do anything. Suppose I come out there for Christmas?'

In the state he was in, it was impossible for him to hear quite how ambiguous a proposition it seemed for a woman living with her parents on the other side of the world and trying to get on with her life. But, hesitantly, she agreed. He booked everything in a sudden explosion of energy, bought presents for Linda, went around the shops with a list of things she wanted. He arranged for Brian Theobald, an old friend of Tubby Hayes' and a one-time road manager who was currently driving a minicab, to pick him up from Elm Park Mansions on the morning of his flight. Seven hours before he was due to leave, Linda rang from Auckland. 'I've been thinking about this, Ronnie,' came the voice on the line. 'I don't really think it's a good idea.' In later years, Ronnie Scott would unhesitatingly acknowledge that she was right. But not on this morning.

Ronnie Scott dissolved. He swallowed everything he could lay his hands on in the flat, left a note for Theobald outside the door telling him to forget it and that he'd be back in touch sometime. When Theobald arrived he was immediately alarmed. He knew only too well how things had been lately. He rang the bell and hammered on the door but there wasn't a sound from the flat.

Theobald rang for Henry Cohen, the giant jazz fan from Dagenham who had become the Frith Street bouncer – 'his shadow's bigger than Asia' his boss used to tell the club's audiences. When Cohen arrived, Theobald told him the score. 'I want you to take the door out,' he told Cohen. The big man shuffled uneasily, edged toward the stairs. 'I can't do that,' he protested. 'I'll get the fuckin' sack.' 'Do it,' Theobald insisted. 'I'll take care of it.' They found Ronnie Scott on the floor beside the bed, the bedclothes lying on top of him. Theobald satisfied himself that Scott was alive and promptly rang Pete King, who summoned Sidney Gottlieb, an ex-East-End doctor who had acquired a West End practice who was a long-standing friend of the club who would help Ronnie and Pete whenever they, or anyone who worked there, were in difficulties. Gottlieb took charge of Scott. The doctor had concluded that whatever the musician's intentions had been before Theobald and Cohen found him, it was senseless to take chances. Scott needed round-the-clock supervision, Gottlieb insisted.

Gottlieb took Scott to his Highgate home, where he rest-lessly stayed for a week or so. He then went to stay with Pete and Stella King and their family at King's comfortable house in Borehamwood, where he would pace the rooms with a cigarette for hours. King's son Christopher would recall the period later, accusing his father of 'doing a Ronnie' whenever he would adopt the same manner of locomotion. King wanted to do what he could to help his partner get straight, and as far as he could see it was mainly a matter of seeing Linda again. He rang her in Auckland, explained what had happened to Ronnie, and bought her an air ticket to come to London. But it wasn't really the remedy King had hoped for, and it was beginning to seem that Scott needed more thorough supervision. Gottlieb had Ronnie Scott admitted to a nursing home in St John's Wood, where he would have a twenty-four hour watch from the male nurses in the home, who weren't supposed to let him out of their sight.

Mary then came over from New York at Pete King's request, and brought Becky with her. When Ronnie knew she was in town he stopped eating the home's meals and would only eat what she would cook for him, taken from the flat to his room twice a day by Theobald. He would try to practise the saxophone nevertheless. The establishment was eventually forced to take his reeds away because he kept the place awake, and Theobald once found him there sitting up in bed and playing his soprano with no reed in the mouth-piece, just to keep his fingering in shape. As he got better, his constant attendants gained more faith in the likelihood that he wouldn't do anything drastic. 'I'm going to take a bath,' Scott said one night to the nurse. 'Don't worry, I'll be all right. Read your book.' The nurse agreed, settled down to read, and nodded off.

Meanwhile, in a downstairs room was one of the home's wealthiest patients, an elderly woman who – refusing to be standardized by the system to the extent of having an electric bell – would communicate with the staff only by vigorously ringing a handbell. Since she had never been known to take a step outside of her room in eight years' residence, it came as something of a surprise to the staff to find her charging volcanically down the corridor like an extra from the 'Ride of the Valkyrie', handbell borne aloft, wailing in fury. They went in to find a good deal of the plasterwork of the ceiling in her bed, and a cascade of water following it. Upstairs, the nurse still dozed outside the bathroom door. One of the home's largest members of staff took a run down the corridor at the door, and it opened unprotestingly to his charge, leaving him prostrate over the lavatory. Ronnie Scott was asleep in the bath with both taps full on. One hand absently held the shower unit above his head. They managed to placate the outraged customer downstairs. They also tried to keep their faces suitably straight when they told the story to the visiting Theobald later on. Nobody managed to.

As he improved, Scott began to consider psychoanalysis. He tried with Dr Gottlieb, but they weren't the right partnership. Gottlieb then recommended a Harley Street psychiatrist. The patient was uncomfortable with the whole idea, but began to tell his story, head in hands. When he looked up the eminent specialist was asleep. 'Excuse me, doctor,' he began despairingly. 'I'm so sorry,' apologized the shrink, waking up with a start. 'It's a little stuffy in here.' Ronnie Scott never went much for psychiatrists since he perceived them rather like unfortunate agents who were blighted by having a string of inept musicians on their books. 'How can you expect them to get it right for everybody?' he would say. 'They must have two dozen people with sob stories coming around every week.'

He couldn't break the habit of thinking that was simply what the problem was. He began to mend, with the help of anti-depressants, and got back to playing again, which was an immense release. But for most of 1974 he was coupling the drugs to heavy drinking. Mary had helped him get back on his feet. She had intended visiting for three weeks and had stayed five months, feeding him and looking after him, preventing the little flat in Elm Park Mansions from becoming the vortex of the downward spiral it had threatened to be. But eventually she and Becky went back to New York. Scott was functioning again, but still flailing.

So many of the steps he wanted to take he knew were crazy but he took them anyway. He booked himself on to a plane to the Antipodes to see Linda again, unannounced, and ended up staying with her and her parents outside Auckland, a stoned-out, drunken Jewish saxophone player nearing fifty with crazed designs on the daughter of a respectable family of Auckland Gentiles, Scott felt himself transplanted into the screenplay of Woody Allen's *Annie Hall*, having supper with Annie's Gentile parents and suddenly believing himself to have changed into a rabbi in mid-sentence.

Scott nevertheless persuaded Linda to leave Auckland with him, even to come back to London to try it again. He tried to lace the journey with the attractive proposition of what almost amounted to a round-the-world tour, returning via the States, adventures unlimited on a Diners Club card for which there was to be a fearsome financial reckoning in the months to come. She came back to Fulham and they tried to start afresh. But nothing much had really changed. The partnership lasted a few more months before Linda Poulton flew home.

Mary and Rebecca kept in touch with him. They would talk on the phone once a week. Mary would hear nothing against Ronnie despite the pain of those years. 'If he hurts other people he never means to, and he hurts himself just as much and maybe more,' she would say. She told him, as the darkest clouds passed and some of that old humour returned that had so charmed her in the Gerrard Street basement years ago, that they should try to put it behind them. And she never forgot all those images of how far into despair he could fall. In the worst months, Scott had sent to Mary all the photographs he had of them and Becky together. He wanted her to have them. It was a way of saying what seemed at the time to be the longest goodbye of all.

12 / Let's Take It From the Top

'Jazz is the expression of fleeting emotions.' (Ronnie Scott to Kitty Grime, *Jazz at Ronnie Scott's*, 1973.)

Gradually, music pulled Ronnie Scott back into the world.

He formed a quartet in the summer following the American tour, with the brilliant Irish guitarist Louis Stewart, Kenny Baldock on bass and Martin Drew on drums. Scott quickly found the band to be exactly what he had wanted for years. He loved having Stewart in the lineup as well. Hearing the guitar always reminded him of those old wild days in the London of years gone by, hearing Django Rheinhardt jamming until dawn with Dave Goldberg in that rabbit-warren of an apartment in Charing Cross Road.

As for the club, it was not the only fish in the sea any more. The Jazz Centre Society, which had started so small, was developing a more adventurous policy of combining home-grown and imported talent than anyone had believed, and was attracting Arts Council funding to do it in proportions that rose healthily through the 1970s. There was also a risk that the booking policy at Frith Street, which was based on a mixture of fondness for saxophonists, the occasional presence of jazz-influenced nightclub singers to appeal to the casual and tourist audience, and great sentimental attachment to artists who were by now regular visitors, was going to be by-passed by the changing times.

Frith Street was by now Ronnie Scott's life. He had no social sphere outside it, didn't need one. Mary wouldn't stay with him now, he knew that, though he believed that she still loved him. And he increasingly took to visiting the establishment's downstairs bar, a tiny room in the basement where the musicians would relax between sets.

The barmaid there was French, another jazz fan and occasional painter called Françoise Venet. Françoise brought her own jazz records to work and played them over the downstairs sound system. Ronnie listened and relaxed. He began to confide in Françoise, tell her what he had been through, try to explain why it had shocked him so much. He distrusted analysis, thought that it might simply become a way of life, like it was for the people you laughed at in Woody Allen movies, but musicianspeak had no vocabulary for coping with what he was feeling. The company of jazz musicians was a Catch 22. It was a predominantly male world, the inhabitants of which tended to be uncomprehending of mental difficulties, if not actually unsympathetic. Ronnie for his part found it harder to relax the cynical, freewheeling image that men admired him for enough to really let his difficulties out. Françoise became the understanding figure he needed. And they were attracted to each other. Françoise was the daughter of a cartoonist, and took to drawing and painting the performers who were coming through the premises. She was a jazz lover, and a skilled photographer. They were soon a couple, and Françoise moved to Elm Park Mansions.

Françoise found that her new partner's sense of humour, self-defence which had never left him even at the worst times, was shared by the professionals whose company he loved. And excellent artists were continuing to come and go in the club through the latter part of the 1970s – like Dexter Gordon, Sarah Vaughan, Dizzy Gillespie, Stan Getz, Art Blakey.

Scott particularly admired Gillespie, one of the pioneers of the music that had taken him over when he was hardly out of his teens. To have visited the 52nd Street clubs when Gillespie's playing, and his mannerisms, and his jokes were the talk of the London jazz circles and to find him there, answering an invitation in the reverse direction thirty years later, was sheer fascination. Gillespie, for all his clowning and bonhomie on stage, was realistic about the jazz business in a way that Ronnie Scott had hardly ever heard before.

One night in the back room, Scott began talking with the trumpeter about the magic of jazz, the pull that kept musicians in thrall to it.

'It happens so seldom,' Scott said to Gillespie. 'Ninety-nine per cent of the time you play within boundaries. Then sometimes something happens and you break through it for a night, or an hour, or eight bars.' 'That's what the incentive is.' Gillespie agreed. 'How often do you think it's happened to you?' the Englishman enquired.

'About once every two years,' Gillespie unhesitatingly returned. It was a reflection of the merciless demands of combining a sophisticated improvised music with the necessity to continually tour to make a living.

The club had become an institution. Spike Milligan regularly visited, a jazz fan and an invaluable friend. Princess Margaret visited the club, once occasioning what was regarded as a highly risqué gag about her friendship with the comic actor Peter Sellers that Milligan got Scott to read out over the microphone. The papers next day were indignant. When the Princess arrived on the premises, doorman Jeff Ellison thought for a moment that at last the club might acquire a status that the music it presented had deserved for so long. 'We're fashionable now,' he said to Scott. 'With visitors like her, it'll make all the difference.' 'Who needs fashionable?' Scott enquired phlegmatically of Ellison. 'It means you're in for five minutes and then people forget all about you. We go on the way we always have done.'

In 1978, Mary sent young Becky over for a holiday. The little girl was by now a self-possessed, independent and funny seven year old, full of mannerisms that reminded her mother of Ronnie – the same crazy jokes, the same hilarious impressions, though Becky's memories of Ronnie were not much more defined than Ronnie's had been of Jock. But the trip was a problem for all of them. Mary, who was receiving money from Ronnie but who was finding single motherhood hard in the States, because she was running a busy jazz booking agency in New York, was in desperate need of rest. Ronnie Scott was working in the club, keeping the same old hours and, though he was intrigued by the personality his daughter had become, had no idea how to handle the relationship. Much of the responsibility for looking after Becky consequently fell on Françoise. She stopped work to look after the little girl. She found a school for her – which Becky was indignant to find herself despatched to – when the visit ran on from a few weeks to three months. By the time Becky went home, life at Elm Park Mansions had become distinctly tense.

Ronnie Scott and Françoise thus took a step that the saxophonist's friends would hitherto have considered unthinkable. He had already put down firmer roots than ever before by buying the Fulham flat, offered to him cheaply as a long-time tenant. Now his relationship with Françoise seemed secure enough to risk re-selling the apartment and deciding to find out what 'settling down' actually meant. After all, Pete King and his family seemed to have an agreeable existence in the suburbs. Maybe those years of rejecting all that had just been punishing himself after all.

Ronnie and Françoise bought a big semi-detached house in West Hampstead. It meant stretching out, practising the saxophone without bothering anybody, keeping a dog and a cat, an end to living in a shoebox. Ronnie Scott, even in the early weeks, wasn't sure. There was something comforting and womb-like about a little flat in a beehive like Elm Park Mansions. The open spaces of comfortable, middle-class territory like Hampstead seemed to shout at him. Nevertheless the couple stayed at the house through 1979, and set about building a life within it. There was to be a music room for Ronnie, the first he had ever had. There was to be a painting room for Françoise. They made plans for the house, chose a decor for it, hired builders. It was not, as it turned out, an ideal conjunction of events. There were too many things to decide that Ronnie Scott had never taken the remotest interest in before, and too little experience of how much time and energy they could take up. Builders filled the house, with noise, dirt and themselves. Ronnie and Françoise found it increasingly trying. The saxophonist was also becoming prey to dark moods again. Françoise was unsure why he had changed and put it down to such a disruption of his former habits of life.

He did defeat some old anxieties as his playing life got back into its stride. He made progress with his fear of aeroplanes, through an unintentional shock therapy occasioned by having to take an air taxi to an arts festival in Ireland during an air strike. As the plane steeply banked over the Republic, Scott asked the pilot in alarm what he meant by heading the tiny craft toward what looked like a bowling green with a wind sock on it. 'That's the airport,' came the reply. Scott was hardly heard to utter another word of protest about planes after that.

Some old habits died hard. He would still gamble ferociously when the impulse took him – though he always insisted that he wasn't an addict of the horses as Uncle Mark had been, or as Jock had been, that there were limits to how far he would go or how much he would lose. But he ran the risks that made it exciting. On a tour of Wales with the quintet he formed in the late seventies, he even lost the wages for the outfit in a Bangor betting shop, bored whilst the others were spending the afternoon talking guitars in a local music store owned by a jazz guitarist. By the last race, he had £40 left out of over £700. He took a flyer on a combination forecast with the last of the money, and though the odds were stacked massively against him the bet came up. He won back the £700 and came out £300 ahead. He would still wistfully say that he wished he had back the money he had lost, willingly swapped for his winnings over the years. But it was too much of a diverting recreation to leave alone. Françoise would watch him glued to the television sports on Saturday afternoons, one hand on the telephone.

Great music continued sporadically to be heard in that smoky, low ceilinged room but Ronnie Scott and Pete King had to face the fact that they were in business and businesses all around the country were ruefully reflecting that they had known better days. The recession was biting and the weakness of the pound against the dollar meant that American artists demanded higher fees just to keep up. Promotion had never been more crucial to the survival of the establishment. Scott would use a gag in his routines in later years that ran: 'We'd like you to eat, drink and enjoy yourselves. Pretend you're on the Titanic.' In 1980, that was exactly the situation they were in.

In the course of trying to sharpen up the club's image, Pete King and Brian Theobald (the man who had broken into Scott's flat in that oblivion of 1974 and who was now running the club's touring arrangements) were having to cope with the mixture of shyness, laziness, diffidence and single-mindedness about simply playing jazz that characterized their front man. It had already become obvious that Scott would hardly ever record, even when the prospects were lucrative, insisting that he hated hearing himself on disc, that he found the studio inhibiting and even disliked live performance when he knew the tapes were running.

He was a good salesman for the club when actually working on the premises, but still maintained that mixture of mischievousness and unwillingness to be obseqious that had been his trademark throughout the club's life. He had done a legendary double take on the black superstar Isaac Hayes one night, who had arrived in the foyer wearing a massive fur hat. Scott didn't recognize Hayes, looked at the hat and remarked, 'When that has puppies, can I have one?' Hayes wasn't amused, and promptly left. Scott's unwillingness to go out of his way to sell himself or the club extended to the Michael Parkinson television chat show, which King and Theobald saw as one of the only peak-viewing showcases for jazz. Parkinson loved it, and usually included jazz acts for the musical interlude. After some wheedling, they managed to persuade Parkinson to include Ronnie as a guest, during a week in which the Woody Herman orchestra was in the club and not doing good business. But when the contract came through for the show, Ronnie Scott didn't want to do it. King rarely tried to talk his partner out of decisions, but sensed that a good performance on the Parkinson show might save Herman's season.

They eventually talked Scott into it. He found himself appearing as a guest with songwriter Arthur Schwarz and the actor Robert Powell, and didn't push himself with them, exhibiting his usual reserve in unfamiliar company. After a while he actually appeared to be asleep, legs crossed, his trousers ridden up above his socks, head lolling back. Parkinson turned the conversation to ambiguous song titles. Powell and Schwarz thrashed around as best they could. Eventually the host sprang it on Scott, convinced his mind was light years away. The saxophonist barely opened his eyes, and without a pause or a change of the loafing pose muttered 'The Party's Over – it's all over my friend.' It wasn't so much the joke as the delivery. Parkinson and his guests cracked up, so did many of the studio staff. Woody Herman's band played a spot on the show, and the club was packed for the rest of his run.

The club's economics had always been such that a short down period would cancel out the virtues of months of good business. In 1980 there was a new and more pressing problem. Value Added Tax had forced King, grumbling furiously, to become a bookeeper for the government when it replaced Purchase Tax in the early 70s, an inconceivable role for an East Ender. King found that though he ought to be saving some of the operation's proceeds for the bill that would one day come, the demands of the artists were more pressing, and easier to sympathize with.

King received an enquiry from a VAT officer to make an inspection of the club's books. He duly set up an appointment for the inspector, then got another call not long afterward, ostensibly for the same business. 'I thought we'd just made an appointment,' King said, mystified. 'Well, who are you expecting to see?' asked the government man. King told him. There was a short silence. 'Ah. That's not us, that's a long way up the hierarchy.'

When the Customs and Excise arrived, they threw the club into crisis. After a long investigation, they left Scott and King with a bill for £40,000, backdated to when VAT began.

It was a crippling blow. The two men could lay hands on £20,000, and undertook to pay the rest in instalments. But business wasn't good enough to keep up with the payments. 'If you'd been shrewd businessmen you'd have seen this coming,' somebody said to King. 'If we were shrewd businessmen we wouldn't be here,' King replied.

The club's accountants could see no other route but receivership. However, if the receiver was open enough to permit the two men to try to buy back their premises once the tangle had been sorted out, it might be possible to stay in the jazz business. The receivers were Martin Spencer and John Pappy, at the time trying to pull the Chelsea Football Club out of its difficulties. Spencer took on the job on 16 July 1980, looked at every detail of the club's operations, suggested ways of cutting costs and stayed with the operation for a year. At the end of that time, things hadn't got much better. 'Look, you're losing this. You'll have to sell,' Spencer eventually informed Scott and King.

The premises went on to the market in the following year. The estate agent's brochure claimed that the club ought to have annual profits of £100,000. Initially Scott and King were surprised by the number of people they had previously regarded as supporters who tried to buy the lease themselves once they knew of the difficulties. But there was an unexpected saving grace. Charles Forte, the original landlord of the premises, had included in the first lease a clause to the effect that it could not be reassigned. Scott and King *had* to be the new owners. They also had to somehow raise the money to cover it. They were looking for £110,000.

For Ronnie Scott, the old gremlins were back in business. His gathering discontent with suburban life had culminated in his usual route out of the frying pan and into the fire. Finding his fits of depression harder and harder to cope with at home, Françoise left to return to France in 1981. There was indeed another younger woman (Scott was fifty-three) who had come to the club with her older sister, who was renting a room in the flat of Joe Green, an old associate of Scott and King. The younger girl played the clarinet, wanted saxophone lessons. That the whole scenario already smacked of a French farce was perfectly obvious to Scott, who this time knew what he wanted to do was crazy and proceeded to dive resolutely in. To begin with the girl was intrigued by the idea of an affair with a middle-aged man who was a legendary saxophone player. Scott soon descended into the depths he thought he had left behind, and as he did, the girl pondered the wisdom of the affair. The close proximity of comedy and tragedy in what followed was of the kind that Scott's own sense of humour was founded on, but it would take time before he was to be able to turn it to account. The newcomer was a student in Brighton and shared a house with college friends. Scott took to visiting there, often getting drunk in the bar on the train. Sometimes he would find himself in desultory conversation with her house-mates, who he began to realise were treating him with a kind of bewildered sympathy. 'Relationships end, you know,' Ronnie Scott heard an eighteen year old boy declaring earnestly to him over the teacups. Another suggested that he ring the Samaritans.

She loved piano music, particularly Chopin, but couldn't afford an instrument of her own. Ronnie Scott bought her a piano in Brighton on the proceeds of a bet, tried to have it delivered without telling her. The boy who ran the household came out of his room as the delivery men were struggling up the stairs. He immediately looked shocked. 'Oh, I don't think so,' he muttered anxiously. 'I don't know if she wants it in her room. I don't know if she wants it at all.' 'All right, if she doesn't want it I'll take it away again. I just want to surprise her, that's all . . .' It was no good. The routine was worthy of Laurel and Hardy. They took it all down again, then brought it back when its intended recipient returned and enthusiastically claimed it. The gift didn't save the relationship. She was tired of it, Ronnie Scott wasn't. Soon after she finished her course, he lost touch with her.

He called Françoise, asked her what she thought about him selling the house and moving back to Fulham. 'It's not up to me, it's up to you,' Françoise said. 'Do what you feel happiest with.'

But Ronnie Scott was hurled back into the dark by the experience. This time it was Ilsa who was on hand to help, coming to Elm Park Mansions to cook for him and look after the flat. Once again he had seriously lost weight. Ilsa was surprised to find that hardly anybody seemed to visit. But Spike Milligan's relationship with Ronnie deepened then. Familiar with mental pain himself the comedian would send cabs to Fulham, ferry Ronnie to his Barnet home to talk, drink, listen to music.

Once again, Ronnie Scott was caught by surprise by his own emotions. Françoise knew, as Mary had known, that he was mortified by the havoc he caused, and that his regrets were not a self-indulgence. She missed him as much as he found he was missing her. Eventually she would come back to England, and back to him though they wouldn't live together again. All these diversions had made things harder for Pete King. He would ruefully shake his head at his partner's preoccupations. 'Every time he gets into something nice, he goes and fucks it up,' he would complain to Stella. She agreed. 'But he stays friends with them, in the end,' the woman pointed out. It was all true. The calls from Mary and from Joan Crewe in America would keep on coming. He and Françoise became very close. But it was hard for Ronnie Scott to concentrate on the crisis in the club. Often he would cast a look of what was very nearly entreaty at King and ask: 'What shall we do?' King was still determined to effect a rescue, somehow.

One night in the autumn of 1981, when the club was playing host to the remarkable teenage gypsy guitarist Bireli Lagrene, Pete King was attending to the club's sound system when a stranger came over to him and said, 'Hi Pete, how are you?' King couldn't place him but knew he was from the record business. The visitor began to ask about the fortunes of the club, said he'd heard that things were bad. King was impatient at first, busy with preparing the premises for the night's work. But he could see that the other man was genuinely interested and didn't simply seem like someone anxious to step into their shoes.

'So you want to buy the club back and carry on?' the man asked. King agreed. 'Are you going to be running it yourself?' 'Yes.' 'Just the same way you always have?' 'We don't know any other way,' King replied. 'If you're going to be running it, then put me down for £25,000.' The speaker was Chris Blackwell, boss of Island Records, who had built his business out of West Indian music and who had been known to Ronnie Scott and Pete King since the Gerrard Street days. King swears he cried as Blackwell walked away.

They tried other avenues too. The Greater London Council under Ken Livingstone had a reputation for interest in the progressive arts, particularly where ethnic groups were concerned, but after several preparatory conversations about it and a meeting with the council's supremo Lord Birkett, nothing was followed up. They went to the Arts Council too, for only the second time in nearly two decades, but got nowhere once again. Despite the nature of the music they presented, Ronnie Scott's Club had a reputation of still being in that Tin Pan Alley sphere. Its proprietors were middle-aged East Enders with no comprehension of the language of arts lobbying, the grasp of committee politics, the limitless patience and detailed reading of minutes and technicalities. They were worlds apart.

Eventually it was the old stagers who came through. The Musicians' Union, partly through the good offices of jazz fans Brian Blain and Johnny Patrick, and with the support of the general secretary John Morton, agreed to lend Scott and King £30,000. With Blackwell's contribution they were halfway there. Then they went to Charrington's the brewery that had had the club franchise. At first, the firm was doubtful, having lost money in the previous trading company, Jazz Ventures, which was wound up by the receiver in July 1980. Eventually they did agree to help, though adding to the obligations the repayment of the outstanding debt, and with a final contribution from the Performing Right Society, the lease was repurchased.

It had been a hair-raising experience.

And slowly they pulled the club round. They tried many ploys to raise its profile, but in the end the best was the one that dispelled the old image of Frith Street as a place that only high-rollers could afford to spend an evening in. The membership scheme devised in the early eighties whereby for a small annual sum members could get very cheap admission on weekdays brought a new and younger public to the place, one that could help to guarantee a future beyond those anxious weekly computations of the take. And as the club stabilized, so it saw some of its most memorable nights of music. Far from the golden age having passed with those magical memories of Sonny Rollins and Dexter Gordon in the Old Place, some of the greatest surviving artists of black music – the tradition on which the club was founded – continued to play there, and some of the most distinctive new developments from black music, white music and further afield came through the door as well. Nina Simone, a dramatic and sometimes spinechilling exponent of both gospel and soul and the European legacy of Weill and Piaf as well, was such a hit with audiences during a three-week stint at Ronnie Scott's in 1983 that she became a regular visitor until a diplomatic crisis early in 1986.

And the proprietors' undimmed instinct for a gamble led to another unexpected offering that was a gratifying hit with the younger public they needed to attract to survive. For six weeks in the summer of 1985, Scott and King booked a group of Cuban bands that Scott had heard play at a music festival in Havana. Like the work of the Afro-Cuban bandleader Machito, who made several visits in the early 1980s and performed the last gig of his life in the club, the younger Cubans delivered a dynamic mixture of African music, jazz, salsa and soul. It was the kind of exposure to the eclectic new descendants of the old jazz legacy that in a sane world would have happened years before.

Two other large ensembles did the same in 1985. One was a young British band called Loose Tubes, whose presiding young genius was a pianist going by the name of Django Bates, an urchin-like figure who would frequently appear on stage wearing frock-coats and outlandish hats and who quickly demonstrated himself to be a keyboard soloist to rival anyone on the instrument in the length and breadth of the land.

The other was the big band that was brought in by the Rolling Stones' drummer Charlie Watts (the project cost Watts, who had been a swing band fan since childhood, £30,000 to stage, and caused him to quip 'I had to buy the club to put this on') turned out to be a virtual summary of everything that Scott and King had lived with and lived by. Three generations of British jazz musicians were included in its lineup. There was Stan Tracey and Bobby Wellins, and the tenorist Danny Moss – looking for all the world like the middle-aged proprietor of a country pub – and Alan Skidmore and Don Weller from the Old Place generation, contemporaries of John Surman and Tony Oxley. And there was Courtney Pine on tenor too, a young black Londoner who loved Coltrane and also loved the incentive of trying to surprise a group of old jazzers who so clearly thought they'd heard it all before.

It was Watts' repertoire, the one he was fulfilling a childhood dream to stage – and so it was something of an anachronism, a kind of private party in which a rich man hired his favourite players to perform an old-fashioned swing book that wouldn't have been out of place in the Savoy Ballroom. But it was a showcase for an extraordinary diversity of British improvisors, of all persuasions and all ages, and the crowds were ecstatic. For Ronnie Scott and Pete King, its players represented what British jazz had been able to become since the days of their apprenticeship when it had no confidence, no experience and no style. It was, however, not to be an occasion for unseemly displays of emotion. King propped up the bar as the band got underway, talking to *The Times* critic, Richard Williams. Watts, whose grasp of jazz drumming was more enthusiastic than expert, had hired two excellent percussionists to flank him – the avantist John Stevens, and the Jazz Couriers' old drummer Bill Eyden. 'What do you think of it?' Williams asked King as the ferocious gallumphing and hammering got into its stride. King gave it weighty consideration, puffing out his considerable chest. 'Needs another couple of drummers,' he finally returned.

13 / Old Times

'Jazz allows you to sound fifty when you are fifty. When you are nineteen you should sound nineteen. Jazz allows you to tell the truth.' (Max Roach to Kitty Grime, *Jazz Voices*.)

Another story was unfolding behind the improving fortunes of the club, behind the shout of confidence that soared up from the brass of a young and home-grown jazz band like Loose Tubes. The passage of time brought many ambiguous signals with it.

In November 1984, Denis Rose had died.

His departure brought a pang even to those old hipsters, to the ageing delinquents who had, as the jargon went, 'lived for kicks' in the war years and the 1950s, who had tried to express – as Bird had involuntarily done – an impassivity to everything but playing. Rose was so much a part of that world, so languidly and expertly a professional at the art of survival in the big city, and so generous and obsessive a teacher of the music he loved, that his loss seemed like a startling resolution of that episode that had begun in the shattered London of 1942 and which had seemed like an everlasting *now*. He had been forgotten by everyone but musicians, but accepted his obscurity, playing piano in Denman Street pubs, teaching occasionally in a room full of music and copies of the *Racing Chronicle*. 'I'm free,' he would say. 'I can play what I like. I don't need to shave, and I don't need to be on the spot all the time like Ronnie.'

The funeral was on a bleak November day in New Southgate, North London, the old stamping ground of Rose and Laurie Morgan. Ronnie Scott was particularly distressed by Rose's death, a man who he felt had set him on the right path when he might never have understood the mechanics

of the music sufficiently to discover it alone. Ronnie Scott
and Laurie Morgan were there as the rain slanted over the
gravestones. So was Tony Crombie, Lennie Bush, Jeff
Ellison, Pete King, and many others. Rose's family put a toy
piano on the mound when the musician was buried, which
remained there for weeks afterwards. It was not a celebration
of Rose's immense virtues, and it was not a wake. It was
a dour, grey occasion, and one to prompt some personal
reflections. Laurie Morgan, staying in the Midlands with
the retired alto saxophonist from Club Eleven days, Johnny
Rogers, had remarked before Rose's death that it was a pity
that so many of the pioneers had gone their separate ways.
'We'll have to be careful that we don't just meet at funerals,'
Morgan had said.

For Ronnie Scott, the reminder came again barely four
months later, when John Haley 'Zoot' Sims, the first American to perform as a guest in that shabby basement in Gerrard
Street twenty-four years before, died of cancer in New York
at the age of fifty-nine. Sims died on a Saturday and Scott,
for whom the American saxophonist held a special place as a
player, a friend, and a milestone in his own life, immediately
decided to fly to the States. The banks were shut, but Scott
and King managed to scrape together the money for the fare
between them. When Ronnie Scott reached New York he
called Mary's number. Becky came on the line. 'Where's your
mummy?' Ronnie asked her. 'She's gone to Zoot's memorial
service,' Becky replied. 'Well, that's where I'm going too,'
Ronnie said. 'If she calls you, don't tell her I'm here.'

Sims' memorial service was at St Peter's Lutheran Church
in Manhattan, and the attendance was massive. Benny
Goodman, Annie Ross and Sims' old employer Woody
Herman were there, and a procession of other jazz artists
included in a gathering that probably numbered eight
hundred. Mary was waiting inside, trying to find Annie Ross,
who she had agreed to meet. A man she knew came over
and remarked 'there's an obituary for Zoot in the *New York
Times* and Ronnie's mentioned several times in it.' In that
instant, she saw him arrive at the church out of the corner
of her eye. Though the occasion was sad, Ronnie had exhibited an old relish for a surprise. But when he and Mary sat
together in the church and the pastor in turn surprised him

– inviting him to come to the lectern to remember Zoot in his own way, Ronnie Scott was frozen to the pew. 'Mary,' he hissed to her in anguish. 'I can't go up there. What am I going to say?' 'Just improvise,' Mary told him. 'You'll find the words.' She reminded him of what it would mean to Louise, Zoot's widow. In the event, he found a way through it. But he couldn't help insisting that he wasn't really the one they should be asking. He didn't really know if words existed to account for the gratitude, love and admiration he felt for Sims, as a player and as a man.

Scott and Sims between them had seen the music world change out of all recognition – and the wider world still more so. The Englishman recalled sitting in the bandroom with Sims when the American astronauts first landed on the moon. Sims remarked: 'Jesus! They're walking on the moon and I'm still playing "Indiana".' In the autumn of 1985, some of the old habitues of Club Eleven decided to stage a reunion gig in its memory. Nearly all of its heroes were still alive – save for Rose, to whom the show would be dedicated, and Tommy Pollard who had died years before. Ronnie Scott himself wasn't keen at the outset. He thought nostalgia wasn't what it used to be.

Jim Godbolt, the ex-promoter, jazz historian and editor of the club's house magazine was the prime mover. He managed to persuade the BBC to include a film of the performance in the schedule for a week of jazz programmes in December 1985. And so on Sunday, 1 September, they got together to play it – two bands with Dankworth and Scott as the leaders, just like it used to be. Crombie, the languid, free-swinging drummer behind Scott's ensemble, Laurie Morgan with his busier and more idiosyncratic style behind Dankworth's. It wasn't just a sentimental occasion, for which allowances would have to be made. Some of the players were rusty, but their own surprise at how much fun it was shone through the music. Dankworth, sometimes a cloistered-sounding and rather unswinging soloist, played magnificently on a swooping, passionate version of 'Lover Man'.

Scott, notably on the classics of the bop repertoire was as loose and flowing with ideas as at any time in his life, as inventive as on some of those out-of-town gigs with his quintet where he often played with less inhibitions than in 'the office'. And he sounded like a performer at ease with his materials. Not simply with bop, because he didn't play the music according to the style of one of the old heroes like Dexter Gordon or Sonny Stitt, but with much of the music that had come after it and which, in his own way, he had absorbed into a way of improvising that was truly his. And at the end of his solos, looking relaxed and comfortable, he smiled with pleasure at his companions. It was a rare sight from the proprietor. He referred to the missing members, Rose and Pollard, in the announcements between tunes, paying a tribute to the contribution of Pollard ('who we regret is no longer with us – in fact he's no longer with anybody') and his mentor Rose, without whom the cause they were all celebrating might never have existed.

Now a rich and varied art-form, jazz has developed many incarnations in the latter half of the twentieth century. Though an Afro-American phenomenon at heart, its many voices have inspired imitation, and eventually creation, all over the world.

Much of this has naturally been due to the highly effective exporting of American culture since the Second World War. But much of it has also been due to the remarkable adaptability of jazz. It came into being as the expression of the resignation and hope of slaves who had discovered the hard way what their emancipation actually amounted to. It readily lent itself – not so much as an articulation of oppression but often as an emblem of it – to the underground cultures of alienated people everywhere. Jazz was prominent in the sound track to teenage movements like the *styliagi* in Russia, the *zazou* movement in France, the beatniks in Britain. The peculiar voicings of the vocabulary and harmonies of jazz became a secret code – not so much for those who went in for organized resistance, but for those whose backgrounds led them naturally toward contracting out.

There was often a strange disparity between the followers of the cult and its heroes in the 1950s. The former might have been the sons and daughters of bankers, doctors, the prosperous and the powerful. The latter were for the most part the sharp working-class youth, the backers of horses, frequenters of low life, familiars of the underworld. So it was with so many of the founders of British modern jazz – musicians like Tony Crombie, Laurie Morgan, Denis Rose, and Ronnie Scott.

Ronnie Scott, though he understands the origins of the music he loves as well as anyone, has always loved it best as an expression of individuality. He has rarely believed it was within his gift to conceive of a radical new direction for the music, to invent a concept that would reshape the way musicians work together, even to be a composer. It has been, for him, a facet of an already highly expressive personality – the one most readily performed before an audience that doesn't necessarily include his closest friends. And it contains within it that ease with vernacular intonation in music that is drawn from blues, from the black American tradition and from Yiddisher wedding-and-barmitzvah culture; the seduction of a kind of professional respectability in the business, engendered also by his Jewish background and by the distant, ambiguous identity of Jock; and a pull in the other direction toward nihilism from such an early and influential membership of that coterie of young rebels in the early 1950s.

Asked if he's considering renovating his current battered tenor, Ronnie Scott will say 'I've thought about making it nice and shiny, but I thought it might make *me* look old.' At fifty-nine, still in good health and in his prime as a player, with the club that bears his name currently reflecting the revival of popular interest in orthodox jazz, he can take stock of a life in which he has gained respect inside and outside 'the business', and created with Pete King (a wit and a jazz-lover whose inclinations are sometimes camouflaged by his leathery mannerisms) an environment in London in which musicians can play at their best and at the same time giving jazz an appropriate home. Some complain that Scott and King are musical conservatives, but Ornette Coleman, Archie Shepp and Cecil Taylor have all played in the club. Many more will testify that those who are serious about music feel that their work is valued by the proprietors, even if the overheads of a West End nightclub have pushed their policies toward a middle road. When Robert Wyatt, the ex-Soft Machine drummer, paralysed his lower limbs for good in an accident in the early seventies, he had only ever played in the club a handful of times, and Ronnie Scott had once or twice jammed with his band. Almost the first piece of correspondence Wyatt received after his accident was a cheque from Scott and King. There are many examples of the same generosity.

Ronnie's son is a student now, a shy, charming and sensitive young man getting to his feet after the obstacles and reverses of that childhood heart condition. Rebecca, who lives with her mother in New York, has turned out to be as inventive, funny and headstrong as her father, and is a budding gymkhana champ. Ronnie has recovered much of his old relaxation, and has thought a good deal about the turmoil of the past decade. He won an OBE for his services to jazz a few years ago, which in a peculiar way reflects the dictum of that great jazz critic Eric Hobsbawm (alias Francis Newton) that jazz may at last have become a subject about which well-informed people at least ought to know enough to hide their ignorance. Ronnie would have dearly loved his mother and grandmother to have been at the investiture, even though for his own part he inclines to the view of his friends that OBE simply stands for 'Other Bastards' Efforts'.

Though jazz is a small world, it has its giant figures – Louis Armstrong, Charlie Parker, Miles Davis, the list of front runners would take up at least two hands, and that of the powerful subsidiary influences far more. And then there are the disciples, the men and women who take more personal visions of what they have learned out into the world, into all the backwaters and tributaries, the welcoming and the hostile climates that jazz has penetrated in this century. In his various roles Ronnie Scott has performed the unique and precious role of bringing confidence, example and first-hand contact with visionaries to the British jazz scene, for so long such a beleagured outpost.

If you ask him about his career, he will usually try to deflect you, tell you that 'It's made a happy man very old'. Probe a little deeper and you find that though the club and its guests have been mostly important to him, it's the saxophone that is his first love, just as it was when Sol and Cissie bought him the Pennsylvania when the bombs still rained on London. 'Sometimes I know that I should never have been a musician' he will say, 'but – occasionally – it's as if somebody else has taken over and everything seems to work. That's when I feel I'm doing what I was meant to do.'

Records/Books

Some early Ronnie Scott recordings on the Esquire label and Tempo labels have now been reissued.

Great Scott – Studio Recordings Volume 1 (Esquire 303)
Battle Royal – Studio Recordings Volume 2 (with Kenny Graham) (Esquire 303)
The Last Word – The Jazz Couriers (Jasmine 2024)
The Jazz Couriers (Jasmine 2004)

The Couriers live album, recorded at the Dominion Theatre in February 1958 is deleted, but can occasionally be found in the second hand racks. *The Jazz Couriers In Concert* (Music For Pleasure 1072). Ronnie Scott's recordings with the Kenny Clarke/Francy Boland Band, mostly recorded for Polydor, are also now regrettably confined to the second hand departments.

It would be impossible to acknowledge all of the references that helped in the completion of this book, but some of the most invaluable were the following:

Bird Lives Ross Russell. Quartet, 1973
Black Nationalism and the Revolution in Music Frank Kofsky, Pathfinder Press, 1970
Drums In My Ears Benny Green, Davis-Poynter, 1973
Encyclopaedia of Jazz in the Seventies Leonard Feather, Quartet, 1978
History of Jazz In Britain 1919–1950 Jim Godbolt, Quartet, 1984
Jazz At Ronnie Scott's Kitty Grime/Val Wilmer, Hale, 1979
Jazz Decade – London Benny Green, King's Road Publishing, 1969
Jazzwomen Sally Placksin, Pluto, 1982
Owning Up George Melly, Weidenfeld & Nicholson, 1965

Red and Hot – The Fate of Jazz in the Soviet Union Frederick Starr, OUP, 1983

Repercussions – A Celebration of African American Music Ed Geoffrey, Haydon & Dennis Marks, C4/Century Publishing, 1985

Some of My Best Friends are Blues Ronnie Scott with Mike Hennessey, W H Allen, 1977

Sound of Surprise Whitney Balliett, Pelican, 1963

Staying Power – History of Black People in Britain Peter Fryer, Pluto, 1984

The Jazz Book Joachim Berendt, Granada Publishing, 1983

The Jazz Scene Francis Newton, Penguin, 1961

The World Is A Wedding Bernard Kops, Valentine Mitchell, 1963

John Fordham is a thirty-eight-year-old London born journalist. He has written about jazz since 1970 for a variety of publications including *Time Out* (of which he was editor until 1981), *Sounds*, *Melody Maker* and the *Sunday Times Magazine*. Since 1978 he has been a regular jazz correspondent for the *Guardian*. He has been a motoring enthusiast since his teens and wrote *The Reluctant Motor Mechanic* in 1977, published by Whittet and Sphere Books. He is currently co-editor of the London magazine *City Limits*.